Also by Nikki Turner

NOVELS

Forever a Hustler's Wife

Death Before Dishonor
with 50 cent

Riding Dirty on I-95

The Glamorous Life

A Project Chick

A Hustler's Wife

EDITOR

Street Chronicles: Girls in the Game

Street Chronicles: Tales from da Hood
contributing author

CONTRIBUTING AUTHOR

Girls from da Hood

Girls from da Hood 2

The Game: Short Stories About the Life

One World

Ballantine Books

New York

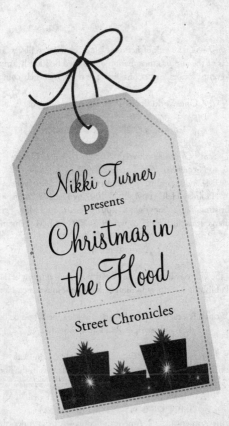

Nikki Turner

presents

Christmas in
the Hood

Street Chronicles

A One World Books Trade Paperback Original

Copyright © 2007 by Nikki Turner

Street Chronicles copyright © 2007 by Nikki Turner
"Secret Santa" copyright © 2007 by K. Elliott
"Me and Grandma" copyright © 2007 by Mo Shines
"Holiday Hell" copyright © 2007 by Dee Blackmon
"A Christmas Song" copyright © 2007 by Seth "Soul Man" Ferranti
"Charge It to the Game" copyright © 2007 by J. M. Benjamin

Published in the United States by One World Books, an imprint of The Random House Publishing Group, a division of Random House, Inc., New York.

ONE WORLD is a registered trademark and the One World colophon is a trademark of Random House, Inc.

Library of Congress Cataloging-in-Publication Data
Nikki Turner presents Street chronicles : Christmas in the hood.
p.   cm.
"A One World Books trade paperback original."
ISBN 978-0-345-49780-2 (trade pbk.)
1. Short stories, American.   2. American fiction—African American authors.
3. African Americans—Fiction.   4. Street life—Fiction.   5. Christmas stories.
I. Title: Street chronicles.   II. Title: Christmas in the hood.   III. Turner, Nikki.
PS647.A35N548   2007
813'.04083552—dc22   2007026536

Printed in the United States of America

www.oneworldbooks.net

2 4 6 8 9 7 5 3

Text design by Laurie Jewell

Dear Loyal Readers
by Nikki Turner

I'm always trying to come up with unique gifts to give to you, my dear readers, and in my heart of hearts, I wish I could be like Oprah and give you all cars but that's not my reality. Then one day the idea came to me: a Christmas book. But not just any Christmas book—this gem would feature five of my favorite authors and be presented as volume three of my Street Chronicles series.

But first, I had to examine the direction I wanted this project to go, which wasn't easy because I have mixed feelings when it comes to Christmas. After all, I don't feel like I should have to wait for Christmas in order for people to bring me gifts! How can we show so much appreciation for one another on one day and be so cutthroat the other 364 days? The commercialism has gotten out of control like a fat man in a pie shop. The vast majority of our confused population will be in debt for six months after Christmas just to fulfill a fantasy that has been indoctrinated in us generation after generation by some capitalistic mastermind.

Black Friday is the day after Thanksgiving and is the biggest and busiest shopping day of the season. Don't let me get started on how uncivilized we can get at those so-called sales. I've seen brawls in some of the department stores that make the De La Hoya and Mayweather fight look like child's play. Tell me, are the four A.M. arrivals, the long lines, and the brutal fights even worth it to get the blue-light and early-bird specials? We've become convinced that we are saving money even though the day after Christmas we are as busted as a broke-dick dog, and all the stuff that we bought (that was supposed to be on sale) is now fifty percent off. How crazy is that?

Each year, at the beginning of the holiday season, I vow that I am not going to get caught up in that madness, but I just can't bring myself to disappoint my children. My parents never let me down; they made sure I had everything on my Christmas list that I asked for and then some. So how could I cheat my kids out of something that I enjoyed so much? I mean that's why we struggle so hard—so our kids can have what we didn't have, right? And for me, that's where the Christmas madness begins: the tree, the cookies, the mistletoe, the fellowshipping, the presents, etc. So, I suppose for me Christmas is ultimately about love and sacrifice.

I hope that in the spirit of the season, you read this book, share this book, but at the end of the day, remember what the holiday is all about.

Happy Holidays and love always,
Nikki Turner

PS. I want to thank the writers of these stories who shared my vision. K. Elliott: I love you so much. You have been such a blessing to me and this project. Even though your plate was full as you were becoming the superstar you are, you still made time for me and this project. Seth: one phone call and you had the rough draft to me the next week or so. You held this project down from behind bars. Mo Shines: thank you for seeing my vision and for wanting to make me happy. Dee: the only girl in this collection, thanks for your patience. J. M. Benjamin: you are indeed one of the hardest workers in this business. Thanks for coming in at the bottom of the ninth and getting things done in a matter of days.

Word on the Street

Dear Loyal Readers by Nikki Turner   vii

Introduction by K'wan   xiii

Secret Santa by K. Elliott   3

Me and Grandma by Mo Shines   33

Holiday Hell by Dee Blackmon   99

A Christmas Song by Seth "Soul Man" Ferranti   169

Charge It to the Game by J. M. Benjamin   245

Acknowledgments   299

Hood Ornaments   301

Introduction

When I think of Christmas, I think of shopping on Thirty-fourth Street in New York City where people of all colors troop through the cold and slush to get that extra-special something for the occasion. All the vendors work overtime trying to push a bunch of bullshit off on you that you really don't need, but you might catch a ten-dollar gift for that aunt you never really felt anyway.

Christmas is the one day of the year when people try to be nice to one another, even if they don't mean it, because of the promise of old St. Nick coming to drop off hope to those who've been good and blocks of coal for the naughty. Picture children with rosy cheeks, tucked heavily into mittens and scarves, learning how to ice-skate for the first time, and in the next breath picture the kids that gotta wake up to nothing because their crackhead uncle stole all their shit to get a holiday blast. Can you picture it?

From suburban America to the most battered slums of Louisiana every kid felt that tingle of excitement when Christmas rolled around, 'cause we were all duped into believing that some fat white dude in a red suit was gonna come drop the latest toys down our chimney, even though most of us didn't have chimneys. Back in the day it made perfect sense, until you got a little older and realized that the life expectancy of an old white man climbing in and out of windows in the hood is short as hell.

Even when the myth was dispelled we still couldn't wait for Christmas. It was all good because no matter whether we got what we wanted or not, it didn't sting so bad because we got something new. That was a rare privilege for someone coming out of a single-parent home where the city kicked in more toward the rent than our biological father did. If you wanted the new one hundred and fifty dollar Jordans but ended up getting long johns, you felt like shit on a stick, but you wouldn't tell your old bird that because you knew what kind of work she had to put in to make that happen.

My most potent Christmas memory was sitting on the lap of a Santa impostor stressing the urgency of me getting a King Kong doll, but instead I got underwear and a cartoon videotape that I couldn't watch because pops took our VCR. I still owe Santa an ass whipping for that one.

I have my own idea of what Christmas is about and what it has meant to me through the years, but in the pages of this book, you'll get several different takes, all with the same conclusion: ain't nothing quite like Christmas in the hood.

K'wan

Bestselling author of *Hood Rat, Eve,* and the forthcoming *Blow*

Secret Santa

by K. Elliott

Shante Morgan aka Foreplay lay on Club Cheetah's center stage with her legs spread like a field-goal post, wearing nothing but a tiny pink G-string. She was a tall slender dancer with a twenty-four-inch waist, a perfect round ass, and small but flawless breasts. Her golden hair and piercing emerald eyes mesmerized the audience as her body glistened under the light from baby oil she rubbed on herself before coming out. A small Mexican guy was on the other side of the stage with a fistful of bills. Shante wanted them all. She danced her way to the edge of the stage, where the man stood, and siezed the bills. She hooked her thumbs into the sides of her G-string and slowly worked her thong down her hips.

The man smiled gratefully and took a sip of his beer before sitting down. A skinny guy with braids yelled, "Make it clap."

"I'll make it clap if you make it rain," Shante said.

The man threw down a five-dollar bill.

She flashed a smile showing her brilliant white teeth.

"Nigga, you made it drizzle. I said make it rain."

"Hell, that's all I got, baby."

Nobody had any money, Shante thought. The money at the club had been slow for the past two weeks, and Shante was sick and tired of working all night and being a circus act for broke-ass niggas who didn't want to pay her. After she finished up onstage, she quickly exited to the locker room. It was time to go home.

Shante Morgan sat on the wooden bench inside the locker room, counting the money she'd made. "Seventy-three dollars," she said. "This shit is pathetic."

Shante thought about earlier that day when she'd taken her children to see Santa Claus at the mall. "So what do you want for Christmas?" Santa had asked her eight-year-old son, Chris.

Chris looked serious, like a grown man. He reminded Shante so much of his father. "I don't want anything; I just want you to bring my mama a house."

A tear trickled down Shante's cheek.

Then Chris pulled out his report card and gave it to Santa. She hadn't even known he'd had his report card with him. "See, I did good, Santa."

The man playing Santa looked at the report card. "Yes, you did great, young man." Santa then turned to her daughter, Makayla, who was nine. "And what about you, young lady?"

"Same thing my brother said, my mama need a house."

Santa smiled, and the crowd around them applauded.

One man yelled, "You have some great kids!"

Shante smiled at the memory of that morning. She knew that she had wonderful kids and that they would be content even if they didn't get anything for Christmas, but she felt obligated—not because they'd made exceptional grades, but because they deserved a good Christmas. But how was she going to get the money? She looked at the bills in her hand. She knew she would get the money some kind of way; she was a hustler. She could try calling her babies' daddy's mother, but she couldn't stand that bitch. She would make it on her own before she lowered herself to begging.

Another stripper, Goldie, walked over to the locker next to Shante, "I didn't even make that much. Consider yourself lucky."

Shante continued to get dressed, putting on her wool socks and her Timberland boots, then her coat and finally her scarf. Even dressed like a boy she was a stunning woman. "You don't have any kids, so consider *yourself* lucky." She smiled. "I have twenty-three days left before Christmas, and my two kids want everything."

Goldie looked sad for Shante, "What about their daddy?"

"That nigga ain't shit. He don't even come around, and they haven't seen his ass in almost two years."

Shante stood and buttoned her coat, thinking about her date with Big Mike. Maybe he could help her with the Christmas gifts. Shante and Big Mike had met two weeks ago at 7-Eleven. He pulled up beside her in his Benz and offered to pump her gas.

She had already taken care of it but thanked him for asking. Big Mike was a huge guy—six feet four and two hundred fifty pounds of dark chocolate. She thought he was cute and charming—and the Mercedes Benz S600 he was driving didn't hurt either—so she gave him her number.

* * *

Now it was two weeks later, and they were about to have another marathon sex session. Big Mike stood over her and smiled, revealing his country-assed gold tooth—the one thing she didn't like about him.

"Put it in, nigga, and quit stalling," Shante said.

"Wait a minute; it ain't all the way hard." Big Mike walked to the dresser and grabbed a bottle out of a paper bag. He opened it up and guzzled down the liquor. "Ahhh," he said, before letting out a loud burp.

Shante turned around. "What the hell was that?" she said, looking disgusted.

"Guinness. This shit makes your dick rock hard." Mike winked. "My brother told me about this shit; it's better than Viagra.

"Nigga, my good pussy is supposed to make your dick hard," Shante teased.

Shante put his manhood in her mouth, and Big Mike looked up toward the ceiling. "Now this is what the fuck I'm talking about," he said, as Shante stroked his dick slowly while licking the head and playing with his balls.

But then she stopped.

"What's wrong?" he said, looking annoyed.

She stood and turned her back toward him. "Mike . . . I really didn't want to get into this with you because I know we just met."

"What are you talking about?" Mike's dick was throbbing.

Shante turned and looked Mike in his eyes. Shante knew from years of experience that men were the most vulnerable when they were about to have sex, and, at that moment, he probably would've built a house for her with his bare hands if she asked him to. "I need help."

"What do you need?"

"I need money to get my kids gifts. I don't have any money this year. The club has been slow, and they want a lot of stuff for Christmas. I want to get my son a PlayStation and my daughter a new computer. I told them if they did good in school this year, I would tell Santa to bring them what they wanted."

"How'd they do?"

"My daughter got all As, and my son, mostly As and Bs and one C," Shante said proudly.

Mike smiled.

He was a hulking man, and even though she'd known him for only a short time, she could tell he was a good person.

"You know what? I'm going to help you. Don't worry about it." He smiled mischievously. "Now, let's get back to work." His member hardened as he moved toward Shante once more.

Shante went down on him again, not really sure if Mike was being honest about his promises. But she was lonely. She was tired of raising the kids on her own. She wanted a man; she wanted a father for her kids. She thought about what it would be like if Mike were a permanent fixture in her and her kids' lives. There would be someone to accompany her to PTA meetings and help her raise her son.

Noticing she was distracted, Mike frowned. "What's wrong now, baby?"

Shante wiped her mouth before she stood and kissed him. "Mike, I'm really starting to like you, and I wish you could be in my life. I want to introduce you to my kids."

Mike looked at his watch. "It's three in the morning."

"Not right now. Maybe tomorrow." She smiled.

"Are you sure? I mean, I don't want to meet the kids unless we're going to be together."

She put her head on his chest. "Don't you want to be with me?"

He took a deep breath but didn't answer her question.

Shante looked into Mike's eyes. It was obvious Mike didn't feel the same way. "Mike, you don't want to be with me, do you?"

"Yeah. Yeah. Course I do," Mike said, but he didn't sound sincere.

It was clear he was lying, and Shante called him on it. "Why not, Mike? Why don't you want to be with me?"

Mike avoided her eyes. "It's not that I don't want to be with you, it's just that I just got out of a relationship. I kind of want some time by myself, you know?"

"I understand," she said, holding back her tears. She figured she was just a piece of ass to Big Mike, just like she was to every other man she had ever met.

Mike put his arms around her and held her for a long time. "It's not like that, shortie, I mean, everything is cool, I just want to chill, you know?"

"Meaning you just wanna fuck," she translated.

"Naw, it ain't like that," Mike said unconvincingly.

She put her arms around him. "It's okay, Mike. I know what you want. It's okay, just keep it real." She forced a smile.

"Seriously, baby, it ain't like that."

Shante dropped to her knees and put his dick in her mouth again. She wondered why niggas lie. Now that she knew that Mike only wanted to fuck her, she would play the game with him and try to get whatever she could out of him. She knew what he wanted, and she would have to use it to get what she needed.

"Don't stop!" he yelled. He was just about to explode when she spit his balls out of her mouth. Big Mike stood up with his dick swinging wildly. "Why did you stop, shortie?"

"I need two hundred dollars, Mike."

"I told you I was going to help you with the kids' Christmas."

"That's cool, but I need the money now."

Mike's dick was still stiff, and she was sure he would have paid any amount of money for the nut at that point.

"How much you need?" he asked.

"Three hundred dollars."

"I thought you said two hundred."

"What the hell did you ask for, if you knew all along?"

"I don't have two hundred dollars."

"Nigga, you driving a eighty-five-thousand-dollar car. What do you mean you don't have two hundred dollars?"

"I don't have it," Mike stated firmly.

Shante stood and went into the bathroom to brush her teeth. She was just about to gargle some Listerine when Big Mike walked in with his dick in one hand and a bunch of bills in the other. She spit the Listerine in the sink, turned to him, and smiled. "You want your little dick sucked, huh?"

He chuckled and, as she reached for the money, pulled back and pointed to his dick.

"No, nigga, put the money in my hand, and only then will you get rewarded."

Mike glanced at himself. His dick had gone down again. Finally he handed her the money.

She counted it. Ten twenty-dollar bills. "I need three hundred dollars."

"I don't have it right now," he stated. "You can take it or leave it."

She took it.

* * *

Club Cheetah's was packed. The Chevy Boyz, a rap group from Atlanta, was making it rain by throwing trash bags of money in the air. Shante had arrived late, but she could tell it was going to be a good night. She was dressed in her sexiest outfit: a green spandex dress with a lime green G-string that highlighted her ass.

Blue was the leader of the Chevy Boyz. He was tall, dark, and lanky, with long cornrows. He stepped to Shante as soon as she left the dressing room. "Goddamn," he said, admiring her ass.

She smiled and looked away. She didn't want to seem like she was a groupie.

"You know who I am, shortie?" Blue asked.

"No, should I?" Shante said, knowing damn well who he was. She'd seen him on BET, but she had to play it cool. She couldn't let the nigga get the big head; then he would expect dances for free. Celebrities were the cheapest customers, usually.

He looked at her skeptically and said, "Yeah, right."

He pointed to his black T-shirt that read: CHEVY BOYZ.

"Okay, I think I've heard of y'all," Shante said, keeping up the charade. "You're a singer or something."

He chuckled. "Damn, you smell good, shortie. What you wearing?"

"Kenzo."

"Never heard of it."

"Yeah? Well, I've never heard of you."

"But you just said you did."

She smiled then laughed out loud. "I did, didn't I?"

"Quit playing games."

"I know who you are, nigga, but still introduce yourself, and don't give me that hip-hop name. What is your government name?" Shante asked playfully.

"You the feds?"

"No, it's just manners. Didn't yo mama teach you manners?"

"Leave my mama out of this."

Hoping she hadn't offended him, Shante rubbed his chest then turned her back toward him and started dancing, pressing her behind against his dick. Just then the DJ announced, "We have the Chevy Boyz in the house!" and put on their song "My Chevy Ride Slow." The crowd went wild.

Blue smiled, revealing a gold grill as he palmed Shante's butt. "Damn, girl, I didn't know Carolina girls had asses like this."

Shante turned and smiled. "This is a one-of-a-kind ass. You can't find this in Carolina, Georgia, or Florida."

"I don't know about all that, but you definitely looking good and smelling good."

"What's stopping you from taking me to VIP then?"

Blue paid for a bottle of champagne, and Shante led the way upstairs.

Inside the VIP lounge, the two sat at a small table in a secluded corner. Blue began to pour her a glass of champagne, but Shante shook her head. "I don't drink."

Blue looked surprised. Shante put her leg over his, and Blue moved her hand to his lap.

"Okay, so what's up, shortie? What do I get in VIP? You giving me head or what?"

"I don't have sex inside clubs. We don't do that here. You'll get thrown out and get me fired."

"What? So what do I get?"

"Just a private dance."

"This shit is whack. In ATL the girls are sucking and fucking."

"This ain't ATL."

She stood, and his eyes zeroed in on her ass. "So what're you about to do?"

"I'm about to give you a dance," Shante said, as she wiggled her ass, which looked like it wanted to bust out of her tight come-fuck-me dress.

"Let's get out of this club, shortie. I got a spot in the Embassy Suites. I want to slide through and unwind."

"After I get off I'll bounce with you; it ain't no problem. But if you want me to spend the night it's going to cost you two Gs."

"Money ain't a thang."

When he said that, Shante felt relieved. Her kids would have a good Christmas after all. "Then you have yourself a date."

. . .

When Shante came out of the bathroom of Blue's hotel suite, she was butt-naked. Blue laid across the bed stroking himself. She slid beside him, and his manhood swelled immediately. She licked it and blew on it. His toes curled.

"Want to place a bet?" she asked him.

"What kind of bet?" he responded.

"That I can make it cum in six minutes, or this one is on me."

He pulled his boxers all the way down to his feet. He had a lot of pubic hair, which made her flesh crawl.

"And if you do make me cum within six minutes?"

She kissed his chest and then his lips. Carressing his sack, she said, "You pay me double."

"That's a bet."

"Can you pay me fifteen hundred now?"

"Why?"

She kissed his sack. "I don't know you, Daddy."

"Imma pay you. You think I'm going to risk my career and get a rape case?"

She decided not to press him because he looked so serious and she didn't want to blow the opportunity. She also thought he was sort of cute; she didn't particularly like skinny men, but Blue was kind of attractive to her.

He rubbed his dick on her chin, causing her to jerk her face away.

"What's the matter? Too freaky for you?"

"No, but you ain't my man, so you can't just do me any kind of way."

"I'd rather be ya N-I-G-G-A," Blue quoted Tupac. "The nigga get treated better than the man."

She smacked her teeth and rolled her eyes. "I don't know about all of that, but are we on or not?"

"You that good, you can make me spit in six minutes?"

"Five, nigga."

"Bet it up, shortie." They shook hands, and she took him deep in the back of her throat. He grabbed her head. She moved his hand and spit on the tip of his dick.

His head fell back.

He looked at the clock: one minute had gone by.

She deep-throated him. He stood, and she grabbed his waist; she met his thrusting with the back of her throat. She cupped his balls. Saliva ran down the sides of her mouth onto his shaft. He sat back on the bed: three minutes had passed. His toes were now pointing up toward the ceiling.

"Damn this shit feels so . . . so good."

Shante kept going.

With a little over one minute remaining, Blue begged. "Please stop! Please stop! You win! I'll pay you!"

She ignored his demands, and seconds later he came and came and came again.

She bounced from her knees, disappeared into the bathroom, and came back with a towel, which she threw to Blue, who was now in a fetal position.

"Damn, girl, that was the best head I ever had."

"Really?"

"Hell, yeah."

"Why don't you give me a bonus then?"

He laughed. "Shortie, you got game and personality. I like you a lot."

Shante was happy she'd pleased him. She wondered what life would be like with a rapper as a boyfriend. "So Blue, why don't you wanna be nobody's man?"

Blue sat up on the bed. "Just don't have time for it. You know with relationships come expectations, and I don't have time for that shit. I like to just chill."

"And buy pussy?"

He looked troubled. "I don't know. My life ain't all what it's cracked up to be. I'd rather just make a deal for sex than have somebody who really only wanted me for my paper pretend they like me."

Shante was confused. "So paying for booty works out good for you?"

"You better believe it." He smiled, revealing his gold-and-diamond grill.

"I see," she said, disappointed, as her dreams of being with a famous rapper disappeared.

After she put her clothes back on, Blue gave Shante her money and kissed her on the cheek.

When Shante got home, the babysitter was asleep on the sofa, and the kids were sleeping on the pullout couch. She kissed her son on the cheek and picked up her little girl. She walked the kids to their bedrooms and tucked them in then hopped in the shower. She couldn't stop thinking about Blue and wondered why it was so easy for him to have sex without attachments. It didn't feel good tricking for cash—even if it was for a good cause: her kids. She felt hopeless and foolish for giving up the jewels to a total stranger, someone who didn't give a damn about her. Though she'd known that it was only business between her and Blue and that she hadn't known him but for a few hours, she had developed a liking for him. She wished he had seen something in her that had made him want to stick around.

. . .

When Big Mike came over he noticed all the gifts under the Christmas tree. "I see you doing okay for yourself."

Shante smiled. "Yes, I got my kids their own shit."

"How'd you do that?" Mike asked, still looking at the gifts.

"The club's been busy."

"That means you won't need my money then, right?"

"Whatever, nigga. You know I need help. I am a single parent, remember?"

"I know. You get them the computer and PlayStation like you said?"

She rubbed his chest. "Yes, and some other things, too."

"Cool, cool," he said. "Are the kids asleep?"

"If they weren't sleep, do you think you would be here?"

"That's what I like about you: you always put your kids first."

"No, this is what you like about me." She rubbed her ass against him.

"You damn right." He smiled again, revealing that country-assed gold tooth.

She kissed him, and he held her. She felt so safe in his arms. He was so big and lovable, she felt that he could protect her from the world. He began to unbutton her blouse.

She buttoned it back up. "Let's just hold each other, Mike."

"What?"

"I just like you being here with me. Do we always have to have sex?"

"I guess not."

"Let's just comfort each other."

Mike looked at her strangely. "Comfort each other?"

She pushed him away and began to cry.

He leaned toward her. "What's wrong now?"

"Nothing."

Mike sat on the sofa. "I swear, women are so damned emotional."

Shante continued to cry. Though she had been able to buy the gifts for her kids, she didn't have a man to share Christmas with. Every year at this time, she'd get sad. She'd see families and wish she had someone to spend Christmas with her and her children.

Mike got down on one knee. "Baby, tell me what's wrong?"

She looked him in his eyes. "Have you ever felt like you have nobody?"

Mike look confused and didn't answer.

"See, you don't understand."

He put his arms around her. "You have me."

She smiled. "If I have you, Mike, just hold me then, no sex. I just want to be held."

He put his arms around her and held her tightly.

· · ·

It was three A.M. when Shante woke up and found that Mike was gone. She walked into the living room to see if the door was locked. Finally, she turned toward the Christmas tree to make sure the lights were out.

All of her gifts were gone.

She looked around. This had to be a mistake, she thought. Her gifts had to be there. Maybe Mike put them in the closet for some reason? She checked. The closet was empty. They weren't in the kitchen, nor in the kids' room. What the hell was going on? She dialed Mike's cell phone number. He didn't pick up, which wasn't like him at all. He almost always picked up. She called him three more times, but there was no answer.

Shante threw her phone across the room as she realized that Big Mike had stolen the presents. But he had done more than that. She had wanted so much to trust him, to believe that there might be something there. And not only did he steal from her, he stole from her children as well. What in the hell was she going to do now?

• • •

Officer Tillman, a tall black man, asked Shante, "Can you describe this man you call Big Mike?"

Tears ran down Shante's face, and she could barely talk. "He was big and burly, about two hundred fifty pounds, with a gold tooth."

A lanky white officer with a name tag that read Diehl scribbled on a notepad. "How tall was he?"

"Six three, maybe six four."

Diehl looked at Shante with serious eyes. "Was he your boyfriend?"

"No."

"Your lover?"

Embarrassed, Shante looked up at the ceiling. She wanted to wake up to find that all this was just a bad dream, but it wasn't. How could she have been such a bad judge of character?

Tillman asked again. "Was he your lover?"

The tears came pouring down her face, leaving a trail. "I guess you could say that."

"So where does he live?" Tillman asked.

"I don't know."

"You've never been to his house?" Diehl asked.

"No."

"Where does he work?"

"I don't know."

"How long did you know him?" Diehl asked.

"About a month." Shante knew she sounded stupid. She felt it.

Diehl looked surprised. "And you brought him home with your kids?"

"Yeah, I know it sounds crazy, but he seemed like a nice guy."

"Where did you and Big Mike meet?" Tillman asked.

"The 7-Eleven. He offered to pump my gas."

The two officers exchanged looks.

"I can see why he wins the Humanitarian of the Year Award," Diehl quipped.

"You shut the fuck up," Shante shouted angrily. "I don't need to be judged by you."

Diehl stopped scribbling. "Ma'am, I'm sorry."

"Do you know his last name?" Tillman probed.

Shante looked in the air as she tried to remember if he had ever told her.

"Think hard," the officer said.

"I can't recall."

"What does he drive?"

"A Benz."

"A Benz?" Diehl said.

"I know. That's why I didn't think he would do something like this," Shante said.

"Just 'cause he drives it doesn't mean it's his," Tillman said.

Someone called Diehl on the radio, and seconds later Shante's kids came running into the living room.

"Mama, what's wrong?" Makayla asked.

"Nothing's wrong."

"Where are our Christmas presents?" her daughter asked.

She pulled the girl close but didn't answer.

"Ma, did someone take the Christmas presents?"

"No, you know I wouldn't let that happen," Shante said, looking at the cops.

Chris started to cry. "Mama, where are the presents?"

"Santa has them," Officer Tillman said.

"That's right, Santa has them," Diehl repeated.

Shante kissed both of her kids on the cheek and then wiped her son's eyes with her shirt. "Take your brother into the room and let me finish talking to the officers."

Makayla grabbed Chris's hand and disappeared into the room.

When the kids were gone, Shante asked, "What am I going to do?"

Diehl shrugged his shoulders. "Try the Salvation Army."

Tillman offered, "Angel Tree is another organization where you can get some help."

Shante couldn't believe this shit had happened to her, nor could she believe she had been so naive. How in the hell could she have been so stupid? And to think that she'd actually wanted him to move in and play daddy to her kids. The tears came again.

"I'll do whatever it takes to make sure my kids have a good Christmas," she said aloud. "Even beg, if I have to."

• • •

Shante swallowed her pride and called her kids' father's mother, who answered on the first ring. "Yeah, this is Janie."

"Ms. Janie, this is Shante."

"Yeah, I know. I saw your name on my caller ID. What do you want?"

"I need some help."

"With what?"

Shante was tempted to hang up. She hated this bitch, but she knew the kids were depending on her to come up with Christmas gifts. "I need help with the kids' Christmas gifts."

"That's your problem."

The nerve of this bitch to be so cold.

"Where is your son?"

"I don't know. I don't keep up with my son." Janie's voice was harsh.

"Listen, Ms. Janie. I had the presents, but I was robbed."

Janie smacked her teeth. "Yeah, right."

Shante took a deep breath, realizing it was a lost cause.

"You're a damn con artist," the older woman continued, "and that's all you will ever be. You conned my son into getting you pregnant, and now you have to pay the price."

"So I put your son's dick inside me, right?"

"You ruined his life. My son was in college until he met your tramp ass."

"How in the hell did I ruin his life? Chris hasn't given me shit for the kids in over two years."

"He has a wife; he don't have time for you."

"Fuck you."

"You just want him back!"

"I could care less about Chris."

Chris was the first man who had ever told her she was attractive. Shante had always known she was sexy, but Chris had made her feel pretty. She had really wanted the relationship to work, but she soon found out she was just a piece of ass on the side. She stopped seeing him for a while, but she missed him so much she ended up going back to him and playing the other woman until the kids came. When he wasn't there for her financially, she finally cut the relationship off.

Shante wanted to cry, but she would not let this bitch mother of his have the pleasure of breaking her spirit. She hung up the phone.

· · ·

Shante was dressed extra-sexy. She wore hot pink spandex pants with the bottom out revealing a pink thong that made her ass look even rounder. She was going to make that money tonight even if it meant getting every customer off in the club. But the club was extremely slow tonight. There were only a few customers, and most were just sitting around not spending money. It was eleven o'clock when an older man with a graying beard and slacks pulled up above his navel walked in. Shante smiled at him. He blushed. He stood at the bar for a few moments, waiting for the soda he'd ordered. When his drink arrived, Shante walked over and smiled again.

The man extended his hand. "I'm John Long."

"Shante."

"So what's up?"

"You tell me," Shante said. "Are you looking for someone to kick it with? You know, have a good time?"

"What do I have to pay?" John asked.

Shante licked her lips and pouted them seductively. "Six hundred dollars for an hour."

"Six hundred dollars is pretty expensive," he said. "How about four hundred."

Shante thought for a minute. She knew he was old and that a lot of times old guys had trouble cumming, so she might have to work extra hard. She couldn't lower her price too much. "Five hundred."

John opened his wallet, skimmed through his bills as if he were counting his money. Finally he agreed. They left the club an hour later.

• • •

Shante and John drove to a Ramada about a mile away from the club. As soon as they got into the room John smiled and touched her hair.

"No."

John looked puzzled.

She looked into his eyes. "Don't try to patronize me."

"I'm sorry," he said. "What's wrong?"

"Nothing," she said, trying to hold back her tears, but she couldn't contain herself. John dug into his wallet and pulled out five one-hundred-dollar bills and gave them to Shante.

"Thanks," she said, looking confused. "What's this for?"

"Nothing."

"Why are you giving me money? I don't understand."

"Just consider it a blessing from the Lord. Merry Christmas," John said.

"Merry Christmas to you, but I have never had this happen to me."

"What?"

"I never had anybody just pay me for *not* having sex with them."

"I'm different."

"Are you?"

"So, tell me about yourself," John said.

"I don't know what to tell you. . . . I'm a dancer, and sometimes I sell sex."

"I know that much, but what led you to dancing?"

"Well, I really don't have any skills. I mean, I want to go back to school and all, but—"

"But what?"

"I have kids."

"And?" His warm smile made Shante feel like opening up.

She turned her head slightly, avoiding his eyes. "I mean, kids kind of make it hard to go back to school."

"Excuses—everybody has them."

She made eye contact with him. "So, John, what do you do."

An awkward silence came over the room.

"You don't have to tell me if you don't want to," she said finally.

He looked into her eyes. "Shante, I'm a minister."

Whoa. What was this world coming to? "I see. . . . What church?"

"Bethel."

"Yeah? You have a big congregation."

"Yeah, I do."

"I attended once."

"So you've seen me?"

"No, they said the pastor was out of town for the week."

"Oh, yeah."

"Said you were in Paris."

"You must have come about four years ago."

"Yeah," she said, and dropped her head.

"Do I disappoint you?"

"No. I mean, the world is what it is. I have no expectations for anyone, not even preachers."

"I'm ashamed."

She smacked her teeth sassily. "Why, because you're a man?"

"No, because I was weak."

"The flesh is always weak," Shante said.

"So you know the Bible?" He smiled.

"Not exactly, but I've heard that before."

"Do you want to study the Bible?"

"When?"

"Now."

"Why do you want to study the Bible with me?"

"I don't know. I think the Lord wants me to help you."

She smiled a polite smile. "Well, I need five hundred more dollars to get my children's Christmas toys."

He chuckled but didn't respond.

"So, John, are you gonna help me?"

"Do you know what Christmas is all about?"

"Yeah, of course I do. But I need money."

John looked puzzled. "That's not what it's all about. Don't you want to go to real estate school?"

Shante had thought about getting her real estate license but hadn't told anybody. "How did you figure that?"

"I have a way of knowing things."

"Lucky guess."

"But again, do you know the meaning of Christmas?"

"Yes. Giving—and it's Jesus's birthday."

"Yes, it is the day our Lord and Savior entered the world."

"We all know this. Are you going to help me now?"

"Shante, if you died tonight, would you go to heaven?"

"I don't know."

"Wrong answer."

She looked confused.

"Shante, you've tried everything else; now try Jesus."

"Is Jesus going to pay my bills?"

"Absolutely!" John took her hand in his. "Trust me."

His hands were warm, and his demeanor was friendly. She believed him, and at that moment she believed in God.

He held her hand tightly and asked her to pray with him. "God, I know that I'm a sinner, and I know that Jesus died for our sins, and I'm asking you to come into my life and take control over it. I'm asking you to save my soul, Father. Amen."

Shante repeated the prayer, John kissed her and left the room. As the door closed behind him, tears rolled down her face. She felt new.

. . .

On Sunday, the day before Christmas, Shante went to John's church. A young man was in the pulpit preaching about angels. He read the lesson from Hebrews 13:2: "Be not forgetful to entertain strangers: for thereby some have entertained unawares angels." Shante wondered where John was as she looked for him after the service was over. Maybe he'd gone on another trip again. Approaching one of the deacons, she asked, "Where is the minister?"

The deacon pointed to the young man who'd just preached the sermon.

"No, I'm talking about John Long."

"John Long died three years ago," the deacon said.

"A tall man with a gray beard?"

"Yes, he was the preacher here for twenty years."

"There must be some mistake."

The deacon led her over to the side of the room and pointed to a picture that hung on the wall. "Is this the man you're looking for?"

Shante examined the picture. "Yes, that's him."

"Yeah, his wife died of lupus more than three years ago, and he died maybe six months later."

Shante was frightened and confused. Had she been talking to a dead man? How was this possible? How had he come to be in the club? Why had this happened to her?

The man asked kindly, "Would you like to join the church?"

"No, not today."

"Are you saved, young lady?" the deacon asked.

"Yeah . . . Yes."

He smiled and nodded. "Merry Christmas."

"Merry Christmas to you," Shante said. While she still didn't know what she was going to do about getting Christmas gifts for the kids and paying next month's rent, she wasn't going to worry about that now. She felt God was showing her signs and that her life would never be the same.

* * *

As Shante was about to unlock the door to her apartment, she noticed a message on the door indicating she had packages at the rental office. She went back down to her car and drove over to the office.

The apartment complex manager, an older white lady, smiled and said, "Hello, Shante. You have about twenty boxes in here."

Shante was surprised. "Really?"

The manager lit a Camel cigarette. "Yeah, it appears you have a Secret Santa."

"Oh yeah?"

"None of the boxes have a return address," the woman said, before blowing out a smoke ring. "I'll help you carry them to the car."

"Thanks."

The manager handed Shante an envelope. "Here, this is for you, too."

Shante tore into the envelope, which contained a note: "Shante Morgan, you are registered for the next session of the Lawrence Real Estate School. Paid in Full."

Shante wanted to cry, this time tears of happiness and gratitude. She looked at the manager and gave her a hug. "Have a Merry Christmas!"

"You too, doll," the manager said with a throaty laugh.

One Year Later

It was the night before Christmas, and Shante and her kids looked around their apartment. It was bare.

"Mommy, how big is my room again?" Makayla asked.

"As big as the living room and kitchen in this apartment put together," Shante said with a smile.

"And I'll have my own room, too?" her son asked.

"Yes, you will," she said, hugging them both, tears in her eyes at the thought of moving her children into their own home.

It had been nine months since she graduated from her real estate program, and even though she was only a sales agent, she had brought her hustling skills to the forefront and had the highest sales of anyone else in her office. High enough to have saved for a down payment on a home and bought a new Mercedes SL500.

"Now hop in the car with me so we can go to the car wash before we go to church tonight."

Shante and the kids drove to a nearby car wash that serviced many luxury cars. She wanted her new ride to look as shiny and new as she was feeling these days.

As they pulled into the car wash a guy stepped up to the car to take down the details of what she wanted done. Fumbling with her purse, Shante didn't look at him right away.

"Hey, shortie, what you need today?"

That voice. Shante glanced up and right into Big Mike's eyes. He looked a far cry from the successful player she once thought he was, in his dirty overalls with his ashy hands. Recognition slowly crept across his face, and he started to look fearful. But as he held her eyes, he couldn't help but be impressed.

"Damn, shortie, you've done well for yourself."

Not wanting to cuss him out with her kids in the car, Shante gripped the wheel and took a deep breath. She closed her eyes briefly and asked God for strength.

"Was it worth it, Mike?" Shante asked quietly.

Not expecting her to approach him in that manner, Mike looked confused. He thought she would go off on him.

"Shortie, I was desperate. I did what I had to do."

"So it was worth stealing from my kids? What's a man driving a Benz doing stealing?"

"That car wasn't mine, baby doll. One of our customers was

storing it here while he did a bid, and I borrowed it on occasion. Shit, I usually take the bus," he admitted.

Shante looked at him again, and, instead of disgust, she started to feel something else. Pity. Any man low enough to steal from a single mother and her kids wasn't man enough for her.

"Mike, I gotta go. I've changed my mind about the wash. Yeah, I recovered, but no thanks to you. You really messed me up, but the good Lord restored my faith. I used to think I needed a man. I felt lonely without one. But I've now learned that I'm never truly alone because I've got the Lord. I hope you find that same peace."

Shante backed her car up and drove out of the car wash, leaving Mike stunned.

Me and Grandma

by Mo Shines

Chapter One

Around six on the morning of December 1, nineteen-year-old Gina "Gigi" Lewis was awakened by the sound of feet storming through the apartment. She thought she was dreaming and turned over to go back to sleep, but the sound of a strange male voice yelling "New York Police Department" let her know that this was not a dream.

Bolting straight up in bed, she grabbed the sheet in fright, looking like a deer caught in headlights. She heard her sixteen-year-old cousin Andrew let out a loud "Oh shit" from the front room, right next to the apartment door.

As Gigi and her grandma scrambled out into the hallway, three police officers were quickly tackling Andrew to the floor. More cops poured into the apartment.

"Hands up! Hands up where I can see them!" one shouted as he grabbed Gigi's grandma by the collar of her nightgown.

Gigi felt a cold metal object on the side of her right temple. The young narc pulled Gigi back into Grandma's room by her white tee and cocked the hammer on his black .38 revolver, still holding it to her head. Her life seemed to flash in front of her eyes.

Grabbing Gigi by the hair, he turned her head and whispered in her ear, "One wrong move, I'll blow your fucking top off." She felt his dry, cracked lips scratch her skin.

The cop jerked Gigi's arms violently behind her back and enclosed tight plastic flex cuffs around her wrists. Then he dragged her into the living room, where they already had Andrew and his grandma restrained with flex cuffs and on the floor. She looked at Andrew with terror in her dark brown eyes. Everything seemed to be happening in slow motion.

Andrew mouthed, Don't worry, as he watched Gigi fight back her tears.

Gigi nodded and turned her face. Her heart was pounding as if it would jump straight out of her chest. It broke her heart to see tears streaming down her grandma's wrinkled face as the cop dropped Gigi down on the floor next to her.

Proceeding to ransack the old woman's nice apartment, the cops flipped over mattresses, threw the dresser drawers on the floor, and tossed clothes everywhere.

"What the fuck is all that P.A.L. shit in the closets?" an angry officer yelled out, searching through the hallway closet.

Andrew replied sarcastically, "That's my uncle's shit. He's a P.A.L. youth counselor."

"Yeah, well, tell your uncle he's a fucking thief."

Andrew looked at him and said, "Whatever, man."

Two cops went into Grandma's bedroom to search it. Gigi heard them yelling.

"Oh . . . shit, oh . . . shit! What the fuck is that?"

"What do they feed that damn thing? That shit is as big as a small dog."

Kitty the Siamese cat always jumped out from under the bed whenever the bedroom door opened. At first glance the cat's glowing green eyes scared anybody who entered the dark room.

A tall, slim black uniformed cop remained in the living room with Gigi, Grandma, and Andrew, badgering them while the rest of the cops searched different areas throughout the apartment, repeatedly asking where the crack was.

Two detectives sporting suits and ties walked into the living room. The black one stared at the trio on the floor. The short, stocky white one turned his attention to the Christmas tree and the wrapped presents resting under it.

"Check the gifts," the white detective ordered the black cop already in the living room.

The younger cop immediately jumped into action. Crossing the room, he knocked over the tree and sent red ornaments rolling across the living room floor.

"Why you fuckin' wit' our tree?" Andrew yelled.

"Shut your trap 'fore I stick my foot in it," the black detective snapped, shifting all his weight onto one leg.

Realizing the detective wasn't just making an idle threat, Andrew kept his lips zipped up.

The uniformed cop grabbed one of the gifts and was about to

rip off the wrapping paper when, suddenly, one of the cops in the kitchen shouted, "Bingo! Bingo!"

Gigi's heart sank as the other cops milling around the house cheered in jubilation. She looked over at Grandma, who just shook her head in despair. A young cop emerged from the kitchen, holding up two ceramic flour canisters he had found sitting on top of the fridge.

"Look what I found," the cop gloated. His hands were covered in flour as he set the canisters down on the coffee table in full view of the other cops.

The bundles were partly visible underneath the flour. Removing them from the canisters, the cop smacked the flour off before bagging them into evidence.

The same two uniformed cops scared by the cat returned to the living room.

"This was in the closet." The tall white one lifted up both hands and showed everyone in the room the huge stash of crack bundles he had found. He had at least six Ziploc bags in each hand.

The skinny white one held up a thin white plastic bag. "There's a little over twenty-seven thousand dollars cash in here—mostly tens and twenties."

Gigi's breath caught in her throat as she watched the cop confiscate the money Grandma had hustled so hard to save for her kidney transplant. The surgery had already been scheduled for January 4. Tears really started streaming down her face.

Grandma had recently been diagnosed with kidney disease, and she was undergoing dialysis three days a week, each session lasting at least three hours. Some days she was in so much pain, she didn't even want to get out of bed, but she never let it stop her.

"Looks like the old lady's doing better than a lot of us. Maybe we all should start slinging dope," the white detective joked, causing all the other cops milling around the apartment to laugh.

"What you talking about?" Gigi yelled. "That ain't drug money. My grandma doesn't sell drugs."

The cops just laughed as they continued searching the apartment. After finding a couple more thousand dollars and a few ounces of marijuana that Andrew had hidden in the closet, the officers finished their search.

The police led them out of the building, one after the other. Gigi and Grandma hung their heads while Andrew scanned the crowd of onlookers with a smile on his face, knowing the arrest earned him stripes in the hood.

Everyone in the neighborhood, including most of Grandma's friends, watched as the cops led them to the paddy wagon that was parked in front of the building.

Deep in her heart, Gigi had known this day would eventually come, having seen it in a dream, but she constantly pushed it out of her mind.

As soon as the trio arrived at the 40th Precinct, the arresting officers quickly put the family into separate holding rooms to interrogate them individually. But someone had a change of heart before they started the questioning, because after a few minutes an officer escorted Gigi into the room where her grandma was being held.

Despite the seriousness of the situation, Gigi had to laugh to herself. These guys couldn't be too bright interviewing them in the same room.

As she sat down, Gigi noticed her grandma didn't look good at all. The older woman's skin was clammy, and she seemed to be having a hard time breathing.

"Grandma, are you okay?" she asked, alarm filling her voice.

Her grandma nodded.

Gigi turned to the door, where the two detectives were just entering the room, and pleaded, "Please, we have to get her medicine. She's sick. . . . She needs a kidney transplant. You gotta help her."

The detectives ignored her and proceeded to question them. "My name's Detective Goldson," the white cop said before motioning toward the tall, dark-skinned guy, "and this is Detective Bettis. We're with Narcotics."

Pulling a chair out from the table, Goldson sat down directly across from Gigi's grandma while his partner remained standing.

"You smoke?" he asked, removing a pack from the inside pocket of his suit jacket.

Grandma nodded.

The detective handed her a cigarette, held out a lighter, and flicked the flame. Grandma leaned forward and lit up; taking a long drag, she sat back.

He offered a cigarette to Gigi, but she refused. Lighting up a smoke of his own, the detective eyed the older woman sitting in front of him.

"So who you selling crack for?" Detective Goldson asked,

leaning in toward the table. "We know somebody's supplying you. Tell us who you work for, and we'll go easy on you."

Gigi opened her mouth to speak, but before she could say anything, her grandma said, "The drugs no Gigi's, and the drugs no mine."

"According to our source, your grandson and granddaughter are selling," the detective stated matter-of-factly, moving closer to the table. "But word is . . . they're selling for you."

Grandma raised her shaky hands palms up. "You can't believe half of what you hear."

"This has the Diaz brothers stamped all over it," the black detective responded, crossing his muscular arms. "Give them up, and we'll cut you and your family slack."

"I don't know what you're talking about," Grandma lied.

Both cops just stared at her for a moment. Finally one of them spoke up. "You sure that's all you wanna tell us?"

Tapping her cigarette ash into the ashtray, Grandma nodded. Lola Lewis was not your typical grandmother. Fifty-five years old, she loved rocking the latest fashions, and she did whatever she needed to do to make sure her grandkids had the best that money could buy.

After questioning the older woman, the detectives left the room. Gigi started to speak, but her grandma quickly shook her head, indicating she should be quiet. She knew the cops kept the recorder running in the interrogation room in hopes of catching some idiot slipping.

Gigi sat there in silence, not believing how her grandma was taking up for her and Andrew. When she saw the other woman lean over on the table, trying to catch her breath, Gigi panicked again.

"Are you okay?" she asked.

Grandma didn't say a word.

"Help," Gigi yelled, running to the door and pounding on it.

When the detectives finally returned a few minutes later, they noticed Ms. Lewis's condition and had her escorted out of the room by another cop.

"Where you taking her?" Gigi asked, tears streaming down her face.

Neither detective bothered to respond as they led her back to the metal table in the center of the small room. Gigi stared out the window, which faced the street.

"So tell me, who does the crack belong to . . . your grand-mother . . . Chico?" the white detective asked, his blue eyes searching her from the feet up.

Turning her attention to him, Gigi readjusted herself in the metal folding chair and then said, "What are you talking about? Grandma doesn't sell drugs . . . and I didn't know there was any in the house. I was just spending the night."

The detective's hardened eyes locked with hers. Undeterred, Gigi didn't give him the satisfaction of looking away. Her stare only grew firmer.

"You're lying. You live in that apartment. We've been watching you come and go for months. We've been watching your grandma, too. Word on the street is Grandma's making crazy dough."

"Fuck what the street say. I know that shit ain't Grandma's. First of all, she's not stupid enough to sell drugs. If she knew drugs were in the house, she would've thrown them out. Second, she's too old. With her bad kidneys, she can barely get outta bed some days."

Before they could respond, another officer came into the room and whispered something to one of the detectives. He looked at the officer in disgust before turning to Gigi. "Your cousin has admitted to everything. You're free to go."

Gigi wasn't one bit surprised. Little did the detectives know the three family members had set a pact when Grandma first started selling crack: if the apartment ever got raided, Andrew would take the blame for the drugs since he lived with Grandma.

Being a minor, Andrew faced minimum jail time, if any, for his first offense. Grandma, on the other hand, was much too old and sickly to do any time, and Gigi was the pride and joy of the family, with her entire life ahead of her.

"Can I see my grandma?" she asked.

"Sure," he said. "They just took her to the hospital. You better hurry. She didn't look too good."

. . .

By the time Gigi arrived at the emergency room, her grandma had already been seen by the doctors and was feeling much better. She looked over and smiled as Gigi entered the room.

"Grandma, are you okay?" she asked, hurrying over to hug the woman.

"I'm fine. I'm fine."

"So they're gonna let you go home with me?" Gigi asked excitedly, sitting down on the edge of the bed.

Grandma shook her head. "They're keeping me overnight for observation."

Growing quiet, Gigi looked around, taking in the new environment.

Grandma patted her on the thigh reassuringly. "Stop worrying," she said. "I'll be outta here by tomorrow afternoon."

"I'm not leaving you here all alone." A part of Gigi felt reassured, but another part of her did not want to leave Grandma in the hospital by herself.

"Nonsense," Grandma replied. "I'll be fine. When you leave here, get some rest."

"I should be telling you that."

They stopped talking long enough for the nurse who had entered the room to check the various machines hooked up to Ms. Lewis. As soon as the white woman left, Gigi and Grandma resumed their conversation.

"What a curse it is to be poor." She sighed as she looked deep into Gigi's brown eyes.

Gigi stared back with a confused expression. "Grandma, we're far from poor."

"I'm sorry for getting you and Andrew mixed up in this mess. This no kinda life to live. I want a better tomorrow for y'all. That's why you have to stay in school, get your degree. I want you to be better than me."

"I know you want the best for me, Grandma," Gigi replied. "I'm gonna be all I can be, trust me. But for now I'm gonna hold you down. That's all there is to it."

At that moment Gigi's mother, Carmen, walked in, followed by her aunt Maria and uncle Tito. With her head held high, Carmen looked sharp in her formfitting business suit. She shot Gigi a stare that let her know Carmen was upset.

Laid back as ever, Uncle Tito planted a kiss on Gigi's cheek. Sporting a five o'clock shadow, he was in need of a shave. "Hey, Ma," he said, leaning in to kiss his mother. "You looking good."

Too busy chasing high after high to care, Maria looked like she didn't want to be there.

"Where's Lulu?" Gigi asked, wondering where her younger sister could be.

"At work," Carmen answered. "I tried to reach her but couldn't get through."

They all crowded around the older woman's bed, making sure she was all right. After all the niceties were out of the way and Carmen realized her mother was fine, she let Grandma and Gigi have it about the drug arrest.

"Gigi, I told you before to move back home with me," Carmen said, "but you wanted to stay with Grandma. Now you'll have a record trailing you the rest of your life. You're so much better than that."

Gigi had already known her mother would fly through the roof once she'd heard the news and was well prepared for her nagging. That was Carmen. It didn't matter that Grandma was sick, Carmen had to speak her mind.

"From the beginning I was against Grandma selling drugs outta the apartment," Carmen continued with her rant.

Andrew's mother, Maria, was in and out of jail so often she wasn't too concerned about his arrest.

"Would you listen to Princess Di," Maria snapped, shooting Carmen a nasty look, "the walking contradiction."

Carmen turned around to glare at her younger sister. "What's that supposed to mean?" she asked, hands on her wide hips.

"You talking holier than thou, but your man's a mule for the Colombians," Maria replied. "What? You thought nobody knew, bitch?"

Even though Carmen didn't approve of Grandma selling drugs, Carmen's boyfriend, Guido, smuggled drugs from Colombia to the United States on commercial flights.

"Mind your business, you crackhead bitch," Carmen shouted. "Fuck you!"

"Not here," Uncle Tito said, stepping between his two sisters. "Have some respect for Ma."

Both women seemed to hate each other. Maria envied her older sister because Carmen had her shit together, holding down a decent-paying job as a secretary.

Thanks to the loud argument, one of the nurses on duty politely asked the family to leave. Everyone said good-bye and left the older woman to her much-needed rest.

The next afternoon Ms. Lewis was back at home, going about her business like nothing had happened. Unfortunately for Andrew, he didn't get out of jail for another two days. When he did get released, he headed right back out on the block that same night, trying to knock off a bundle.

Gigi hated to admit it, but her grandma's decision to hustle had had a big impact on Andrew, and he took to hustling with a passion, even though she was against it.

Chapter Two

When Gigi's alarm sounded at eight o'clock, she woke up and hopped out of bed, more excited than if it was Christmas Day. Three days had passed since the raid, and the family was getting on with life.

After taking a quick shower and throwing on a pair of jeans and a sweatshirt, Gigi headed down the long hallway, where she found Grandma in the kitchen making a hot breakfast.

"Good morning, Grandma," she said, kissing her on the cheek. Not only did her grandkids call her Grandma, so did everybody else on the block.

"Hey, baby," Grandma said, giving her a bright smile. "You ready to go shopping?"

Gigi couldn't help but laugh. "Why you messing with me?" she said. "You know the cops took all our money."

"I know . . . I know," Grandma said, her Spanglish accent coming through, "but I still got my disability check. Hurry up . . . eat. You gonna need your energy."

Grandma hadn't worked since being diagnosed with kidney disease at the age of fifty. She depended on the disability check she received every month, but she knew how to stretch the money. Even after her own kids were all grown, she helped raise Gigi and Andrew.

"I don't want you wasting money buying me clothes."

"Hush," Grandma said. "No argue with a sick old lady." She was determined to make sure her grandkids got everything they wanted for Christmas.

Gigi grinned as she sat down to pancakes, sausages, and eggs. She had already taken a few bites when she looked at her grandmother. Despite the smile the older woman always wore, Gigi realized she wasn't looking too good.

"How you feeling today?" Gigi asked.

"I'm fine," Grandma said, settling down to a plate of wheat toast and tea.

Gigi stared at the food. "That's all you're eating?" she asked, knowing something was definitely wrong. "Grandma, you know I understand if you don't wanna go shopping today."

Before she could even get the words out, her grandmother was shaking her head. "We're going," she said. "I been waiting weeks for this." She reached over and stole a piece of bacon off Gigi's plate and popped it in her mouth, making a show of chewing it.

"You sure?" Gigi asked worriedly.

"Hurry up," her grandma said, ignoring her question.

Gigi finished eating, all the while keeping an eye on Grandma, who seemed to feel better after she had eaten. Once the dishes were washed, they bundled up and were just about to head out the door when Andrew came out of his bedroom.

"Where you two headed?" he asked sleepily.

Gigi tried not to groan. She was looking forward to spending the day alone with Grandma, but she knew if Andrew decided he wanted to come, her grandmother wouldn't stop him.

"Out," she said with an attitude.

Andrew didn't bother to ask any more questions. "See ya," he said, heading toward the kitchen, where Grandma had left him a plate in the microwave.

"Andrew, don't get in any trouble," Grandma said.

Smirking, Andrew didn't bother to respond.

By the time they made it to the shopping strip on Third Avenue in the Bronx, the streets were already bustling with people headed to work. Gigi took in all the activity and the Christmas decorations and smiled. She loved this time of year. She looked over at Grandma, whose thin arm was wrapped around hers, and patted her gloved hand.

"Where to?" she asked.

Grandma pointed to a clothing store, and they headed inside.

They spent hours trying on clothes and buying so much that Gigi knew they would have to catch a cab back to the block. They bought gifts for the entire family: Andrew; her younger sister, Lulu; her mother, Carmen; and Andrew's mother, Maria.

By the time they were done, Gigi was exhausted, and although Grandma looked exhausted, too, Gigi had never seen her look happier.

People were getting off work as they were headed home, so it took them a while to catch a cab. They finally decided to stop at a bodega, where they both ordered hot chocolate.

"So you got everything you wanted?" Grandma asked after taking a sip.

Gigi grabbed a napkin from the dispenser and wiped whipped cream off Grandma's upper lip.

"Yep," she said.

"What about your tuition?" Grandma asked, looking down as she stomped snow off one of her Timberland boots. "How do you plan to pay it?"

"With the money from my job," Gigi said, shrugging as she took another sip of her hot chocolate. "The school lets me make deferred payments."

"I'll get the money for your tuition," Grandma insisted.

Gigi knew that if her grandmother said it, it was just as good as done. She felt bad because her grandma always put them first. "But what about your operation?" she asked.

Grandma just smiled, patting her hand. "Now, baby, you just let me worry about that," she said.

Gigi sighed. Grandma did everything possible to make sure her family was all right. Still, Gigi couldn't help but feel guilty.

"What you want for Christmas, Grandma?" she asked as she gathered their bags so they could catch a cab.

"I just wanna see both y'all happy," she said simply.

Gigi smiled. "Come on," she said. "There's gotta be something."

Grandma thought for a minute. "It would be nice to get these old kidneys fixed," she admitted.

Gigi felt like crying. Her grandmother never complained about her condition, and to hear her admit that she was bothered by it made Gigi more determined than ever to find a way to get Grandma the one thing she wanted for Christmas.

* * *

Back on the block, residents braved the cold weather even though over two inches of snow had fallen earlier. The freezing wind carried with it the rotten stench from the garbage bags piled at the curb in front of the six-story tenement building.

Sporting a bubble North Face jacket, Andrew chilled in the lobby, awaiting the night rush. He watched as a cab dropped Grandma and Gigi off in front of the building.

Two pimped-out BMW 525s, one red, one black, pulled up. The Diaz brothers hopped out like they owned the block. Though they didn't hold the deed, in the drug game, 141st Street was their prized possession. Their deadly crew had the area on lock. Chico was the head, and naturally Joe fell second in command. Everybody on the block stayed on point when the Diaz brothers came through.

Grandma knew the siblings well. She had babysat both brothers when they were toddlers. As a result, both men treated Grandma and her two grandkids as if they were family.

Tall, rail thin, with a baby face, Chico definitely didn't look like the monster people knew him to be. Greeting them with a warm smile, Chico planted a kiss on Grandma's cheek and tossed Gigi a nod. "Hey, ma."

"Let me help you wit' that, Grandma," Chico insisted, taking the bags from Grandma's hand. The trio disappeared into the building while Joe waited on the stoop, chatting it up with Andrew.

Upstairs in the apartment, Gigi watched as Chico followed Grandma into the bedroom and closed the door. A few minutes later, Chico emerged from the room, waved at Gigi, and left the apartment.

"He dropped off more bundles?" Gigi asked.

Grandma nodded. She had been working for the Diaz brothers for the last five months.

Gigi could remember the day Grandma first told her she needed to have surgery. Soon after, Gigi noticed things started to change. Grandma seemed to have way too much money. At first she told Gigi she had gotten an increase in her disability check.

Gigi also noticed Chico and Joe had started stopping by more frequently than ever before, and they always went into Grandma's room and closed the door. And right around that time, fiends from the neighborhood started popping up at the apartment looking for Grandma. Gigi knew the disability story wasn't adding up. Grandma was definitely hiding something.

The more Gigi questioned her grandmother about the strange visits, the more evasive Grandma became. Finally one day she broke down and told Gigi what Gigi had already figured out: Grandma was selling crack for the Diaz brothers. With Medicare covering only half the cost of the operation, Grandma had approached the two brothers about working for them, and they'd accepted her with open arms.

. . .

The next evening Gigi arrived home from work to find she had the house to herself. Figuring Grandma was still out for her dialysis treatment and her cousin Andrew was running the streets, she decided to give her new boyfriend, Mel, a call.

"Hey, papi," she said the minute he picked up.

"What up, ma?" he asked.

"Just thinking about you. I thought I'd call to see what you're up to. I miss you," she said.

Final exams were the next week, and Gigi had spent the last few days studying.

"You wanna get together tonight?" Mel asked.

"That sounds good," she said, realizing she needed a break. "You want me to come over to your place?"

"Most definitely," Mel said in his deep, sexy voice, and Gigi felt a tingle go down her spine. "I'll come scoop you."

"Don't be speeding," she said. "You already have more than enough tickets."

Mel laughed. "See you in a minute," he said before hanging up.

Gigi was just about to change clothes when the phone rang. Sighing, she went to answer it and tried not to groan when she heard the familiar greeting: "You have a call from a prison inmate, Rasheed Hall. To accept the charges, press one. . . ."

Gigi reluctantly accepted the call and settled on the sofa. She hadn't talked to her ex in a while. He was a drug dealer who had been sentenced to forty-five years in prison for murdering a set of twins, and she realized she hadn't missed him.

"Hey, mami," Rasheed greeted.

"Hey," she said drily, studying her nails before she grabbed the television remote and began flipping through the channels.

"You miss me?" he asked.

"Why you always ask me that?" she said, avoiding the question.

He laughed. "Yo, ma, I just wanted to check on you . . . make sure you didn't need anything. You all right?"

"I'm fine," she said.

"My boy, Big Ben, tell me you're still refusing the love I'm sending you," he said.

"Yes," she said, being as vague as he was about the money he sent her.

Although he was in jail, he was still making as much as he had when he was out, if not more.

"You need anything, let me know," he said.

"I gotta go," she said suddenly, realizing she had no desire to talk to him.

"Wait," he screamed before she hung up.

She put the phone back to her ear. "What?" she said.

"When you coming to see me?"

"I don't know," she said. "Now isn't a good time. I'm getting ready for finals, and you know the holidays are coming up."

"Can't you come this week? My cousin has a package for me, and she can't bring it because the doctor put her on bed rest."

"Get someone else to do it," she said.

"Gigi, can you do this one thing for me?" he pleaded.

She sighed, mentally kicking herself for agreeing to what he was asking. She couldn't believe that he still had that effect on her after being in prison for almost three years.

"I'll come after the holiday," she said.

"No, I need you to come this week," he insisted.

"Can't she mail it?" she asked.

"No, it's too important. Just do me this one favor. I promise I won't ask you for anything else," he said.

She snorted, knowing that wasn't true.

"I'll see what I can do," she said before hanging up.

After relaxing for a little while, Gigi decided to fix dinner since she knew Grandma would be tired after her dialysis treatment. Just as she got the food started, her cousin Andrew walked in.

"What's up?" he said, heading straight to the refrigerator.

He grabbed a forty and took a huge swallow before turning to her.

"Hey, Andrew," she said, getting up to check the steaks.

"Where's Grandma?" he asked.

"She had dialysis today," Gigi said, flipping the sizzling meat. Sometimes she went with Grandma to keep her company, but Grandma preferred for her to stay home and keep the sales rolling in.

Andrew didn't respond. He had never said it, but Gigi knew he couldn't stand to see their grandmother in pain.

As Grandma grew sicker, reluctantly she started depending on Gigi and Andrew to hold her down whenever she was too tired to serve the fiends. She made them promise they would never sell drugs outside of the apartment and for no one else but her. Gigi took pride in helping her grandma.

Suddenly, someone knocked on the apartment door. At six-thirty in the evening Gigi figured it had to be a crackhead. Throughout the day and night a steady flow of fiends came through. Most were straight-up junkies; others were truckers and blue-collar workers.

Gigi loved the truck drivers because they were more likely to buy one or more bundles in a single transaction. Sometimes they copped the entire stash, leaving Grandma sold out for the night.

Gigi made a beeline for the closet in Grandma's room. She grabbed an open bundle from the stash and hightailed it to the front door.

Removing a .45 from his waistband, Andrew followed Gigi. He always held her down during transactions. Positioning himself behind the door, Andrew racked the slide, ready to blast if anything jumped off. Then he signaled Gigi to open up.

Clutching a wrinkled twenty-dollar bill, a Hispanic fiend stuck his bony hand through the crack in the door.

"One or two?" Gigi asked. The price of each crack vial was ten dollars.

"Two . . . let me get two."

Gigi dropped two white-top vials into the fiend's open palm and shut the door, locking both dead bolts.

Thank God nothing ever pops off, Gigi thought as she watched her cousin kiss the barrel. *Andrew's way too trigger happy.* Thanks to the Diaz brothers, Grandma had the building on lock. They put word out on the block that no one but Grandma and her grandkids could move work out of the building.

"Have you thought about what you're getting Grandma for Christmas?" she asked as they returned to the kitchen.

Andrew shrugged and took another sip of his drink. "Nah," he said nonchalantly.

Gigi threw down the fork she was using to turn the meat and stared at him. "How can you be so selfish?" she asked. "Grandma went out and spent hundreds—maybe thousands—of dollars on you for Christmas, and you haven't thought of one measly thing you can get her?"

"Yo, what's your problem?" Andrew asked, looking at her like she was crazy.

Gigi sighed and took a seat at the table. "I'm sorry," she finally said softly.

Andrew took a seat across from her. "What's going on?" he asked.

Although they were cousins, Grandma had raised them both, so in a lot of ways they were closer than most brothers and sisters.

"Grandma told me the only thing she really wants for Christmas is new kidneys," she said, finding herself near tears again.

"So we'll make the money back," Andrew said. It was the closest he had ever come to admitting that Grandma was sick.

"How?" Gigi asked. "How the hell we gonna make twenty-five thousand dollars in, like, three weeks?"

"I don't care. I'll make the money," Andrew said, getting up from the table. He pulled up his jeans, which were sagging around his butt, tucked the gun on his waist, and headed toward the front door.

Gigi ran over to stop him. "What you gonna do?" she asked.

"I'ma get some paper," he said, trying to step around her.

"How?" she asked.

Andrew looked her in the eye. "Trust me, you don't wanna know," he said.

"You promised Grandma you were gonna stop robbing people, Andrew," she said sharply.

"Yeah, whatever," he said as the front door opened.

Grandma walked in, looking tired, and Gigi hurried over to help her.

"How was dialysis, Grandma?" she asked, kissing her on the cheek before helping her out of her coat.

"It was fine, baby," her grandma said, giving her a tight smile.

Gigi helped her over to the sofa then went to get her a glass of water. When she came back, Andrew was gone, and she made a mental note to talk to him about his thieving ways. There had to be another way to help Grandma.

Gigi got dressed for her date with Mel, although she really wasn't in the mood to go out.

Chapter Three

$\mathcal{B}$y the time Gigi returned home the next morning from spending the night at Mel's place, Grandma was still asleep, and it looked as though Andrew hadn't been home.

After checking on Grandma, Gigi thought about going to bed, but she realized she wasn't sleepy, so she studied instead. It was around nine o'clock in the morning when she finally heard Andrew come in.

"Where have you been?" she asked before the front door could even close.

"Where you think?" he said, barely able to catch his breath. His round face was red and sweaty.

"What happened?" she asked.

"These dudes were chasing me," he said.

"Why?" she asked, peeping out the window.

"Get away from there," Andrew yelled as he snatched her back. "Someone might see you."

After they settled on the sofa, Gigi turned to him. "You know Grandma doesn't like you stealing," she said.

"Grandma's the reason I'm doing what I do," he said, removing a balled-up handkerchief from his baggy jeans. He opened it on the cushion, revealing three crack bundles.

"Where'd you get that?"

"I stole it from some bitch-ass nigga's stash two blocks over."

Gigi didn't know what to say. While she didn't agree with what Andrew was doing, she understood why he was doing it. His heart was in the right place. She was willing to do anything for Grandma, too.

As though reading her thoughts, Andrew turned to her. "This would be a lot easier if you helped me," he said.

"Help you?" she repeated. "What . . . rob cats?"

"Nah, I ain't talking 'bout that," he said. "If we both hit the block and bump off them bundles, we'd make the money for Grandma's kidney transplant twice as fast."

Gigi realized Andrew made sense, but she didn't like the idea of standing on a corner making drug sales. It was nerve-racking enough doing it from the comfort of Grandma's apartment. Plus she had seen how badly things could turn out when her ex-boyfriend went to jail, and she had vowed never to put herself in that position.

"Do it for Grandma," Andrew pleaded, knowing good and well Gigi would do anything for her.

Gigi sat thinking for a while. She thought about all Grandma had done for her and was still doing for her despite being sick. She tried to think of another way to get the money, but she couldn't come up with anything else.

"Well, if we plan on making twenty-five grand, we need more work than that," she said. "We gotta get our hands on some more white."

"I'ma step to Chico."

"There's no way he's gonna do it," she said. "He know Grandma don't want us hustling unless she approves of it. And you know she ain't."

"Quit tripping," Andrew said. "It don't hurt to ask."

Thinking of a way to get their hands on the product they needed, Gigi's ex popped into mind. Asking him was almost as bad as hustling. She sighed and turned to her cousin.

"Let me holla at Rasheed first," she said. "If it doesn't work out, then you can ask Chico."

"A'ight . . . bet," Andrew said.

* * *

Gigi got up *really* early on a cold Thursday morning and spent hours trying to sleep as she traveled to Attica. After making her way through security, Gigi waited anxiously in the drafty visitor's area of the prison.

Not wanting to hear anyone's mouth, she had lied and told Grandma and her boyfriend, Mel, that she had to work when she really had the day off. She shivered as she wondered why it was taking longer than usual for them to call Rasheed's name. It had begun snowing hard a few minutes after she arrived, so she was ready to get her visit over with and get started on the long trip back home.

She still couldn't believe she was asking her ex for his help. The thought of having to rely on Rasheed didn't appeal to her, but she figured with her ex's street connections, he would be able to get her what she needed.

Finally, Rasheed walked into the visiting room sporting a

state-issued orange jumpsuit. Gigi noticed the angry expression on his face as he sat on the plastic chair facing her.

"What's good?" Rasheed mumbled.

"What's up wit' you?" Gigi asked, adjusting her chair closer.

Rasheed shrugged. "I keep hearing you too good for my money now."

Although she and Rasheed weren't together anymore, he still tried to look out for her. He had his people bring her money a few times a month, but she always refused to accept it. Since she lived with Grandma, her expenses were low, so the money she made from her part-time job took care of all her needs.

"I don't need any handouts," Gigi replied, leaning in closer, "but I do need a big favor."

"What?" Rasheed snapped, annoyed she wasn't there for the sole purpose of seeing him.

"I need you to hook me up with one of your connects."

"Why?" Rasheed asked more out of curiosity than concern. "You wanna be a hustla all a sudden?"

Gigi shook her head. "This is serious. I gotta pay for Grandma's kidney transplant," she answered with a concerned expression. "She's real sick."

"I'm sorry to hear that," Rasheed said, immediately changing his attitude. "Don't worry. I'll set it up for you."

They talked a few more minutes before a corrections officer tapped Rasheed on the shoulder, advising him the visit was over. They hugged each other good-bye.

When Gigi got home late that night, Grandma was already

sleeping soundly. She checked Andrew's room and was surprised to find him holed up in there flipping through the TV channels.

"Hey," she said.

"What's up, Gigi?" he said, never taking his eyes off the TV screen.

"It's done," she said simply, as she stood in the doorway.

"What's done?" he asked, finally looking at her.

She just stared at him a second before rolling her eyes. "Rasheed's gonna hook it up."

Andrew's eyes got big as he realized what she was saying. He jumped off the bed, ran over to her, grabbed her by the hand, and dragged her into the room. "Yo, we about to get paid," he said excitedly.

"Look, we only doing this for Grandma," she insisted. "Once we make the money we need to pay for her transplant, we're out. Agreed?"

Andrew nodded, but Gigi knew he wasn't listening to her.

She got in his face. "Agreed?" she repeated.

He finally looked at her. "Whatever," he said.

"Andrew, we aren't gonna do anything stupid," she warned. "I'm serious. No dumb shit. We just gonna make this paper. This ain't about us. It's about Grandma. Promise me we're finished after Christmas."

"Okay, Gigi," he finally agreed.

· · ·

Two weeks before Christmas, Rasheed made good on his promise. Gigi was headed to work one morning when Rasheed's best friend, Big Ben, met her at the corner.

Without even bothering to greet her, Ben handed her a back-pack and turned and walked in the other direction. Gigi knew what was inside and nervously looked up and down the street, wondering why he would do something so out in the open. After realizing she was alone on the street, she shouldered the backpack and headed back to the building.

"Back so soon?" Grandma asked, making her way down the hallway.

Gigi nodded, trying not to look guilty. "I forgot something."

"It looks like you found something," Grandma said, nodding at the backpack. "I didn't see you leave with that."

"Oh, I left it upstairs at my friend Tiffany's apartment yester-day," Gigi lied nervously.

Grandma looked at her suspiciously. "What did you forget?" she asked.

"Oh . . . uh, I hafta tell Andrew something," she said, inching past Grandma and making her way to her cousin's room. She didn't look back, but she could feel Grandma's eyes on her back.

Once she made it to her cousin's room, she closed the door and leaned against it, trying to calm down. She hated lying to Grandma, but she knew the older woman wouldn't approve of what she was doing.

Andrew was still asleep, so she shook him. It wasn't until he sat up that she noticed the naked female lying next to him. "Get dressed. Meet me in my room," she ordered, ignoring the girl.

It took Andrew a good five minutes to make it to her room, and by the time he did, Gigi had thought of several reasons why she shouldn't do what she was about to do. Each time she would change her mind, as though led by some unseen force, her gaze would wander to Grandma's picture, and she would think of all that Grandma had done for her. She couldn't even begin to repay her, but she could try.

"What?" Andrew asked the minute he walked into the room.

"Where's your friend?" she asked, not really caring.

"Gone," he said.

Gigi went to the door and looked up and down the hall to make sure all was clear before coming back into the room and locking the door. She grabbed the backpack and emptied its contents on the bed.

Andrew's eyes grew big as he examined the quarter brick of cocaine wrapped in cellophane.

"We need to flip all this in two weeks if we still wanna get all the money for Grandma. Remember, her surgery is January fourth. You down?"

Andrew nodded.

"Okay, then now I need you to show me how to cook this up. I have a hard enough time boiling water." Even though she handled crack almost every day, she had never took part in the cooking process.

For the next two hours, Andrew explained more than she ever wanted to know about cooking up coke. After they were done, he took her to a friend's house and began the laborious process of turning the cocaine into crack.

They agreed they would start selling the next morning. Gigi spent the night tossing and turning, trying to tell herself that what she was doing really wasn't hurting anyone. By the time it was six A.M. she was still awake.

Andrew came bounding through her door at six-thirty, already dressed.

"What you doing up so early?" she asked.

"I'm trying to catch the morning rush," he said, grinning. "It's time to get paid."

Gigi sighed. "I'm serious, Andrew. Once we reach the goal, we're out. It's bad enough we're doing this when we promised Grandma we never would. I don't wanna get in any trouble."

"Whatever," he said. "You coming? The fiends need their medicine before they go to work."

Gigi reluctantly got dressed. By the time she made it down the hall, Andrew was sitting at the table while Grandma prepared him breakfast.

"Good morning," she said, hoping the guilt over what she was about to do didn't show on her face.

"Hey, baby," Grandma said, smiling and giving her a kiss.

"Hey, Grandma. How you feeling today?" Gigi asked.

"Just fine," Grandma said.

Something in her voice made Gigi look at her. Grandma looked a little pale, and she seemed tired.

"No, you're not," Gigi said, leading her over to a chair.

"I'll be fine," Grandma insisted, but Gigi ignored her as she went to finish preparing breakfast.

"Do you have a treatment today?" she asked. She immediately felt guilty at having to ask the question. There used to be a time when she knew Grandma's dialysis schedule better than Grandma did, but the last week had been so crazy, she couldn't remember.

Grandma nodded. "Do you think you could take me?" she asked.

Andrew's eyes grew big. "Uh, she can't take you today, Grandma," he stuttered when he saw Gigi about to give in. "She promised me she was gonna help me with something."

Gigi felt horrible. She knew that Grandma really wasn't feeling well if she had even asked for Gigi's help.

"I'm sorry," she said. "Can I call Access-a-Ride for you?"

"Thank you, baby," Grandma said, leaning heavily in her chair.

She looked as though she was having trouble breathing, and Gigi hurried the few steps to her. "Are you sure you're okay?" she asked.

Grandma just nodded.

Gigi threw Andrew a look. Hustling would have to wait. There was no way she was going to leave Grandma alone.

"I'll take you," she said, ignoring Andrew shaking his head.

Grandma smiled her thanks, and Gigi went back to the bedroom to grab her purse.

"You go on without me," she said to Andrew as she helped Grandma into her coat. "I'll get with you later."

Andrew headed out the door without saying a word.

• • •

By the time Gigi made it home that afternoon she was depressed. After Grandma's dialysis treatment, they had seen a doctor, and things were not looking good. Grandma definitely needed the kidney transplant. Gigi knew she had to do whatever it took to get the money.

After she made sure Grandma was comfortable, Gigi grabbed

some product and headed out. She joined her cousin, who was now standing on the stoop. "Damn, it's cold out here," she said.

"You just came back outside, and you already bitching," Andrew replied, sucking his teeth.

Gigi rolled her eyes at Andrew. "Why don't you mind your business?"

Suddenly, gunshots rang out as a gunman chased a fleeing teenager into the middle of the street. The intended target was headed straight in Gigi and Andrew's direction.

"Get down! Get down!" Andrew yelled as bullets went buzzing over their heads. They both ducked, quickly crawling into the lobby of the building.

From the vestibule, Gigi and Andrew watched in horror as a bullet slammed into the back of the slender teen's back, sending him sprawling a few feet away from the stoop. The hooded gunman aimed the revolver at the teen's head and shot him point-blank. His body jerked violently for a few seconds before going limp. A pool of blood ran along the sidewalk, spilling into the gutter.

Still in shock, Gigi knew from the blank look in the guy's eyes that he was dead. Making matters worse, Gigi recognized both the killer and the victim. They had been her classmates in high school.

The responding officers pushed their way through the growing crowd gathered around the corpse.

Watching from the stoop, Gigi bowed her head, saying a silent prayer for his soul and asking God to forgive her for not coming forward as a witness because she wasn't the snitch type. What happened on the block stayed on the block; Grandma had instilled that in Gigi.

Gigi was an eighties baby, raised in the South Bronx during the wild crack era. By the time she turned nineteen, Gigi had seen more drug dealing and bloodshed than most of the police officers working her neighborhood.

Now she realized selling on the block wasn't as easy as it looked, but before long she got the hang of it, and, despite the murder, by the end of the night she had made close to a thousand dollars.

Although it was a decent amount, she knew it wasn't nearly enough to help Grandma, so she decided she had to step up her game the next day.

Between school and her part-time job, Gigi barely had time to hustle, so she was relieved now that winter break had arrived and she could focus on making money at night. She thought about taking time off from her job in a local dentist's office, but she didn't want to arouse Grandma's suspicion.

By the time Andrew made it in, she had fallen asleep, and when she got up the next morning, he was already gone—if he had come home at all.

Chapter Four

Grandma looked much better the next day. Gigi made her some bacon and eggs and kept her company while she ate, all the while thinking of how she could make more money.

It had occurred to Gigi the night before that she was wasting her time trying to sell crack or coke in her Bronx neighborhood. The block was already saturated with hustlers. She had to go to where the big money was—Manhattan—but she didn't know how she could get access to the people who had the kind of cash she needed.

She was so deep in thought it took her a second to notice the box wrapped in red paper Grandma had placed on her breakfast plate.

"Grandma, whose gift is that?" she asked curiously.

"I don't know," Grandma said, unable to contain her denture-filled smile.

"Yes, you do," Gigi said excitedly. "Is it for me?"

"Open it and find out," Grandma urged, looking just as excited.

"Oh, my God, is this what I think it is, Grandma?" Gigi asked as she peered into the box. She had ripped the bow off and tore off the paper without waiting for her to answer.

Gigi's face lit up as she spotted a shiny gold chain with a Lazarus medallion. Tears welled up in her eyes as she looked up at Grandma.

"Thank you," she said, barely getting the words out as she started to choke up.

Gigi knew her grandmother understood just how much the Lazarus chain meant to her. Grandma was a God-fearing Catholic and had always taught Gigi that Saint Lazarus would protect her from all evil.

"You're welcome," Grandma answered. "Christmas came early."

Every year Grandma surprised Gigi and Andrew with an early Christmas present, and every year Gigi was genuinely surprised.

Gigi gave her grandma a long bear hug, then gestured for help putting the chain on. Once it was on, she admired herself in the mirror. "It's beautiful," she said, gently stroking the chain. "Thank you, Grandma."

"You're welcome, baby."

"Do you know how much I love you?" Gigi said suddenly.

"Sure do," Grandma said, "but it's still not as much as I love you. I'd do anything for my grandbabies."

"And I'd do anything for you, Grandma," Gigi said.

Grandma's words gave Gigi the motivation to get on her grind, and at that moment an idea hit her.

A young white guy, Scott, from her accounting class worked down on Wall Street as a junior broker with a bunch of big spenders. According to him, his business associates worked hard and partied even harder, especially when it came to snorting coke.

Gigi found Scott's number in her spiral notebook and gave him a call. She told Scott she had something for him but couldn't talk about it over the phone. He invited her to stop by his office.

She made sure Grandma was settled, then she grabbed her backpack and headed out. As Gigi waited for the train, she wondered how many customers Scott would introduce her to. No matter what, she knew she had to make it happen.

The panoramic windows in the brokerage firm's office gave a great view of Manhattan's skyscraper-filled skyline. Entering Scott's cubicle, Gigi noticed Scott appeared stressed out, even though it was barely eleven A.M. Only twenty-two years old, he looked more like thirty-two.

"You okay?" she asked, trying to appear concerned.

Scott looked at her strangely. "Why you ask?"

"Just noticed you seemed a little stressed," she said.

"Shit . . . my performance rate has fallen short the last two months. Now, my boss is riding my ass. If I don't turn things around quick, my job's down the toilet."

Gigi nodded understandingly. "It'll work out."

"Maybe," he said. "I know you didn't come all this way to play Dr. Phil."

"Whatever." Gigi chuckled.

Scott smiled slightly, motioning to a chair. "Take a load off. Let's get down to the nitty-gritty."

Gigi sat down.

"For you to be in the city and it ain't even a school day, this must be important."

"You know it," Gigi said as she unzipped the backpack and pulled out a glassine bag filled with a gram of powdered cocaine. "I got coke for sale."

Scott's face, redder than a ripe tomato, suddenly brightened. "Well, why didn't you just say so? What's the damage?"

"For you . . . a hundred."

He reached into his pocket, retrieved his wallet, and pulled out five crisp twenty-dollar bills, handing them to her. "This stuff good, right?" he asked.

"The best."

"Okay, then let's see what you're working with," he said, finally managing a full smile.

Gigi tossed him the glassine bag.

Scott tapped some coke onto a glass coaster resting on his desk and used a business card to cut up two lines. Using a rolled-up fifty he snorted a line. Welcoming the oncoming high, he tilted his head back for a few moments.

"Oh yeah, Gigi," Scott said, straightening up. "Best believe I have quite a few friends that'd love to make your acquaintance. Unless you wanna introduce me straight to your connect."

She gave him a small smile. "If I did that, you wouldn't need me."

Scott stood and stretched his arms. "Give me a few minutes while I see how many takers we have," he said, before hurrying out of the cubicle.

Gigi breathed a sigh of relief. She had made her first sale, and it looked like a few more sales were on the way.

With Scott hooking her up with more customers, the rest of the day went pretty smoothly. By the time she made it home that evening, she had made almost three thousand dollars, and she had a bunch of business cards from various Wall Street brokers. She had a feeling she was going to get a lot of repeat business.

Apparently Wall Street stressed out a lot of its employees because in a week's time Gigi had dozens of repeat customers, and after reupping twice she had managed to put away almost thirteen thousand dollars.

Andrew hadn't been so lucky. He had managed to make only a thousand dollars, despite Gigi's advice to move his business out of the Bronx. One night, in frustration, Gigi decided to accompany Andrew to see why he wasn't making much money.

That night, Andrew headed out to one of his usual spots. He

posted up on the corner of 141st Street and Saint Ann's in front of the corner bodega, trying to knock off a bundle.

"Got that fire, mami," Andrew said to a passing woman who looked like she could have been a fiend or a wino.

The woman looked interested and staggered over to him.

"Yo, baby, give me another free hit," she begged as though Gigi wasn't there. "I'll make you feel good again."

Andrew looked embarrassed. "Not tonight," he said, pushing her on down the street.

"So that's why you haven't been making money," Gigi said angrily. "You've been giving the shit away?"

"I don't know what you're talking about," Andrew said, gazing down the street.

"You gotta stay focused. We're out here for Grandma."

He offered a few more passersby product, and only one agreed.

After Gigi calmed down a little, she focused on the task at hand. "Have you sold any of the coke?" she asked.

Andrew shrugged. "A little," he said. "It's too hard to move. Fiends checking for that rock."

Gigi popped him upside the head. "Have you lost your mind?" she asked. "The coke ain't moving 'cause you're pushing it to these junkies who can't afford it. I told you you gotta hit Manhattan where them white folks at," she said. "You claim to be a hustler, but you sure getting hustled. You're probably giving away more product than you selling."

Andrew looked at the ground guiltily.

"Did you forget we're doing this for Grandma?"

Before he could respond, a shadow fell over them.

"Get yo' faggot ass up off my corna, nigga," a dark-skinned

man in his early twenties demanded as he strode up to Andrew. A black do-rag covered his nappy afro, and the latest urban fashion hung off his medium-build frame.

"Fuck you, Rob," Andrew shouted. "This ain't yo corner, bitch!"

Without warning, Rob slugged Andrew in the mouth. The impact sent Andrew stumbling backward into the brick wall of the grocery store, which was the only thing that kept him from falling flat on his ass. Gigi stared in shock for a moment before she rushed over to aid her cousin.

Before she could check to see if he was okay, Andrew pushed her aside and pulled a knife out of his back pocket, flicked open the blade, and charged Rob, who tried to sidestep him. He still managed to plunge the blade halfway into Rob's left thigh.

"Ahhhhh . . . shit," Rob said, staring down at the blood trickling from the gaping hole in his pant leg. "Why the fuck you stab me, muthafucka?" He covered his wound with his hand, trying to stem the flow of blood.

Gigi grabbed her cousin's arm.

Stepping between the trio, Chico seemed to pop up out of thin air.

"Both y'all niggas betta stop causin' a scene on my block." Chico pulled out a fifty-dollar bill and slid it into Rob's free hand. "Go get that stitched up."

"This shit ain't over," Rob warned, shooting Andrew a death stare.

Chico decided to send a warning of his own. "Don't even think 'bout retaliating or you gonna deal wit' me. You hear me, Rob?"

Rob nodded reluctantly.

"Now take yo' ass to the hospital," Chico ordered, staring Rob down. "And you better catch a bad case of amnesia when they ask you what happened."

With his head hung low, Rob limped over to the curb and hailed the first gypsy cab to pass by. He climbed into the back-seat, still holding his wounded leg.

"That nigga's getting his," Andrew snapped, still clutching the knife tightly. "Watch."

"Put that away. What's wrong with you?" Chico asked, grabbing the knife from him and tossing it into the sewage drain on the corner.

"I didn't come out looking for problems," Andrew fumed. "That nigga put his hands on me. Tryin' to put fear in my heart. Fuck that. I'll stab his ass again."

"Just chill," Gigi demanded. "You too hardheaded."

Chico added his two cents. "I'm telling you for yo' own good, leave that shit alone."

Andrew balled up both fists angrily. "Long as he don't say shit, it's all good."

"You too hardheaded and ambitious," Chico said. "I gotta keep my eye on you. Next thing you know you'll be coming for my spot," he said playfully. "Do Grandma even know you out here pumping?"

Andrew stared at the ground.

"Do she?" Chico asked forcefully.

"Nah."

"A'ight, then take y'all asses upstairs."

"Look, Chico, you know Grandma's very sick," Gigi blurted

out. "When the cops raided the crib, they took the money she had saved for the surgery."

"Damn. Why didn't she tell me?" Chico replied, rubbing his chin.

"You know how she is."

"How much the operation cost again?"

"Twenty-five thousand."

Chico's mouth seemed wired shut for a moment or two. "When she need it?"

"Before January fourth."

"I'll see what I can do," Chico assured her before turning to Andrew. "I don't wanna see you on this corner. Stick to that stoop of yours like a fly on shit."

"Whatever," Andrew snapped, as if he wasn't frightened by Chico's ruthless reputation.

"Never take my kindness for weakness. You family, and I'd never cause you no real harm," Chico said, anger flashing in his eyes. "But I'll slap fire out yo' ass if you disrespect me again."

Andrew had the good sense to look nervous. "My bad," he said, before walking off with Gigi.

Chapter Five

The week leading up to Christmas, Gigi worked harder than she had ever worked before. Although she knew Andrew was doing the best he could, she realized he was fine selling to the dope fiends on their block while she was determined to sell to a higher clientele.

Through sheer determination she had already managed to stack eighteen thousand dollars, thanks to the stockbrokers, which left them only seven grand shy of their goal.

With only three days left until Christmas Day, Gigi and Grandma lay sleeping one night when they were awakened by a gunshot in the apartment.

Not knowing what was happening in the living room, Gigi knew her cousin was in trouble because he was asleep on the couch when she last saw him. She dashed into Andrew's room, searching for the gun her cousin kept hidden there.

Gigi heard the intruder bump into the wall as he ran past Andrew's room toward the front door. The intruder yelled "Fuck, fuck!" as he struggled with the locks. Just as she found the gun under the mattress, she heard the apartment door slam into the wall as the man made his escape. She turned in time to see Andrew fly by. Clutching the .45 tightly, she quickly followed, ready to bust her gun if necessary.

The intruder hit the stairwell like a bat out of hell, almost tripping as he descended the staircase, two steps at a time. Andrew busted through the stairwell door just as the intruder reached the half landing. Raising a .380, Andrew let off two rounds that just missed their mark. The man barely dodged death as he dipped around the partition separating the lower staircase from the upper one.

Dashing out the building the intruder almost knocked over a fiend and leaped into a black sedan idling at the curb. The car squealed off before the intruder could shut the door.

Flying onto the stoop, Andrew took aim at the car disappearing down the street and unloaded the rest of the clip.

Hearing the wail of police sirens in the distance, Gigi knew it was just a matter of time before the cops pulled up. She grabbed Andrew by the shoulder.

"Let's go," she yelled, running back inside the building. "We gotta get rid of the drugs before the cops get here."

As they reached the second-floor hallway, Grandma was standing halfway in the apartment doorway and halfway in the hall.

"Andrew, you bleeding!" she cried out when she spotted her grandson's bloody head. Bloodstains soiled the right half of his shirt.

"I'm okay, Grandma," Andrew assured her as Gigi spun around to look. "He just grazed me."

"Thank God," Grandma said, rubbing the rosary beads hanging around her neck.

Caught up in the moment, Gigi hadn't realized her cousin had been hurt. "You sure you okay?" she asked.

"Yes," Andrew replied, shoving her forward. "Let's clear the house 'fore we all end up back in jail."

As Andrew's words sunk in, the trio rushed into the apartment and tossed all the drugs, money, and guns into two book bags.

Gigi grabbed both bags and hurried out of the apartment, running up one flight to her friend's place. She pounded on the door, her leg shaking nervously as she waited. Finally she heard footsteps growing closer.

"Who is it?" a woman asked through the door.

"It's me," Gigi said, trying not to shout.

Gigi heard a series of latches being unlocked before the door swung open.

"What's wrong, girl?" a slender female asked as Gigi rushed into the apartment. "Is everything okay? I thought I heard gunshots."

Gigi didn't answer until she reached the living room and made sure no one else was around. "Someone tried to rob us, Tiffany. My cousin got grazed, but he's all right."

"Oh shit," Tiffany replied, dumbfounded.

"I need you to stash this," Gigi said, dropping both book bags on the couch.

"What's in the bags?"

"Trust me, you don't wanna know," Gigi replied, before turning on her heels and heading for the door. "I'll be back for them later."

No sooner than Gigi returned to the apartment, the police were ringing the bell. Answering the door, Gigi recognized the two detectives standing in the hallway with four uniformed cops. The same two detectives that had questioned her at the precinct the day Grandma's apartment was raided. The two plainclothes narcs invited themselves inside.

Minutes later, EMS arrived and attended to Andrew's wound in the living room while the detectives questioned Gigi and Grandma in the hallway.

"Way I figure, word must've leaked Grandma has large sums of cash and drugs stashed in the apartment," the white detective said, staring at Grandma before turning his cold blue gaze on Gigi. "Why else would someone break in?"

"It definitely wasn't for the fine art," the black detective added.

"Grandma already told you, my cousin stopped selling drugs," Gigi snapped, glaring right back at the white detective, showing no signs of fear. "Andrew almost died, and y'all treating us like the criminals. There ain't no drugs in the house. You and your dumb-ass partner can look."

The black detective's nostrils flared as he spoke up. "You got such a fresh mouth for a young lady."

"Damn right," Gigi replied, rolling her eyes.

"I can't help people who refuse to help themselves," the white detective said, shaking his head in frustration as he glanced over at his angered partner. "Let's get outta here."

"Yeah, good idea," Gigi said, as the two detectives made a bee-line for the staircase.

• • •

When the Diaz brothers found out about the home invasion, both drug dealers were livid. Chico and Joe couldn't believe someone had had the balls to fuck with Grandma and her family.

Grandma pounded the coffee table with her fist. "Nobody fucks with my blood," she said, through clenched teeth. "I want y'all to find that bastard and make him pay."

"We got you," Chico said, rubbing his palms together. "We gonna make an example outta this muthafucka."

Joe cut in. "Only problem, we don't have the slightest idea who the hell we looking for."

"It's only a matter of time before the 'hood starts talking," Chico replied.

In Grandma's bedroom, Gigi and Andrew had their ears

pressed to the closed door, eavesdropping on the conversation taking place in the living room. They had never heard Grandma curse before. Matter of fact, they had never seen her lose her cool. But that night, they saw a side of Grandma they'd never expected.

Chapter Six

On Christmas Eve, Gigi sat counting all the money she had made. She couldn't believe she had actually managed to make close to twenty-eight thousand dollars in such a short time. She would be able to give Grandma just what she wanted for Christmas: a new life with new kidneys.

. . .

Christmas morning, Gigi got up and decided she just wanted to spend the holiday with her family in peace.

She smiled to herself as she turned off the hot shower and stepped out of the tub to dry herself off.

. . .

Up bright and early, Grandma was already busy cooking Christmas dinner. The aroma from the cooking food radiated throughout the apartment. All the noise Grandma was making in the kitchen finally woke up Andrew.

A few seconds later, he walked into the kitchen with his head still bandaged, rubbing his red eyes. "Mmmm . . . that shit smells good," he said with a yawn. "I can't wait to eat."

"It does smell good," Gigi said, as she joined them in the crowded kitchen. "Merry Christmas."

Planting a kiss on Grandma's cheek, she glanced at the pots and pans cooking on the stove and then greeted her cousin. "Morning, knucklehead. Merry Christmas to you, too."

"By the time everyone gets here in a few hours, the food'll be ready, and we can all eat," Grandma said over her shoulder as she stirred the collard greens bubbling in one of the pots.

"Grandma, that's still hours away. I'm starvin'," Andrew said, rubbing his fat belly for emphasis.

Following her cousin's lead, Gigi held her washboard stomach and added, "You ain't the only one."

Grandma laughed. "I knew you two would be hungry," she said, reaching into the microwave and pulling out two plates overflowing with breakfast food. She placed one in front of each of her grandchildren then went back to bustling around the kitchen.

"Aren't you going to eat?" Gigi asked, cutting into a sausage link.

"I'm not really hungry. I ate a little earlier," she said.

"You're feeling okay, right?" Gigi asked.

"I'm fine, baby. It's Christmas Day. I couldn't be better."

They spent the morning laughing and talking, and Gigi thought several times about giving Grandma her present before the family arrived. Now that she had the money, it occurred to her that Grandma would ask all kinds of questions about where she had gotten it, and she didn't know how to explain it.

Finally, she decided that she wasn't going to tell her grandma where she'd gotten the money, but she was going to insist she take it.

Later that afternoon, Gigi and Andrew were glued to the TV, playing one of his new PlayStation games, when the doorbell rang. Pausing the video game, Gigi glanced at the clock hanging on the living room wall. It was five minutes after two. She skipped down the hallway and opened the front door to find her mother and younger sister, Lulu, standing in the dim hallway. They had several containers of food and plenty of gifts sticking out of their bags.

"Merry Christmas," they said, greeting Gigi in unison.

They exchanged hugs and kisses as she hustled them inside the apartment.

"Give me your coats," Gigi said, holding out her hand.

"I'm ready to open my presents," Lulu said, as she stepped past Gigi and then stopped to take off her North Face jacket. Lulu lived with their mother, Carmen, even though Gigi preferred to stay with Grandma. Carmen and her older daughter couldn't get along. They butted heads because they shared the same type of temperament.

Sniffing the air, Carmen smiled at Gigi and added, "I'm ready to eat dinner."

"Remember that we have to kiss under the mistletoe," Gigi announced, motioning to the mistletoe hanging above the door frame. After kissing her sister and mother on the cheek, she skipped to the doorway of Andrew's bedroom and tossed their coats onto the bed. "Who wants eggnog?"

"Dag, Gigi, calm down," Lulu replied with a laugh. "We just

walked in." Heading into the living room, she placed the bag of gifts down and greeted everyone else.

Singing "Santa Baby," Gigi happily passed out decorative Christmas mugs filled with eggnog. Just as she handed out the last cup, the doorbell rang again, and once again Gigi skipped down the hallway to answer it. This time it was Uncle Tito and his kids. Gigi greeted them with a jovial "Merry Christmas," grabbed a camera from a side table, then snapped a picture, blinding them momentarily with the bright flash.

Gigi was the life of the party. She was already tipsy from drinking two glasses of Coquito, a mixed drink made of coconut and spiked with Puerto Rican rum. She happily handed out everybody's presents and forced everyone to kiss under the mistletoe at some point during the evening, all the while snapping pictures.

Her boyfriend, Mel, stopped by. He couldn't stay long because he had to have Christmas dinner with his mom and little brother. Before he left, Gigi dragged him to the mistletoe to give him a juicy kiss.

"You get your Christmas present later," she whispered in his ear.

"Santa got a yule log for you, too," he whispered in hers.

Ten minutes later, the entire family was seated around the dining room table enjoying the huge Christmas dinner Grandma had slaved over most of the day. The table was cluttered with all kinds of dishes—turkey, *pernil,* macaroni and cheese, apple pie, stuffing, chicken. Name it and Grandma had it on the table. Everyone was caught up in conversation, stacking their plates full of food. Grabbing the remote control, Gigi turned on the stereo in the living room to a station playing Christmas carols and raised the volume up high.

Slowly but surely the Christmas songs took the place of conversation as the family dug deeper into their meals. Every now and then a few of them stopped stuffing their mouths long enough to make light chat. For the next thirty minutes or so the family filled their bellies before each one slowly drifted away from the table into the living room, where they opened their gifts.

Gigi was so nervous about how Grandma would react to her present, she ignored the pile in front of her. When Grandma finally opened Gigi's gift, she didn't say a word. Tears filled her eyes as she read the note Gigi had attached.

"Something wrong, Grandma?" Lulu asked, seeing her grandmother's expression.

Grandma could only nod.

"What'd she get you?" Carmen asked curiously.

Grandma just stared at the box, shielding the contents from view and she softly whispered, "A second chance."

She walked over to Gigi and hugged her tight. "Thank you, baby," she said. "Thank you so much."

"You're welcome," Gigi said, hugging her back, relieved she wasn't upset about the gift. "You know there's nothing I wouldn't do for you."

"And there's nothing I wouldn't do for you," Grandma said.

She picked up a neatly wrapped box off Gigi's pile and handed it to her. "Merry Christmas, baby," she said.

Gigi shook the gift, trying to figure out what it might be. Finally, curiosity got the best of her, and she ripped the paper off and tore into the box. She frowned when she saw the red-and-white Santa hat.

"Thanks, Grandma," she said, trying to act as if she really liked it.

Grandma didn't say a word as Gigi pulled the hat out of the box and revealed a diamond tennis bracelet resting on a personal check. Gigi's mouth fell open when she spotted the shiny piece of jewelry.

"Grandma, I love it!" she screamed. Jumping to her feet, she gave the older woman a big hug.

"You're welcome, baby. Merry Christmas." Grandma smiled triumphantly. "Now, try it on."

After putting on the bracelet, Gigi shook her wrist beneath the light, watching the diamonds sparkle. Grandma's gift had caught her by surprise.

Gigi picked up the check, written out for four thousand dollars, more than enough to cover her tuition, expenses, and books.

All she had been expecting was the Lazarus chain, but the expensive bracelet and tuition money surpassed all that.

By the time they finished opening presents, the entire family was caught up in the Christmas spirit. Grandma had really delivered on gifts for everyone. Uncle Tito and Carmen were dancing away to Spanish music without a care in the world, while the little kids played with one of the PlayStation 3s, although Grandma had bought one for each of them. Worn out by the long day, Grandma remained seated at the table, enjoying the moment.

The doorbell rang and Gigi answered it. Carmen's boyfriend, Guido, stood there. "What's up, Guido?" Gigi said as she motioned him in.

He strolled into the apartment with his usual swagger. He always sported a long leather trench coat with a button-down shirt and slacks underneath. Nobody would know by looking at the short, lanky Colombian with slicked-back hair that he smuggled cocaine into the United States for the cartels back home.

"Merry Christmas, Gigi," he said, heading to the living room. "Hey, Ma, how you doing?"

"I'm okay. What about you?" Grandma asked.

"Can't complain," Guido replied. He always seemed to be in a good mood, thanks to his booming business, and he always showered Grandma with money and gifts. He treated her as if she were his own mother.

"I need to speak to you before you leave," Grandma said, anxious to talk to him privately.

Happy to see her man, Carmen greeted Guido with a peck on the cheek before he had a chance to answer Grandma. "Merry Christmas, baby."

"Hey, sexy. You look hot," he replied, causing Carmen to blush.

"I hate to break up your little love connection, but I wanna talk to him in private," Grandma said, getting to her feet. "Give us a few minutes." She motioned for him to follow her to the bedroom.

. . .

The celebration finally died down around one A.M. Gigi kissed her younger sister and her mother, who were the last to leave, good-bye. She wished Grandma a Merry Christmas once more and sent her off to bed, then she cleaned up the mess her family had left behind.

It was almost three o'clock in the morning when Gigi finally made her way to bed. She was just drifting off when her cell phone vibrated. By now she had gotten used to the late-night phone calls and figured it was one of her customers. This time she didn't answer the call. She had reached her goal. She smiled, realizing it was all over and she didn't have to hustle anymore.

The expression on Grandma's face when she had seen the money for the kidney transplant had been worth every moment Gigi spent hustling. She thought about the stash she still had left and tried to figure out how to get rid of it, but sleep overcame her.

The next day, Grandma began feeling ill to the point she could hardly get out of bed. Already weak and experiencing shortness of breath, Grandma's heart palpitations had started up again.

"Grandma, I really think you should go to the hospital," Gigi said. "I'll keep you company."

"No," Grandma refused. "It'll go away."

For two days, Grandma lingered around the apartment in the same condition. Concerned about her health, Gigi and Andrew finally convinced Grandma to go to the hospital. Reluctantly, she agreed.

At the hospital doctors put Grandma through a battery of tests. A few hours later, the test results were back, and the news was grim. Wasting no time, the doctor admitted Grandma to the hospital.

"Her kidneys are failing fast, thanks to her poor diet," the doctor informed Gigi and Carmen, who stood in the hallway outside of the older woman's hospital room. "Not to mention, the disease has weakened all her major organs, including her heart." He paused to look at the chart. "And I see here, she was already suffering from palpitations. She needs that transplant."

"Will she get better after the operation?" Carmen asked, almost pleading.

The doctor shook his head. "I can't make any guarantees," he said.

"Why not?" Gigi asked.

"Her body could reject the new kidneys."

"So she could die after the surgery?" Gigi asked.

The doctor frowned. "I'm sorry, but there's always a risk associated with this kind of surgery."

"Isn't there anything we can do?" Gigi asked, starting to grow hysterical. "I wanna speak to the fucking head of the hospital."

Carmen did her best to calm down her emotional daughter. "No matter what, we have to remain positive."

Gigi wanted to spend the night, but she and her mother agreed that Carmen would stay and Gigi would come back the next day to relieve her.

• • •

Later that same night, Chico's black BMW rolled through the tollbooth headed to Randalls Island, a desolate strip nestled between three boroughs—the Bronx, Queens, and Manhattan. The place was frequented as a lover's lane because of its remoteness.

Slowing down near a baseball field at the south end of the island, Chico pulled off the asphalt road and drove onto the snow-covered grass. He parked near a stand of trees.

Andrew was in the passenger seat and right away noticed Joe's red BMW sitting a few feet away. He scanned the dark deserted park, noticing the huge trees lining the field were casting even darker shadows.

Fighting the bitter winds blowing across the open field, Chico pulled the knitted cap over his ears as he stepped out. He glanced at Andrew, who was already out the car. "Ready to earn yo' stripes?"

"No doubt," Andrew replied without hesitation.

Chico screwed a silencer onto the barrel of a .38 special and then passed it to Andrew. "Don't use it 'til I say."

Andrew was so busy eyeing the revolver, he didn't bother to acknowledge him.

"You deaf?" Chico asked.

"Nah, I got you."

About twenty feet from where they stood, to the right of the baseball field, was a small cinder-block structure. On the left side of the unit was the women's bathroom and on the right side was the men's.

When Chico and Andrew entered the dimly lit men's room, Joe had Rob seated on the dirty toilet with one arm handcuffed to the metal drainpipe. Standing in front of the stall, Joe kept a watchful eye on him.

Seeing Chico, Rob's blackened eyes widened, and a shudder racked his body. "Yo, Chico, w-wh-what the fuck's going on?" he asked, his voice cracking in fear.

"Get a load of this nigga," Chico said, looking at his younger brother, Joe. "Like he don't know." He turned his attention back to Rob. "The day you violated Grandma, you should've slit yo' own wrist and saved me the time."

"C-Ch-Chico, I swear to God, it wasn't me," Rob pleaded.

"You fucked up—told the wrong nigga yo' business. Now it's come back to bite you in the ass."

Rob had made the mistake of telling one of his boys from the block about the foiled robbery attempt. That person had then ratted him out to get in good with Chico and Joe's team.

"Looks like yo' friends are worse than yo' enemies," Joe added.

"I-I-I know I fucked up, man," Rob stuttered, "but let me make it right. Don't kill me. I'll make it right, Chico."

"How you gonna make it right?" Chico asked, pointing to the gun-toting Andrew. "You shot poor little Andrew in the head. He's blood to me."

"You saw how he stabbed me. You would've done the same thing if you was in my shoes."

"I told you to leave it alone," Chico said, cutting off the pleading man, "but you didn't heed my advice. Now you gotta suffer the consequences."

Rob looked to Joe for help. "Come on, Joe. What about all the work I done put in? That shit don't mean nothin'?" he pleaded, tears rolling off his chin.

"It means you should've known better," Joe said. "When you violated Grandma, you violated us."

"Andrew, put this nigga out his misery," Chico said, giving the trigger-happy teen a nod.

Rob braced himself as Andrew stepped forward and pressed the silencer to his forehead.

"Please, man . . ." Rob managed to say before Andrew pulled the trigger. A small red flower-shaped hole blossomed right above his brow, leaving blood splatter on the stall's dingy white tiles.

Chico spit on the slumped corpse. "Now that's what I like to see," he exclaimed, getting a rush from the bloodshed. "Straight to the point. No boring speeches and shit."

. . .

Gigi and Andrew went to see Grandma the next day.

The large hospital bed seemed to swallow their grandmother as she rested. *Grandma does look sick,* Gigi thought as she studied the older woman closely. Her rosy cheeks and bright complexion were now pale. Gigi could tell her grandmother was in a lot of pain, but, no matter what, Grandma never complained. Forcing a smile, she just lay there, suffering in silence.

Gigi sat on the edge of the bed and leaned in to kiss her grandma's sweaty forehead.

Grandma looked up at her grandkids with tender love in her eyes, and said, "I'm glad y'all are here."

After a few minutes, Andrew excused himself, claiming he had to use the bathroom.

When he left the room, Grandma cupped Gigi's hand in her own. "Gigi, I need you to do something for me. I want to see Andrew's lawyer. I wanna make a statement," Grandma said.

"Why?" Gigi asked.

"Don't ask questions," Grandma said. "Just do it. Please."

Gigi made the call, and Andrew's lawyer dropped whatever he was doing and made it to the hospital within an hour.

"Now, you take this down," Grandma said to the lawyer, pulling herself up to a sitting position. "I want to make it known that *I* was the one selling the crack. My grandson didn't have nothing to do with it."

Andrew inhaled sharply. "Grandma, I told you, you don't have to do this. I already took the rap for it. It's not like we haven't been hustling anyway. How you think we got the money for your surgery."

"Is that true, Gigi?"

Gigi nodded.

"My heart was right." Grandma sighed, and she beckoned for Gigi to come over. After Gigi was settled on the bed, Grandma gave her a hug. "Didn't I tell y'all not to sell drugs on your own?" she asked.

Gigi nodded. "We did it for you," she said.

Grandma sighed. "Promise me you'll never do it again. You're a smart girl. I don't want y'all to go down the same path I did. You can make something of yourself. Promise me you'll do that. Both of you."

"Okay," Gigi said.

Andrew nodded reluctantly.

"I'll need you to act as a witness to this statement," the attorney said, turning to Gigi. Gigi nodded.

Grandma finished giving her statement, and when the lawyer left, Gigi looked at Grandma.

"You shouldn't have done that, Grandma," Gigi said, choking back her tears. "You're gonna get better, and when you do, they're gonna send you to jail."

"Gigi, I can't let Andrew end up in prison for my drugs," Grandma said. "I was trying to make a better life for you and your cousin, not make it worse."

"And you did," Gigi replied. "If it wasn't for you, I wouldn't have money for college."

Grandma shook her head. "What about Andrew? My poor baby's facing time 'cause of me. I failed you both."

"It's okay, Grandma," Andrew said. "You did what you had to do, just like I did what I had to do. Trust me, I'll be okay."

"When you get better, we'll all put this behind us," Gigi said, tears running down her cheeks.

"No, Gigi, I'm not getting better."

"Don't be ridiculous."

"Promise me . . . when this is over, you'll leave this crack shit alone and finish college," Grandma said. "Promise me, you'll live your life the right way. Don't do what I did. I never wanted this for ya'll. Look at me, cursed with this illness for all the wrong I've caused, at least when I'm gone, no one—in hell or on Earth—can ever say I didn't keep food on our table."

"I promise, Grandma. Believe me, I was only in the game to help you out. I know this ain't the way."

Suddenly, Andrew punched his fist into the wall. "Shut up!" he barked, fighting back tears.

"Calm down, Andrew," Gigi demanded.

"Grandma's coming home and shit's gonna continue like it was. We gonna keep making this money!" Andrew shouted, before storming out the room.

Gigi knew this was the beginning of the end. She knew there was a chance Grandma would not survive after the operation.

"Andrew's right. You're gonna be fine," Gigi assured her, struggling to believe her own words. Praying for the best, she hugged Grandma tightly.

. . .

Gigi lay in bed with Mel that night, and, long after he had fallen asleep, she thought about Grandma and all that the older woman had done for them. Grandma was right. They all deserved better. She vowed that she was going to finish school and get her life together, and take care of Andrew.

The next day, Gigi arrived at the hospital for her daily visit, carrying a beautiful bouquet of flowers and two huge Get Well balloons. Stepping out of the elevator, she headed down the long corridor toward her grandmother's hospital room. She walked into the room and found Grandma's bed empty. Taking a deep breath, she tried to stop her racing heart from beating so fast.

She must be getting her dialysis treatment, Gigi thought as she left the room and walked down to the nurse's station.

Approaching the nurse seated there, Gigi rubbed her sweaty palms on her blue jeans and asked, "Is Lola Lewis being treated for dialysis? She's not in her room." Gigi bit her lip, impatiently awaiting the nurse's reply.

"Are you a relative?" the nurse asked solemnly.

"I'm her granddaughter. Why?"

"Hold on just a second."

Rolling back from the desk, the nurse wheeled around in her swivel chair and spoke to a doctor standing behind the station. The older man glanced up from the chart he had been examining and stared at Gigi over his thin-rimmed glasses with sorrow in his dark eyes. The grim expression on the doctor's pale face said it all.

With tears rolling down her face, Gigi already knew what he was about to tell her before he said a word.

"Come with me, please," the doctor said, nodding toward a spot off to the side where they could have more privacy.

Squinting, Gigi tried to stop the flow of tears. She tried to keep the doctor from speaking by tossing her hand up and turning her face away from him. Gripping the ribbon on the balloons tightly, Gigi braced herself for the bad news.

"I'm sorry, Miss Lewis, but your grandmother had a fatal heart attack. She expired early this morning. We tried to reach you—"

Unable to contain herself, Gigi dropped the flowers she was holding and collapsed on the floor sobbing. The balloons floated up to the ceiling. Deep wails racked her body as she curled up into a fetal position.

With solemn expressions on their faces, the doctor and a hospital orderly helped Gigi back to her feet. Waving away the orderly, the doctor let her cry on his shoulder. Gasping for air, Gigi was inconsolable as a continuous flow of tears fell from her face onto his white coat.

Finally finding the strength, she pulled away, her eyes red and teary, staring blankly at the doctor as he gave her his condolences.

"I'm sorry, dear. I wish there had been something I could have done."

"Thank you," Gigi managed as she turned to walk away.

Lost in a daze, Gigi trailed through the hallways, then stepped into an enclosed phone booth in the hospital's main lobby. Pulling the glass door shut, she sat on the metal stool and wept hard again. The pain of losing Grandma was just too much to bear. She was doubled over, lost in her grief.

"Grandma, Grandma," Gigi cried out repeatedly, knowing she would never see the older woman again. "What am I gonna do now?"

Gigi wished she could hear her grandmother's loving voice one more time. Then the thought hit her, Grandma died without any family by her side. Gigi wished she had been there, holding Grandma's hand when she took her last breath. The last thing she had wanted was for her grandmother to die alone.

After grieving a few more minutes, Gigi tried to regain her composure for the walk back to the train station. *Grandma's in a much better place,* Gigi thought, pulling herself together.

Exiting the hospital, Gigi still didn't know what she would do without Grandma. A car horn beeped, and she looked up to see Chico's black BMW waiting at the curb.

"How's Grandma?" Chico asked as she approached, then he saw the agony etched on her face. "Aww, don't tell me."

"She's gone," Gigi said.

Chico dropped his head into his palms. When he finally looked up again, tears were rolling down his cheeks. "I loved that woman. You know she was like a mother to me."

Gigi nodded. "You gonna be okay?"

Chico grimaced. "I should be the one asking you that. But I know you'll be all right. You're strong. You know that, right?"

Gigi nodded.

He reached into the glove compartment, grabbed a manila envelope stuffed with something, and handed it to Gigi. "I know this can't replace your loss, but I want you to have it."

She glanced curiously at the package before opening it. To her surprise, it was filled with money, mostly fifties and hundreds. "I can't take this."

"Don't talk crazy. That's thirty grand. It was for Grandma's transplant. I was on my way to give it to her. Now it's yours. It's the least I can do. If it wasn't for Grandma, we'd probably still be in a drought."

Gigi tucked the cash into the inside pocket of her Woolrich coat. "What you mean?"

"Our regular supplier got busted a few months back, and we needed a new connect. Grandma tried to hook us up with ya mother's boyfriend, Guido, but he would only deal with Grandma, so she ended up supplying us."

"Damn . . . so you were really working for Grandma?" Gigi asked.

"Well, I wouldn't say that. But she was our new connect," Chico said.

Shaking her head, Gigi couldn't help but smile. "I'm always the last to find out."

"I know this ain't a good time, but now that Grandma's dead, I'ma need you to holla at Guido for me when it's time to reup."

Gigi nodded. "I got you."

"Hop in. I'll give you a ride back to the block."

"Nah, that's all right. I need time to think. The train ride should do me some good."

"A'ight . . . holla when you need me. I mean that," Chico said, before pulling away from the sidewalk.

With tears still staining her cheeks, Gigi couldn't help but smile as she fingered her Lazarus chain. Even in death, Grandma was making sure she was taken care of. She dried her tears and headed for her mother's house to tell the rest of her family that Grandma was gone. Grandma had done everything for Gigi, and Gigi was going to do everything for her grandma, starting with never selling drugs again.

Holiday Hell
by Dee Blackmon

Chapter One

Roberta Holiday flew down the speckled Berber-carpeted stairs as fast as her shaky legs would take her. She wobbled on the last three stairs but managed to right herself immediately. If she showed any signs of her addiction, then Carlos would never give her the money. He never dealt with hypes because he knew they weren't reliable. But everything would be okay once she got the money. Life would be great once she got her fix.

She took a deep breath, stopped at the hallway mirror to put on lipstick and fluff her dull, flat, lifeless hair, then entered Carlos's office. His handsome, muscular, mahogany body was hunched over his desk, the telephone pressed to his ear. She glanced around his office quickly. The office's once stark white walls were now a creamy beige, and earth-tone accents had been strategically placed around the room. Plush throw rugs with beige, green, and brown hues were strewn across the hardwood floor. It looked rugged. It looked like 'Los.

Carlos's voice rose above what Roberta knew for a fact was Christmas music. She distinctly heard the Temptations' version of "Silent Night." Roberta wasn't sure if she was hearing things during her drug-induced craze, but she thought she heard one of the Temptations tell baby Jesus to "relax his mind." If her situation wasn't so fucked up, she may have considered laughing, because a man telling Jesus to relax was funny as hell.

"I don't give a fuck about Christmas. The motherfucker better have my money by tomorrow or he can start looking for a wheelchair because I'm breaking both his legs."

Carlos slammed the cordless phone down in its cradle, rolled his shoulders to relieve the tension, and looked up at Roberta. At least a shell of Roberta. His six-foot frame moved gracefully as he paced back and forth while looking at Roberta. He ran his hand across his short curly hair as he often did when he was in deep thought. Something was up with her. He intended to find out what it was, but he'd keep playing along like the fucking idiot she thought he was. So, since she asked for a loan of ten thousand dollars, he was going to give it to her. Now, whether she was telling the truth—about being in the process of refinancing her house and expecting the equity to be deposited three days before Christmas—had yet to be proved. Carlos had two weeks. So did Roberta.

Carlos sat back down and asked smoothly, "You show my cousin a good time, Bobbie?" In exchange for the loan, Carlos asked Roberta to sex his cousin, who he said hadn't had sex in a while. Roberta had let his fat fuck of a cousin pump into her upstairs for a good half hour, and, while a part of her was disgusted, she chose to focus on her goal—money for drugs.

"Yes," Roberta replied, thinking how much Carlos looked like the original *Miami Vice* star, Philip Michael Thomas. It was too bad his cousin hadn't inherited such good looks.

"Now, what did you need the money for?" Carlos asked, as he rested his right palm on a pile of money.

Roberta licked her lips nervously and replied, "It's just a loan until I refinance."

When Carlos looked as if he was going to renege on the deal, Roberta hastily added, "I have the appraisal paperwork right here in my purse. The amount more than covers the loan."

Roberta rummaged through her purse and produced a wad of crinkled-up papers. She handed them to Carlos for a quick glance. The papers were legit, but she didn't want him to have too much time to think about it and change his mind.

Carlos handed the appraisal papers back to Roberta and said, "Take the money." He slid a stack of bills across his desk and watched her place the money in her bag, with what he thought were shaking hands.

"Two weeks, Bobbie. Two goddamn weeks. Not a day more. You fuck around with my money, and I'm coming for whatever you hold near and dear," he threatened.

"Thank you, Carlos."

Carlos stared at her so intently that she felt like he knew she was getting higher than a helium-filled balloon released on a windy day. But he couldn't have known. She was being ever so careful. Her own kids didn't know, so there was no way Carlos could. She made certain to cover her tracks . . . literally.

When the black cordless phone rang again, although it startled her, she was grateful for the interruption.

Carlos jabbed his index finger in the air and said into the phone, "Either I get my money by Christmas Eve, or you tell that son of a bitch I'll string him up by his balls and hang him on the Christmas tree downtown at the Monument. That will be his Merry-fucking-Christmas!"

The life of a loan shark, Roberta thought to herself.

Carlos stood angrily and walked to the lone window in the wood-paneled office. Christmas lights shone through the window and danced on the walls and the floor.

It was the reflection of a blue blinking light that drew Roberta's attention to the floor. The blue reflection that blinked right beside a black duffel bag. A bag filled to capacity with cold hard cash.

Don't fucking do it, Roberta thought to herself. *Don't do it!*

Even as the admonition entered her mind, Roberta found herself leaning forward, reaching for the money in the bag while keeping an eye on Carlos's back.

She thought about all the crack she could buy. Hell, all the heroin she could shoot into her veins. She could taste it even as she thought about it. Even her teeth began to tingle. She could even buy her daughters Christmas presents for a change. Life for a little while would be great.

Roberta didn't think twice about it. She grabbed three handfuls of cash and stuffed them into her purse. She knew she grabbed more than what Carlos had given her. No, not given, *loaned*. She had better remember that. She would be able to pay him back in a couple weeks, so she didn't feel bad at all. Well, she felt bad, but not about taking the money. She had already convinced herself that she'd give it back before he ever truly missed it.

Roberta stood up when she heard Carlos end his call.

As he turned back around to face her, she barely looked into his eyes and said, "I appreciate it, Carlos. I'll have it back to you in a couple weeks. I promise."

She even gave him a hug as he stood there looking at her and not responding. She wished like hell she could read his mind. She needed Carlos to believe everything she was saying.

"Bobbie, I've known you for a lot of years. At any point have you considered me to be stupid?"

"Not at all 'Los," Roberta mumbled, and tried to avert her eyes.

"Are you willing to risk your daughter's life on this loan? Because this time, if you don't pay me back, I'm coming after her."

Roberta fumbled with her purse straps then nibbled a piece of dry cuticle on her index finger.

"I swear I'll pay you back. Just don't hurt my daughters. Either of them."

"Now that part's up to you, isn't it?"

Chapter Two

*N*oelle Holiday shivered as the chill night air raised goose pimples on her café au lait–colored skin. She pulled her sky blue terry robe tighter and cinched it at the waist, making a double knot. Old Man Winter had hit early in Baltimore, and he wasn't wasting any time.

Noelle peered out the window and saw Christmas decorations and lights on her neighbors' lawns. At the age of twenty-four she was anti-Christmas. For starters, Noelle had been born on Christmas Eve, and for some strange twisted reason her mother had decided to name her after the Christmas song playing on the radio at the time of her birth. Secondly, why her mother would doom her to a life of teasing by naming her Noelle when their last name was Holiday was beyond her understanding.

And to make matters worse, Roberta Holiday still didn't get it when she named Noelle's eleven-year-old sister Paris. According to their mother, her youngest daughter was the closest she would ever get to having a real Paris holiday.

Noelle wondered where her mother was at three A.M. She prayed to God that she wasn't with her demons. Said demons being crack, cocaine, and heroin.

Roberta had ninety days' clean. Or so Noelle thought. She hadn't had time to really check on her mother's progress like she should. Hell, Noelle barely had time for herself. She was working three jobs to help her mother catch up on some of their bills, plus she was basically raising her sister. Noelle was exhausted.

Her every day started at five A.M., rain or shine. Noelle taught a six A.M. hourlong aerobics dance class, then rushed back home to cook breakfast for her sister and get her off to school. She showered and sped downtown by nine A.M. to Focal Point Barbershop, where she braided and twisted men's hair. And if that wasn't enough, she left the barbershop at two P.M. to pick up Paris from school, help her with homework, fix a quick dinner, then back to the barbershop from four P.M. to six P.M. And how could she forget her third job as a waitress?

Exhausted was an understatement.

Yet here she was, awake at three A.M., worried about her mother, even though her alarm would be chirping in exactly two hours.

Noelle slipped her cell phone from the pocket in her robe and dialed her mother's cell for the third time. And for the third time the phone went right to voice mail.

"Is everything okay, Noelle?"

"Paris, sweetheart, what are you doing awake?"

Paris shrugged her shoulders. As she did so, the action reminded Noelle that she had to twist the new growth in her sister's hair. Paris's double-strand twist looked adorable on her. She was growing up so fast. Even though they had different fathers, Noelle and Paris looked a lot alike. They had the same high cheekbones, big chocolate brown doe eyes, and full pouty lips. Since neither of them knew who her father was, or what he looked like, each had to have taken after someone on their mother's side of the family.

"Mom's using again, isn't she?" Paris asked.

Noelle turned from the window abruptly and walked over to the stairs.

"What makes you say that, Paris?"

"It's three in the morning, she's not home, and you have that worried look on your face. You want to go get her, don't you?"

"Do you think I should?"

"Yes," Paris replied. "I'll go get dressed. We both know where she is."

Noelle tightened the black scrunchie around her copper-colored curly locs.

"Okay, let's go get Mom. But this time, promise me you'll wait in the car."

"I promise," Paris replied with a lot of spunk and an attitude well beyond her years. "But if anybody bothers you, I'm coming in with the Club swinging. That thing can do more than lock the steering wheel."

Noelle smiled. She wished she had had half the smarts and confidence at eleven that Paris had. The young girl was turning out to be a ride-or-die female all the way.

"Okay, Paris. Deal."

Chapter Three

Noelle cruised down one of the worst streets in Baltimore. Her ten-year-old red Toyota Camry threatened to announce her arrival because of a small hole in her muffler. Just as soon as she had some extra money, she was planning to have it fixed.

Noelle felt like a character on HBO's hit series *The Wire*. It was certainly a familiar story line. And since the show was filmed on the streets of Baltimore, it was almost surreal. Inside one of the cruddy dilapidated houses was her mother. Noelle was just having trouble remembering which house it was.

"That one, Noelle," Paris stated quietly. "The one with the green shutters. Remember?"

"Yes, I remember."

Noelle pulled over in front of the white house with the green shutters and cut the Camry's engine. It was déjà vu. How many times had she played out this exact scene? She couldn't count.

To the ordinary eye, nothing about the house remotely looked like it was a crack house—other than its being in a bad neighborhood. There were no neon signs announcing "Crack House Here." Noelle forced herself to keep the memories at bay. The last time she had been here it was a living hell. A goddamn nightmare. She took a deep breath and tried to calm herself.

"Wait here, Paris. If you have any trouble, blow the horn."

"Okay."

Paris looked at the house then at her sister again. She *hated* this part. They never knew if their mother was dead or alive. At times Paris hated her mother for putting Noelle through such hell. She didn't really worry about herself because as long as Noelle breathed air she would make sure Paris had everything she needed.

"Maybe we should leave, Noelle. If Mom wants a shitty life, then that's on her."

"Watch your mouth, Paris. Now stay here."

Paris closed her mouth immediately. She instantly regretted

using the curse word. She knew Noelle hated for her to curse, but she got so angry about her mother. Lately she was angry all day, every day.

Before Noelle got out of the Camry, she zipped her coat and looked around. The street was empty, but she knew it had eyes. Plenty of them. The streets were always watching.

Before Noelle closed her car door she handed the Club to her sister. Paris had the right idea about their mother, but Noelle felt obligated to help. This was, however, going to be the last time. She'd done one too many of these pickups. If her mother wanted to stay high and nod, tricking in and out of cars while constantly on the city streets, then she could damn well do it on her own. Noelle planned to take Paris and move to another city or, even better, another state. She knew how to hustle hard and make a home anywhere. Besides that, she had a job interview in New York in just a few days. If things worked out, she would take Paris and leave sooner rather than later.

Noelle didn't even bother knocking on the door. The people who were in the house were always too damn high to notice anything, let alone answer the door. Soft lamplight barely illuminated the rooms as she passed through. She couldn't really see anything, but she didn't need to.

The strong foul stench of urine assaulted her nostrils. Dark brown shit stains covered the lower part of various walls, because druggies often couldn't hold their bowels. Noelle had learned that the hard way the last time she had come to fetch her mother. On the way out of the house her mother had just stopped, dropped her pants, bent over, and explosively shit on the pea green peeling wallpaper.

She thought for a moment and tried to remember where her mother had been the last time she was here. Upstairs bedroom, Noelle thought. Last time she had gone upstairs and walked in on her mother performing a blow job with a ten-dollar bill in her hand. With the constant need to get high, pussy was a bargain.

Just as she climbed the first two stairs, she heard voices coming from the basement. Noelle changed directions and headed there instead.

The rickety stairs creaked beneath her feet but didn't alarm anyone. She was careful not to touch the broken wooden banister for fear of getting splinters from the jagged edges or getting punctured by one of the many rusty nails. An odor mixed with smoke and liquor and something else that was unidentifiable assaulted her.

The basement was barely lit. Night-lights were plugged into a few of the electrical outlets. But it was bright enough for Noelle to see the faces of the men, women, and teenagers sitting together in various corners.

Noelle's heart sank. She had hoped against hope that her search wouldn't produce anything. And when she hadn't seen her mother's car in the area, she had an even greater hope. Hope, however, had turned into her own personal hell.

Huddled together with a group of men was her mother, completely naked. Roberta Holiday didn't even have on a pair of underwear. Her body was filthy with a mixture of dirt, blood, and dried semen, probably from several different men. Noelle followed the trail of blood up to its source. It seemed that someone had bitten her mother on her right breast, and the wound was still slowly oozing blood. Her hair was tangled and all over her head, like a wild woman's. Roberta Holiday looked ridiculously horrible.

How could you do this to me, Noelle thought. She was so pissed off, so fucking tired of being angry all the time. She was tired, period. She was supposed to be the child, but instead here she was being the parent yet again. All she ever wanted was a mother who baked chocolate chip cookies and gave a fuck about her day. Instead, she had a mother who would rather parade herself around high, naked, and kissing any Tom, Dick, or Harry—literally— than be with her children.

She walked straight over to her mother and lifted her up as if she were a small child. "Come on, Mom. It's time to go home."

Her mother just smiled and laughed. "But I don't wanna go home. I wanna stay with my friends and play," Roberta slurred.

"I said, it's time to go home," Noelle repeated forcefully.

"But I have so many friends. And this."

Roberta produced a glass pipe virtually out of thin air. It was still cloudy with smoke, as if it had just been used.

"Where are your clothes? Where's your purse?"

Roberta just laughed, which made all her new "friends" laugh as well.

"I don't know," she replied. "I don't fucking know."

"Leave Bobbie alone," a man slurred at Noelle and staggered toward her.

Noelle was a quick thinker. She always had been. That was the only way she had managed to survive and keep her sister safe in the process. So when the asshole began coming toward her, she didn't hesitate. She grabbed the wooden banister, twisted, and was happy when the splintered wood gave way. She swung hard and was rewarded when she heard the dull thump of the wood against the side of the asshole's head. His shriek of pain and the blood on his cheek was further confirmation that a few of the protruding nails had met their mark.

"Let's get the hell out of here," Noelle whispered, and literally dragged her mother behind her. She looked back for any signs of her mother's belongings but saw nothing. No shoes, clothes, purse . . . nothing. All she saw were men's dicks flapping as they tried to stand but kept falling on their asses.

And of course she heard the screams of the asshole who now had more than his personal wood to play with.

Paris jumped out of the car with the Club in her hand when she saw her sister nearly running out of the house. Then she took a closer look and realized that the woman behind Noelle was their mother. She didn't have a stitch of clothing on, and she was laughing even louder with each step. When the older woman tripped over an uneven section of the walkway, Noelle literally dragged her mother along by the arm.

"Hey, what the fuck you doin'? It ain't time for Bobbie to leave yet. She owes me another round of pussy. Another goddamn round," a man yelled after them. "You're not fuckin' leavin' yet. You hear me, you bitch?"

Noelle shoved her mother into the car and hurried around to the driver's side just as the man came running toward the car.

"Paris, put your seat belt on."

Noelle's tires screeched as she sped away from the curb. She tilted the rearview mirror to get a better view of her mother in the backseat. Well, at least the woman who was supposed to be her mother. At the moment, Noelle was looking at a stranger.

Roberta Holiday looked as if she didn't have a care in the world. She sat smiling and staring out the window as if it were a perfect summer day. That pissed Noelle off. Their mother had no right to disrupt their lives. It was all a bunch of bullshit, and Noelle was so goddamn tired of it all.

She had considered giving her mother her coat, but thought better about it. Since her mother was high enough to think and act like a coat didn't matter, then Noelle sure as hell wasn't going to act like it mattered either.

She was *so* angry. Angry for herself and angry that Paris had to be exposed to such a sickening disease. It hurt for Noelle to see her mother in such a condition, let alone for an eleven-year-old to see it all.

Changes have to be made, Noelle thought. She had to take her sister away from this hell they were dealing with. New York was starting to look better every day. All she had to do was get the job.

Paris looked up at her sister with her big chocolate eyes and uttered, "Thank you, Noelle."

"You're welcome, baby girl."

Noelle fought to keep the tears out of her voice. They weren't sad tears. They were tears of utter frustration. She had finally just accepted her mother's fate. After all these years, Noelle realized her mother was simply a member of the walking dead.

Chapter Four

As soon as Noelle ushered her mother into the house she started issuing orders then began to make a pot of coffee.

"Paris, can you get Mom's robe, please? Then I want you back in bed. You can still catch a few hours sleep before school."

"Sure," Paris relented. "But don't you want my help with Mom? I'll be okay for school. I'm not a little kid anymore, Noelle. You know I can handle it."

"Thank you, baby girl, but we'll be fine. I know you're growing up, but I'll get Mom situated then get myself ready for work."

"Okay. But let me know if you need anything else."

Paris darted quickly up the stairs and retrieved her mother's red silk robe. Then she did as she was told and went back to bed. Reluctantly.

* * *

Roberta's high was starting to come down, and reality was setting in. For the first time in nearly twenty-four hours she realized the gravity of the situation. Or at least she thought she did. She wasn't quite sure. She was fighting through a thick fog to clear her mind. And attempts at doing that were making her want another hit. There was no way she was going to make herself dope sick. She couldn't handle that. Not right now. Anything but that . . . anything. She sat at her oak dining table and fought like hell to hold on to her high, but reality was crashing down on her too quickly.

She hung her head and looked down at her robe. Where the

hell were her clothes? she wondered. She barely remembered anything. She fought hard to think and remember the events of the past day. If her life wasn't so pathetic, she would laugh. Despite the chill of her skin, she was drenched in sweat. She cradled the mug filled to the brim with black coffee that Noelle had given her.

Roberta could barely look her daughter in the eye. What could she say? Sorry? She didn't think Noelle would fall for that one again. So she remained silent and thought about a likely excuse to give her daughter, and most of all she tried to remember what had happened.

Dammit Roberta, think!

Roberta remembered going to the ATM machine the previous morning and finding out that her account was overdrawn by four hundred dollars. She was feeling so sick, and she needed a fix so badly. She remembered coming back home and searching both her daughters' rooms for any money whatsoever. She'd found twenty dollars on Noelle's nightstand and had taken it and bought a couple rocks, but they weren't enough even to take the edge off. They were just enough to keep her from puking her guts out and getting the shakes.

But she needed more money, so she went . . . she went . . .

Where? Where would I go for money?

The memory froze her face in agonizing terror.

Carlos!

"Noelle, where's my purse?"

"I don't fucking know. You tell me. I'm not the one who got high and can't remember a goddamn thing."

"What the hell do you mean you don't fucking know? Where

the fuck is my purse?" Roberta jumped up from the table and started searching. She looked in stupid, odd places such as under the dining room table and inside the china cabinet.

She couldn't have lost the money. *She had to have the money.*

Oh Lord! All that money. Roberta had the original ten thousand that Carlos had loaned her, plus the money she had taken, which was another nearly fourteen thousand dollars. She got down on her hands and knees so she could look underneath the furniture.

"He'll kill me," she whimpered as she lay her head down on the carpet and openly sobbed. "I'm fucking dead!"

Noelle's blood ran cold. Time stood still as she watched her mother sobbing frantically on the floor. Just when she thought things couldn't get any worse. What had her mother done now?

"Mom, what are you talking about? Who's going to kill you?"

"Noelle, where the hell is my purse? Why didn't you bring it with us?" Roberta stood and screamed at the top of her lungs. She was beyond frantic. She was hysterical.

Noelle screamed right back at her. "I didn't see your purse. I looked. No purse, no clothes, nothing. You didn't have anything. Only a crack pipe, Mom. A fucking crack pipe!"

There was no way she was going to be blamed for her mother's actions. It was ridiculous. Once she would have taken responsibility for whatever went wrong during her mother's drug trips, but never again. Things were definitely different now.

Roberta rubbed a hand across her face and wiped her tears. She needed another fix. Just enough to allow her to think again. Just enough to take the pain away. Enough to erase the thoughts of Carlos killing her. But she knew she would have no such luck.

At least, not with her judgmental bitch daughter hovering over her, asking her to remember things that she couldn't. If Noelle was a good daughter she would have paid attention to all the details and found her purse.

"What about my car?" she asked. Maybe her purse and the money were in her car.

"Hell if I know," Noelle replied. "I didn't see your car and believe me I looked."

"What am I going to do?"

Noelle stood up from her chair and questioned her mother one last time. She had to know what was going on so that she could protect Paris if necessary.

"Mom, you are going to tell me what's going on and you're going to tell me right now."

Roberta's hand shook as she lifted her coffee mug to her lips. After taking one sip bile rushed from her stomach to her throat. It took everything she had not to vomit on the table in front of her daughter. The back of her throat burned, but she managed to take a deep breath and swallow.

"Get it together, Mom and start explaining."

"I . . . uh . . . I borrowed some money. Christmas is coming up and . . . and I wanted to buy you two presents."

"Cut the bullshit. How much money, Mom?"

"Ten . . . no, twenty thousand . . . maybe."

"What! Twenty thousand? There's no way you can pay that back. What the hell were you thinking?"

Noelle grabbed her midsection to steady herself from the shock of it all. Where was her mother going to get twenty thousand dollars?

"What happened to the money?"

"I don't remember," Roberta whispered. "I know you don't believe me, but I'm telling the truth. I don't remember. I was stoned, okay. I was stoned!"

"Think dammit!" Noelle yelled. "What happened to the god-damn money?"

"I just needed a little something to take the edge off, Noelle. Things have been so hard lately, and I just wanted to relieve a little stress. I had the money when I went to get something. It was in my purse. My car keys, too. I don't remember after that," she confessed.

Roberta's entire body began to spasm, she was shaking so hard. For the first time in her life she was scared. Terrified, actually.

Noelle shook her head in disgust. *Twenty thousand dollars. Unfuckingbelievable!*

"So you got high and your purse was stolen," Noelle reasoned.

"I guess."

"And your car," Noelle added.

"He'll kill me, Noelle. You have to help me get that money back. You have to."

"Mom, go to hell."

"How can I go somewhere I already am, Noelle? Tell me, since you know it all. How?"

Chapter Five

Noelle walked into Focal Point Barbershop twenty minutes late. Her client had already called to say that he'd be late as well, so she didn't feel too bad. It had already been one hell of a morning. She couldn't stop thinking about her mother's twenty-thousand-dollar debt.

She hung up her coat on the chrome coatrack then stepped around men's outstretched feet as they sat on the wooden benches waiting for their turn and watching ESPN's *SportsCenter*. The air was filled with the smell of paint. A fresh coat of sunny yellow, with cleverly placed accent stripes of forest green and gold, covered the walls. The shop looked cozy and comfortable.

"What's up, Noelle," Terrence called out as she passed his station to get to her own. Terrence owned Focal Point and the boutique next door but still cut hair. He was cool toward everyone. He had to be if he wanted to keep a good staff and clientele in the shop.

"Nothin' good, that's for damn sure."

"Yo, my boy left outta here tighter than a mug yesterday. You did a good job, yo," Terrence told her.

"Thanks, T."

Just as Noelle got her supplies situated at her station, her client, Marcus, walked into the shop.

"Hey, Marcus. How are you today?"

"I'm straight. I'll be better when I get this bush of mine braided, though. I can't be lookin' all crazy in front of the ladies."

"I hear you. Have a seat in my chair."

Noelle took a deep breath and went to work parting his hair

and plaiting it. She was trying like hell to clear her mind and focus, but her mother's tear-streaked face kept popping up every couple of minutes. She couldn't shake the image of her mother crying at the dining room table and mumbling over and over again that she was going to die. Even though she knew she shouldn't give a damn about her mother, she still couldn't get that shit out of her mind and her heart. After all that had happened, Noelle still felt as if she owed it to her mother to help. After all, the bitch did birth her.

But so fucking what! You deserve to have a good life. You're not your mother.

Thoughts raced through Noelle's mind quickly. She didn't know what she would do. But in the end, she was afraid that she did know. In the end, she knew that she would help her mother. No matter what.

"Yo, T, have you seen these before? These joints are tight," Marcus called out, his voice snapping Noelle out of her working trance.

She looked up and saw Marcus holding a new pair of Nikes in his hand. The bootlegger who brought them in was confident that he'd unload them easily. He was a cocky young cat with cornrows, a tight shape up, and designer everything. He was obviously doing well at his profession of boosting merchandise.

"Those are nice," Terrence commented, and set his clippers down to take a closer look at the shoes.

"They a buck-fifty in the stores but I'll give 'em to you, yo, for seventy-five. That's half price," the bootlegger offered.

"You better get 'em, son," Terrence told Marcus. "And they are size tens. Scoop 'em up before someone else does."

"All right, I'll take 'em," Marcus told the bootlegger.

"I also got CDs and DVDs," the bootlegger said.

"I'm good, man. Just the shoes."

Just like that, the bootlegger made seventy-five dollars. There was no telling how much stuff he had "acquired" and was now selling in all the downtown barbershops. A good bootlegger made bank. Period.

"Yo, T, how much does he really make in a day?" Noelle asked Terrence.

"Yo is 'bout his shit," Terrence informed her. "He just bought a brand-new BMW fresh off the lot. Yo makes bank fo' sho.'"

"How much longer, Noelle, 'cause now I gotta go buy a shirt to match my new kicks," Marcus asked, interrupting Noelle's thoughts once again.

"Fifteen minutes," she replied.

Noelle continued plaiting Marcus's hair all the while wondering how hard it would be to boost men's clothing. And how much money could she make, and how fast?

Chapter Six

Roberta pulled on an old gray sweatshirt and a pair of jeans. If she could just get a little something, she would be in good shape. She had to come up with a plan to pay Carlos back. But how?

The mortgage company had left a message on her cell phone to say that her refinancing the house wouldn't be possible after all.

Apparently the late payments she'd made had really messed up her credit. Carlos wasn't going to accept that. The company apologized and said that they hoped she had a good holiday. How was she going to have a good holiday with no money? Carlos didn't give a shit about what time of year it was. He would kill her if Jesus himself stood by as a witness. All Carlos cared about was that she paid him his money.

Dammit, she needed a hit. First things first.

Roberta bypassed Noelle's room and went straight to Paris's door and opened it. She easily found the bright pink pig with purple polka dots on it in her daughter's underwear drawer. It was one of those ceramic piggy banks that had a horizontal slot on top, but no way to get the money out other than breaking it.

So Roberta did what any junkie would do. She slammed her daughter's piggy bank on the corner of her nightstand. Coins and bills fell out, and Roberta scooped them up, smiling as if she had struck gold. She counted the bills quickly then added up the coins. Thirty-seven dollars and forty-three cents.

It was enough. Enough to hold her until she could figure out a way to get more money later. At least if she got a little something she could come up with a plan to get Carlos his money.

She had already come up with one good-ass idea. But that would take Noelle's cooperation, and she didn't think her daughter would help her at all. Not like before. They'd been closer before—before the drugs.

Paris, on the other hand, was the perfect age. Maybe . . . just maybe . . .

Roberta left the house quickly and started walking since her car was still missing. She didn't care, though. All she could focus on at the moment was that weightless, floating feeling she would get with her first hit. She wished that feeling lasted forever.

A green older-model minivan slowed to her walking speed and kept pace with her for several steps. She looked over once, didn't see anyone she recognized, and kept walking. Roberta didn't even get alarmed when a man jumped out of the minivan's sliding door and approached her.

"You looking for this?" the man asked her, and held out a crack pipe.

She looked into his face as if he were an angel sent from God to help her. He knew exactly what she needed when she needed it. That was surely divine intervention.

"Oh, thank you," Roberta replied.

"Come on, get in," he coaxed. "I'll give you a private party in the van."

Roberta's smile grew even wider. This was her lucky day. Things were definitely going to change for the better.

She climbed into the minivan, and, as soon as the door slammed shut, she realized her mistake. Carlos sat in the middle row of seats, smiling in her face, along with his cousin from Alabama, a driver she didn't recognize, and her new friend. Roberta pulled on the door handle, but the doors were already locked. She tried to unlock the door manually, but Carlos grabbed her by the arm and flung her into the last row of seats beside him.

"How you feelin', Bobbie," Carlos crooned as he smoothed down the hair around her face.

"I'm okay, 'Los. Thanks for asking."

Roberta tried to remain calm and still the shaking that was inevitable from the combination of her craving and her fear. The fact that Carlos showed up meant she was in deep shit. She was either going to be really hurt or dead. She didn't know which one would be better, truth be told.

"You want this real bad, don't you, Bobbie?"

Carlos held out the crack pipe with a lighter and watched Roberta's eyes widen and glaze over. He used to like Bobbie. But she should never, ever have fucked with his money.

"That's okay, 'Los. I'm fine."

That was the toughest statement she had ever made. Roberta wanted to light that pipe very badly. She literally twitched at the thought of the pipe touching her lips. God, she needed a hit.

"Come on, girl. My treat."

Carlos held the flame to the pipe and set the tip of the mouthpiece right on Roberta's lip. She shut her eyes at first trying to resist, but the temptation was too strong.

Roberta closed her mouth around the pipe and experienced true bliss.

"Have at her," Carlos told his cousin as they traded places in the backseat.

His cousin positioned Roberta on her knees so her ass faced him in the middle of the seat and shoved her facedown into the seat. She saw bits and pieces of food crumbs buried in the crevices of the upholstery. She couldn't seem to make herself care. Roberta had what she really needed, and it was wonderful.

He slid her baggy jeans down over her hips and got even more excited when he realized she wasn't wearing any panties. Freeing himself quickly, he spread Roberta's butt cheeks and shoved his dick inside her ass.

Roberta's brief intake of breath was the only indication she gave of her discomfort. She would have been in greater pain had she not just had a hit.

He came immediately, then heard Carlos and the other two guys laughing at him.

"So you're a two-minute brother," Carlos joked.

"Hell, 'Los, I ain't never fucked a woman in the ass before," he drawled in his lazy southern accent. "That shit was supertight. Like I was fuckin' a virgin. I had to nut or lose my damn mind, 'Los."

"Where to, 'Los," the driver asked.

"Go back to Roberta's house. Since she can't pay back the twenty-two thousand, three hundred dollars she owes me, we'll wait for someone that will."

Chapter Seven

Noelle walked through downtown Baltimore going into store after store. She was trying to work up enough courage to walk into one and actually steal something. She had never stolen anything before in her life. But then again she had never needed twenty grand before either.

Noelle entered another men's store and saw only one female cashier in the entire store. And luck would have it that the cashier was completely entertained by the man who was trying to holla at her. She hadn't even seen Noelle walk in.

Noelle went to a rack with some very expensive men's shirts that were currently hot on the streets. She slid one, then two shirts off of hangers and stuffed them into her oversized gym bag. Just for good measure she placed the two empty hangers on the floor beneath the rack so it wouldn't be obvious that shirts were missing. She turned and headed for the door, but stopped suddenly when she heard the cashier's voice.

"Can I help you with anything?"

Noelle took a deep breath and turned around slowly. She prayed that she didn't look guilty. "No, thanks. Just out Christmas shopping."

"Well, yell if you need anything," the cashier said, then promptly went back to talking to the man, a big smile on her face.

Even though her heart was pounding, Noelle walked out of the store as casually as possible. She had gone to one of the more expensive stores that didn't use antitheft devices on their clothing. Stupid on their part, but good for her.

Once she had gotten a good distance away from the store, she took a deep breath. She had done it. The shirts had a ticket price of ninety dollars. She could sell them for fifty at the shop and make a quick hundred. She thought she would feel bad about stealing, but she was numb. Numb to everything except the need to come up with the twenty grand.

Noelle reached into her bag and ripped the price tags off the shirts, but kept the designer tags intact. She walked back to the barbershop. She had thirty minutes before she had to pick up Paris from school. She could unload the shirts by then. She had to.

"Hey, everybody," she called out to barbers and clients alike.

"What's up, Noelle," a couple of the clients replied.

"Hey, girl," Terrence greeted her.

"Yo, T, my boy came by and dropped off a couple shirts. They go for ninety in the stores, but he's selling them for fifty." Noelle came up with the lie at the spur of the moment. It gave her a good sound reason for having boosted clothing.

Terrence set his clippers down and took the shirts Noelle pulled out of her gym bag.

"Yo, I been lookin' for this shirt. That's what's up." Terrence reached in his pocket and handed Noelle a crisp fifty-dollar bill.

"I'll take the other one," Terrence's client said as he peeled off a few bills for her.

"When you gonna have more stuff, Noelle?" Terrence asked. "These shirts been flyin' off the shelves, yo. I'm surprised your boy managed to even get two of 'em."

"I'll talk to him later," she replied. "I'll see if I can get more stuff to bring in tomorrow."

Just that fast, in a matter of twenty-six minutes to be exact, she had made one hundred dollars.

Now all she needed to do was steal nineteen thousand, nine hundred more dollars' worth of merchandise. What the fuck?

Chapter Eight

Paris wrapped her black wool scarf around her neck. It seemed the weather had gotten colder since earlier that morning. Or maybe it was just her heart that had grown colder. She didn't think her friends at school had to worry about whether or not this was the day that their mother would never come home again. She wanted to cry so badly, but she blinked back the tears.

Noelle had told her to go back to bed, but Paris had listened to everything from the top of the stairs. She knew her mother owed somebody a lot of money. She was so upset that her mother would risk everything for drugs. It hurt mostly because Paris thought she had been clean. It was all a lie. That's all her mother knew how to do—lie.

Paris didn't know what she would do without her sister, Noelle. Her mother sure didn't take care of her or pick her up from school. But there was Noelle waiting for her across the street, like clockwork.

"Hey, baby girl, how was school?"

"It was okay," Paris replied. "How was your day?"

Noelle thought about the shirts she had boosted. She most certainly wasn't going to tell Paris about that. She didn't need to know about the twenty-thousand-dollar debt. Truth be told, Noelle didn't know why she was worried about it either. She hadn't taken the money. Her mother had. Yet still she felt some crazy unexplainable sense of obligation to help with the bullshit. Maybe somewhere deep down she didn't want her mother to die, even though she was on a definite path to self-destruction.

"My day was fine," she replied.

"How's Mom? Have you talked to her?"

"I tried to call, but she didn't answer."

Paris shook her head and sighed.

"We aren't going to get her back this time, are we?"

"I don't know, Paris."

The rest of the ride was filled with silence. Noelle finally turned on the radio to Magic 95.9 FM. At least the DJ's voice was better than the silence in the car. Neither sister thought too deeply with the distraction.

Noelle pulled into the driveway and cut the ignition. She wondered if her mother was even home. She wasn't chained to the bed, even though Noelle had thought about it before she left.

"Homework today?" she asked as they got out of the car and climbed the porch stairs.

"It's Friday Noelle."

"Paris, do you have homework?"

"I did all of it already except start on my book for my book report. It's not due until we come back from Christmas break, though."

Noelle unlocked the front door and ushered Paris inside. The girl had a tendency to stop all action when she thought she had to talk herself out of trouble.

"Well, at least start on the book today so you can get a head start. Christmas will be over before you know it."

"Yes ma'am, *Scroogette*."

Paris flew past Noelle and headed to the kitchen for something to eat as most kids did right after school.

That's when Noelle noticed the smell in the air. She distinctly smelled the cologne Eternity. She worked around so many men every day she could identify most fragrances.

"Wait a minute, Paris," Noelle called out, but it was too late. She spotted the two men in the kitchen just as Paris ran in there.

"Well, well, well. What do we have here?"

Paris stopped abruptly and stared at the men. She hadn't heard anything when she came into the kitchen, yet there sat two men eating pretzels and drinking sodas.

"You must be Paris," Carlos said approvingly. The little girl was beautiful. She looked like Roberta's former self.

"Yes. And who the hell are you?" Paris asked, sounding quite indignant for her eleven years.

"What are you doing here?" Noelle asked breathlessly. She came up behind Paris and placed her hands on her sister's shoulders in a protective gesture. She had a bad feeling, and she was willing to bet it was all because of her mother.

"Well, it seems, Noelle, that you and I have some business to take care of," Carlos informed her.

"What business? What are you talking about? And how did you get in here?"

"Your dearly departed mother let us in," he replied smugly.

"Dearly departed," Noelle repeated in horror. "What the fuck are you talking about?"

She guided Paris toward the stairs and yelled for their mother. She heard a few movements and was almost relieved, except a huge man came bounding down the stairs. She called for her mother again, but got no answer. *Dearly departed?*

"Mom, Mom," Carlos mimicked. "She is up there, but I'm afraid she overdosed about an hour ago."

Noelle's hand flew to her mouth in shock, and Paris pressed against her even closer. Noelle's eyes filled with tears, and she willed herself to talk.

"She was a fucking junkie," Carlos said with a sneer. "Don't waste your tears."

"Why are you still here?"

"I told you, we have business. Your mother owes me twenty-two thousand, three hundred dollars. Now that she's dead, *you* owe me that money."

Noelle's heart fell to the pit of her stomach. What the fuck was she going to do? At that moment she wished that she could resuscitate her mother just to kill her again.

"And to make sure you pay up, I've decided to take some insurance." Carlos snatched Paris from Noelle's grasp.

Noelle reached out for her sister, but it was too late. The man who had eaten their ice cream took Paris from Carlos and tried to subdue her.

"Let me go," Paris screamed as she kicked and clawed at the man. He was way too strong. It was like kicking a brick wall.

"This one has fire in her," Carlos said, and laughed. "She isn't anything like her mother."

"Leave her alone," Noelle shouted. Tears slid down her cheeks, and her entire body shook with fear. "I'll get you the money, but only if you'll leave her here with me."

Carlos shook his head and smiled. He pulled out a 9 mm semiautomatic and caressed Noelle's right cheek with the tip of it.

Noelle wished like hell she could get to the straight razor that she kept in her purse. Then just maybe Carlos wouldn't be having such an enjoyable time.

"You *will* pay me my money, and I *will* keep the girl until you do. Now whether she lives or dies is going to be completely up to you."

Noelle let out a sob. "I'm begging you," she pleaded.

"Let's go," Carlos told his men. They moved toward the front door with Paris. "Christmas Eve, Noelle. You have until Christmas Eve, or the girl is dead."

Carlos closed the door behind him, and Noelle ran to the window. She could hear Paris's screams. She turned when the front door opened again.

Carlos stuck his head back in and looked at her. "I almost forgot. No police, or the girl dies." The door closed again.

Moments later Noelle watched as the minivan pulled off, and she memorized the license plate number. She then took the stairs two at a time and found her mother nude and lifeless on the bathroom's cold blue-and-white tile floor.

Sitting like a beacon on her mother's chest was an off-white business card with Carlos's name and phone number.

Bastard!

Falling to her knees, Noelle felt for a pulse on the side of her mother's neck. A deep wave of sorrow washed over her. She put her head in her hands and sobbed, rocking back and forth. After about fifteen minutes of crying, a voice in her head instructed: *"Pull it together, Noelle, and think!"*

Shakily, Noelle took a deep breath then stood up. She had to call an ambulance. Then, as soon as they took her mother away, she had to figure out a way to get Carlos's money. Paris's life depended on it.

Chapter Nine

*I*f the police and the medics thought Noelle was a bit impatient, they didn't comment on it. They had chalked her behavior up to the fact that she had found her mother overdosed in the bathroom. They thought she was in shock.

She answered all of their questions as if she were on autopilot. Her mind was focused on just one thing: Paris. She didn't even know if her sister was being fed. It was dinnertime, and Paris wouldn't be home to eat. She prayed to God that her sister wouldn't go hungry.

Once the last police officer had left the house, Noelle pulled Carlos's business card out of her back jeans pocket and dialed the number. He answered on the third ring.

"It's dinnertime, and Paris needs to eat. How do I know you're taking care of her? Can't you let her come home? I'll still get you your money."

"I'm not stupid, Noelle. She had a burger and fries. Don't worry about the cost of food. I'll pick up the tab. She'll be fine until Christmas Eve. But the clock is ticking."

Noelle hung up and grabbed her purse and keys. She had to get downtown. She didn't have a lot of time. She would have to boost a lot of merchandise for some quick cash. She was sorry about her mother, but she loved her sister more. Carlos wouldn't get the opportunity to harm Paris. If that meant resorting to stealing, then so be it. She would do what she had to do.

* * *

Noelle parked downtown and deposited quarters in the parking meter before she remembered it was after six P.M. The meters were free after six. She had one client's hair to twist, and then she was hitting the mall. She decided to steal more men's clothing and bring it to the barbershop. Hell, she would sell to anyone who would buy.

She waited thirty minutes for her client to show up. After he was officially thirty-one minutes late, she left and headed to the mall. She thought it was good that it was the end of the day because people would be tired of working and ready to go home. Noelle counted on that to help her get past the sales-people.

As she parked in the garage she thought about what stores she would hit first. She wouldn't bother to pay for a funeral for her mother. Hell, the state could bury her. She didn't give a fuck. The only thing on her mind was trying like hell to get the money to bring her sister home.

The first clothing store she approached was completely empty, and the sales associates stood directly in the center of the store talking. Then like clockwork they started going through each rack to check for loose hangers.

The second store she stopped at looked like a much easier mark. One employee left the store to go on break, which left one cashier on the floor. Like her first experience that afternoon downtown, there was a man trying to pick up the female cashier. *Perfect,* she thought.

Before long, Noelle had two shirts, a watch, and three bottles of cologne in her bag. They were all expensive items, so that was good. Her spirits were dampened, however, when she thought about the amount of stuff she would have to steal in order to reach her goal.

She would have to first sell nearly everything in her house and her car for starters. That would get her a few thousand dollars. Her credit wasn't good enough to get a loan for that amount of money, so Noelle would have to hustle and hustle hard.

There had to be a better way to get her hands on twenty grand before Christmas Eve.

Chapter Ten

Working until the wee hours of the morning, Noelle gathered all the salable items from her house and put them in the dining room. Every television, radio, and DVD player would be sold. Even pieces of jewelry that she thought would fetch a price went into Ziploc bags. With her last bit of energy she took the clothing from her mother's closet, along with all their leather coats, and hefted all of those items onto the pile.

At some point she must have dozed off because the sun shining through the living room window woke her up. When she checked the clock on the wall she realized she had missed teaching her aerobics class. She couldn't muster the energy to care. Her mother was dead, and her sister had been kidnapped. Aerobics wasn't a high priority right now. Her priorities were to get downtown—since stores would open in less than an hour—and steal as much as she could. Every little bit of money would add up.

* * *

Noelle zipped her bulky black winter coat halfway up. It wasn't so cold outside that a goose down coat was warranted, but she could get away with it because it was December. She figured that she could stuff clothing down her coat, and the bulkiness would conceal it all. She was going to find out momentarily as she walked down Howard Street toward one of the hottest stores in Baltimore, Longevity. Anything that was hot on the street was sold at that store, and most often hot meant designer lines.

She took a deep breath then entered the store. The motorcycle in the middle of the floor was a definite showpiece, as were the crocodiles in a tank on the side wall. The store screamed exclusivity.

Noelle saw a few men in the back, but they really didn't pay her any attention. They were trying to do something at the crocodile tank, feed the crocs, perhaps.

She picked up a few A. Tiziano shirts and shoved them down her coat. Next were a couple of Ed Hardy hats that carried hefty price tags. The hats were one-of-a-kind designs, and men loved them. Just as she was about to reach for another batch of shirts, one strong hand grabbed her arm and spun her around and another strong hand unzipped her coat. Shirts and hats fell at her feet.

"What the fuck do you think you're doing?"

Noelle peered through narrowing eyes at the tall milk chocolate man with locs as she weighed her options. Going to jail certainly wasn't an option. Paris would die if she ended up behind bars. That meant talking her way out of this situation. Visiting central booking wasn't a factor in her plan to get twenty grand.

"I'm sorry," she replied.

"I don't want to hear 'I'm sorry.' I want the truth. You don't seem the type to steal. In fact, I've seen you around somewhere. Now tell me why you're stealing from my homeboy's store, or I'm calling Five-oh."

Noelle's eyes filled with tears as she stared at him. She didn't need this shit right now. She needed money to get Paris, and this man was stopping her.

She stared at him a few moments longer. He was right about having seen her around. She was almost certain that he'd come into the barbershop once or twice to see Terrence. Besides, she was too damn tired to come up with a good lie. The drama in her life at the moment was worse than any fiction she'd ever read.

"You want the truth," she began with attitude, "well, here it is. My mother, who just overdosed and died yesterday, went to a loan shark for money. She must have pissed him off because he killed her. But anyway, here's the kicker. Said loan shark wants his twenty grand, or my eleven-year-old sister dies. So, since I don't have an extra twenty grand sitting around, I've been boosting stuff on the streets. You wanted the truth—well, you just got it."

"Everything all right, Parker?" the owner of Longevity called out, coming toward them.

"Yeah, man, everything is fine. Seems I made a mess trying to show Ms.—" Parker looked at her expectantly.

"Holiday," Noelle supplied, wiping at her tears.

"Trying to show Ms. Holiday a few things," he lied smoothly.

Noelle picked up the shirts and hats and put them back on the tables.

"What's your first name?" Parker inquired.

"Noelle."

"Yeah, right," Parker laughed. "It's Christmas, and your name is Noelle Holiday? Try again."

"Look, don't make fun of my name," Noelle told him. "You think I haven't heard that one before?" She reached into her bag, pulled out her driver's license, and showed it to him.

He glanced at it quickly. "I want you to wait out front for me while I grab my coat. Then we're going to Lexington Market, where I'll treat you to breakfast and give you a solution to your problems."

"You believe my story?"

"Yes."

"Why would you help me? You don't even know me."

"Because I have a soft spot for women in trouble; you're beautiful; and you obviously love your sister a great deal."

"But how do you know I'm not some nutcase off the street? My sister means absolutely nothing to you," Noelle told him.

"I'm guessing you're not a nutcase, and you're right, I don't know your sister, but I don't want her to die. No one deserves that, especially not an innocent child. Your love for her makes me want to help you."

Noelle didn't know whether to jump for joy or run like hell.

Chapter Eleven

"*T*oday is Saturday," Parker told her when they arrived at Lexington Market amid the hustle and bustle. "When's the last time you ate something?"

Noelle stared blankly at Parker. She opened her mouth to answer him but closed it when an answer didn't come immediately to mind. After a pause, she replied, "I don't know. Thursday, maybe, when things were still normal."

"I thought you'd say something like that."

Parker kept a hand at the small of Noelle's back as he purchased two bowls of mixed fruit; two platters of sausage, scrambled eggs, grits, toast; and two coffees. He then seated Noelle at a table for two by the window and took the other seat.

"Eat first, talk second," Parker instructed.

Parker didn't have to repeat himself. She was suddenly ravenous. She really hadn't thought about eating since dragging her mother out of a drug house. *Her mother.* She was actually dead.

"What are you thinking?" Parker asked, while polishing off the last of his sausage.

"I can't believe any of this is happening. My mother is dead. My sister has been kidnapped. I don't know where to begin. . . ."

"First, we need to get your sister back home, which means getting you twenty thousand dollars."

"Twenty-three thousand to be exact."

Parker nodded his head and stared out the window for a moment. He hadn't always been a savory character. In his early twenties he'd been a hellion and a mastermind at white-collar crimes. He had given up that lifestyle, though. Now he was just an ordinary citizen who observed way too much and knew a whole lot of crooked shit.

"What's your sister's name?"

"Paris. She's such a good kid. Most days I feel like she's mine. I guess she is now, actually."

"Do you know who has her?" he asked around a mouthful of toast and grits.

Noelle blew on her coffee before she took her first sip.

"A loan shark named Carlos," she replied, then took another sip.

"Fuck! Goddammit!"

"You know him," Noelle stated sadly. No friend of Carlos's would help her.

"Yeah, I know the bastard. All too well. How long did he give you to come up with the money?"

" 'Til Christmas Eve."

"You don't have that long. It's not about the money to 'Los. It's the principle. He's going to kill Paris just to make a point. If he gave you two weeks, you have only *one*."

Noelle felt like a fist had slammed into her chest. What the fuck? This was all just a game to the asshole. Her sister's life was at stake, and it was just a *game*.

"Shit. The key to getting Paris back is to get Carlos first."

Fresh tears spilled down Noelle's cheeks. So she had even less time than she'd thought.

"Please, if you know of a way to save my sister, tell me. I can't let her die. She hasn't done anything to deserve this."

"The only way to handle 'Los is to kill him before he kills her."

"Oh my God," she gasped. "How in the hell do I get close enough to him to kill him?"

"You won't have to. Meet me for dinner. That will give me enough time to check out a few things and come up with a plan."

Noelle nodded okay.

"Where and what time?"

"Seven at Ruth's Chris downtown."

Despite the seriousness of the situation, Noelle couldn't help but be impressed, and a little intimidated, by the prospect of going to one of the most expensive steak houses in Baltimore.

"Take my number," Parker said, before rattling off his cell number.

"Call if you get into any trouble. And stop stealing clothes."

"I don't even know your last name."

"Norman. Parker Norman. I know, it's not quite James Bond, is it?" he joked, and left her sitting at their table to start coordinating a plan to get Paris back.

• • •

Paris sat in a bedroom eating a bowl of Frosted Flakes and watching cartoons. She couldn't really hear or see anything out the window. A black velvet covering was nailed across the windowframe. The man named Carlos must have known she would try to escape out of a second-floor window. The only way she knew the time of day was by the television programming.

Paris heard her door being unlocked and set her bowl of cereal down on the floor. She never knew what to expect. Sometimes the man Carlos would come into her room and just laugh at her.

Other times the man who looked like Wesley Snipes would bring her food.

"You want something else to eat?"

Paris looked up at "Wesley." He had been the only one who had been kind to her. No one else cared if she ate or not. Carlos sure didn't. She was afraid of Carlos, actually. He looked as if he would kill her at any moment. She tried not to piss him off, but he always seemed to be pissed off.

"You look like Wesley Snipes."

He smiled and said, "You know, I've been told that lately. I think it's the haircut."

Paris eyed the cell phone clipped to his belt. She wanted to call Noelle. If she could just speak with her, she'd know she was going to get out of this nightmare.

"Could I please use your phone for two minutes?" When it seemed as if he was going to deny her, she forged ahead.

"Please. I just need to hear my sister's voice. I'm just a kid. It would make me feel better."

"Two minutes," he replied, and closed the bedroom door. He unhooked his phone and handed it to her.

"What's your name?" she asked as she accepted the phone.

"Ronald."

"Thank you, Ronald."

Paris dialed Noelle's number with lightning speed, afraid Ronald might change his mind. She breathed a sigh of relief when her sister answered on the third ring.

"Noelle, I'm okay." She knew Noelle was worried and choked back her tears so she wouldn't add to the stress of the situation.

"Paris, I am so glad to hear your voice. Are you hurt? Have you eaten? Baby girl, where are you?"

"I'm eating, and I'm not hurt. I just really wanted to hear your voice 'cause I'm a little scared. Are you going to get the money to get me out of here?"

"You know I am, Paris. Just hang in there a couple more days. I promise you'll be home soon, baby girl."

Ronald signaled for Paris to end the call, so she did. She at least wanted to keep him on her good side. She was grateful that he had even allowed her to make the call. Carlos wouldn't have done it. She was sure of that.

"Thank you, Ronald," Paris said, wiping her eyes.

"Sure. Hey I bought some cinnamon rolls. Would you like one?"

"Yes, thank you."

As Ronald left the bedroom, Paris prayed that Noelle was right. She wanted to go home.

Chapter Twelve

Noelle showed up at Ruth's Chris Steak House with five minutes to spare. It was an effort for her actually to leave the house after Paris's call. She couldn't stop crying long enough to get dressed. But crying wasn't going to bring her sister home.

So, clad in a slinky black dress, Noelle was prepared to accept whatever advice and help Parker Norman had to offer. She milled around the lobby for a couple minutes and began to worry when she didn't see Parker approaching the entrance.

"Good evening, welcome to Ruth's Chris Steak House," the hostess greeted her.

"Hi, I'm meeting Parker Norman. Is he here, by any chance?"

The hostess motioned Noelle forward and said, "Yes, he's here. Please follow me."

Noelle spotted Parker immediately. The man had a presence about him and commanded the space quite well. And he was extremely attractive. He looked like he had just stepped off of the cover of *Essence* or *Ebony*. His dark brown skin hinted at a five o'clock shadow, and as she neared him she knew the heady musky fragrance was his cologne. He smelled really good.

She was certainly curious about him. What he did for a living . . . how he knew Carlos . . . whether she could trust him. For now, however, she *had* to trust him. She didn't have a choice. He was her only real chance to get Paris home.

Parker stood as she approached. He'd traded in his casual attire from earlier for a blue pinstripe suit. He looked like a Wall Street power broker and fit in beautifully with the posh atmosphere. He was, however, the type of man who looked good in anything.

"I'm glad you made it," Parker said, and kissed her cheek.

"I wouldn't have missed anything that would help Paris." Noelle fidgeted with her strand of pearls. She had a terrible habit of playing with her jewelry when she was nervous. She just wished she knew what to expect. She was coming into this dinner meeting blind as a bat.

"Paris will be home sooner than you think, so stop worrying," he stated confidently.

"How's that going to happen?"

"Let's order first, then I'll explain everything."

After ordering, Noelle was barely patient until the wine was poured. She wanted to grab the bottle from the waiter and finish the task herself. The waiter seemed to draw out every action with a flourish, no doubt in hope of a big tip.

As soon as the waiter took his leave, she launched into all of her questions. "So, what's the plan? And how am I going to get the money?"

Parker scooted his chair closer to the table and leaned toward her. He had done a lot of thinking and had made a select few phone calls.

"There's a man by the name of Phillip Grayson. Everyone calls him Gray. Ever heard of him?"

"No, can't say that I have."

"Well, Gray has two jewelry stores. One downtown Baltimore and one in Pikesville. He specializes in rare precious stones."

"He's a black man?"

"Yes," Parker replied, impressed that Noelle was picking up on the little things he hadn't stated.

"A black man with a diamond store in Pikesville? That's unheard of. It's a strong Jewish community."

"Exactly. That lets you know how powerful he is."

Noelle took two sips of her wine then downed the entire glass.

Parker refilled it before she had a chance to ask. "Gray and Carlos are enemies."

"Why?" she asked, drinking more wine.

"That I don't know. I'm still waiting for that bit of info."

Parker paused while the waiter placed their food in front of them. He waited a few minutes before resuming their conversation. He wanted Noelle to enjoy that first bite of steak. He watched as she daintily cut into the steak then brought the fork to her mouth. He felt himself stiffen when he saw her tongue dart out. He kept telling himself to focus on the conversation, but it was damn hard. The woman was very beautiful.

Parker cut into his steak as well, but he noticed that Noelle had put down her fork and knife. She was anxiously waiting for him to stop chewing.

"Go ahead and eat, Noelle. Your food is getting cold."

"So what does Gray have to do with me getting Paris back?" she asked. The steak was really good, but she was having trouble eating. She just wanted all the details as quickly as possible.

"You are going to attempt to steal diamonds and emeralds out of his safe at home."

"*What?*" Noelle nearly choked on her food. Parker handed her wineglass to her so she could take a sip.

"Notice I said *attempt* to steal. I'm going to help you get inside his house."

"But if I don't steal the stones, I won't have the money."

"My plan is to set Carlos up. Since Gray and Carlos are known enemies, think about what's going to happen when you get caught and tell Gray that Carlos sent you to steal the stones."

"Why would Gray believe me? And how will that benefit Paris? Coming between two enemies won't get her home."

Parker liked Noelle more and more by the minute. She asked all the right questions at the right time. He took a bite of his baked potato before he continued. "There are only three people who know about that safe in Gray's home. Carlos is one of them. Gray will believe Carlos sent you because the other two people would never talk about the safe."

"If the other two would never talk, how do you know about the safe?"

"I'm one of the two," Parker revealed, and smiled. "And the only reason I'm telling you is because I don't want your sister to be killed."

Noelle's head was spinning. Whether it was from the plan or the wine, she didn't know. All she kept seeing was Paris's sweet face, her bright smile, and hearing her voice which lacked its usual melodic tone as she replayed their earlier phone conversation.

If Parker thought the plan would work, then she was willing to try it. Nothing ventured . . . but she had everything to gain.

"So if I'm not really stealing the jewels, how do I get the money to get Paris back?"

"You are going to tell Gray that you will give him proof that Carlos sent you. You tell him that, and Gray will take care of the rest. Be honest with him. Tell him it's your mother's debt, and Carlos murdered your mother and kidnapped your sister for ransom."

"Gray will believe me? And help me?"

"Yes, I'm positive."

"How can you be so sure?"

"Because I'll be there. I'll make sure he believes you," Parker stated matter-of-factly.

That statement sent Noelle for a loop. She had been following along until that revelation popped out. "Wait. Why would you be there? You're losing me."

"Gray will call me the moment he catches you because I'm one of the two other people who know about the safe, like I said earlier."

"How do you know about it?"

"Because I designed it."

Chapter Thirteen

*N*oelle showed up bright and early at Parker's downtown brownstone. Apparently he did quite well for himself. She had seen the silver BMW the valet had delivered curbside the previous night as they left Ruth's Chris. And after learning that he designed impenetrable security systems for wealthy individuals, she knew that he had money.

Parker had explained that he could give her the money, but Carlos wouldn't stop until he had what he *really* wanted, which was another murdered innocent life on his hands. The man seemed to get off on shit like that, Parker had told her. And when he was done with Paris, he would come for Noelle. Straight like that.

"Good morning, beautiful," Parker greeted her as he opened the door and ushered Noelle inside. "Welcome to my humble abode."

Parker's crib was anything but humble. Expensive artwork adorned the walls, and authentic African masks and sculptures were placed strategically throughout the rooms. Both the architecture and the furniture had sleek lines, which fit his personality to a tee.

"I took the liberty of fixing you some breakfast. After we eat, then we get to work."

"Okay, thank you," she said, as she admired his paintings.

Parker guided her through the house to the kitchen, where he'd set two places at the island in the center. Once Noelle saw perfect crepes on a platter, her mouth started watering. She hadn't had such delicious home cooking in a long time.

Parker filled their plates, and poured two mugs of coffee and two glasses of orange juice.

"I like your shirt," she remarked. "I thought you'd been to Focal Point before."

Parker laughed. "I told you I'd seen you somewhere before. Terrence is a friend of mine."

Noelle eyed the newest SHYO (Stop Hating Your Own) shirt on the market. The shirts Terrence designed to sell in his own boutique next door to the barbershop sold like hotcakes. It had been a smart business venture. Parker must be very good friends with Terrence, because SHYO couture shirts went only to a certain few VIPs.

"You've been to the shop and never asked me to twist your hair? I should be offended."

"Well, now I know better. Eat up. It's going to be a long day."

Noelle started in on her breakfast with gusto, because the sooner she finished eating, the sooner Parker could begin teaching her how to break into Gray's home and his safe. She would be one step closer to rescuing her sister.

Thirty minutes later, Parker took her by the hand and led her to the study.

The room looked masculine, with chocolate brown leather wingback chairs, a huge cherry desk, and more African artwork. A map of Africa was framed on a side wall.

"How many times have you been to Africa?" she asked, eyeing a picture of him with Nelson Mandela.

"Four times for business, once for pleasure. It's gorgeous there. I'll take you and Paris once the fiasco with this asshole is over."

"What did Carlos ever do to you?" she asked, sensing a personal vendetta.

Parker was silent a moment, but decided to tell her the truth.

"My mother went to Carlos for money ten years ago. When she met him to pay it back, he raped her. The money was for my college tuition, but I didn't know she was struggling at the time. She became so depressed and withdrawn that she took her own life. I found out everything six months later when I finally had the strength to go through her things before I sold the house. She kept a detailed journal."

Parker worked as he talked, pulling out blueprints of Gray's house and a miniature replica of the safe in the closet.

"I'm sorry for your loss," she told him.

"Well, now we have a chance to kill the bastard, so let's get started."

Noelle thought about everything Carlos had done and realized that she actually wanted the man dead. He had taken the one thing in life that was most precious to her: Paris. The only way she would feel safe for the rest of their lives was if he were dead.

For the next several hours Parker explained how the safe was designed and how to disable all the built-in security mechanisms. She asked question after question about which wires did what, which buttons were located where, and how the voice recognition program should be disabled.

Parker gave her a pair of tiny wire cutters so that she could get familiar with using them. He explained that, before she made it to the safe, she would have to bypass the alarm system to get into the house.

Bypassing the alarm actually seemed to be easy. It was the safe she was worried about. She kept forgetting the part where she was supposed to disable the voice recognition. It was crucial. The plan depended on her getting her hands on the jewels to make a hard case against Carlos. Gray had to believe Carlos was setting him up.

"Let's take a ten-minute break," Parker told her after seeing her frustration. He knew the design for the safe was intricate. Hell, it was one of his best designs. But Noelle was doing a good job learning everything. They were just going to have to practice a lot more, but they had all day.

"No, I'm fine," she said. "Let's keep going so I can get this right. Paris's life depends on it."

"Baby, it's okay. You'll get it right."

Parker took Noelle's wire cutters out of her hand and set them on top of the desk. Then he gathered her into his arms and held her as her tears fell.

"We are going to get Paris home. *I promise.* Now, let's take a break, and you'll feel a lot better when we get back to work. It's what helps me."

Parker slowly stroked her back and breathed in her scent. Before he realized what he was about to do, he dipped his head and kissed her gently on the lips. She responded with a kiss of her own that had his loins aching by the time they separated.

"Now is a good time for that break," Noelle said, and backed away flustered. "Where's your restroom?"

"Down the hall on your left," he replied. "And I really meant what I said about Africa, Noelle. I want to take you and Paris with me."

Noelle could do nothing more than nod her head. She couldn't understand how such good and bad could happen all at once.

Chapter Fourteen

Paris watched the end of her favorite soap opera, *Days of Our Lives*. It was hard to focus on the show because she was so hungry, and she cried the whole time. It was Christmastime, and everyone on the soap was with their families, baking cookies or preparing turkeys or wrapping presents. She wanted nothing more than to eat in her own kitchen with her sister.

Ronald usually brought her three meals a day, and sometimes snacks, but she hadn't seen him since he let her use his cell phone. Some fat man had brought her dinner the night before, and that had been it.

She wanted out of the room. She wanted food, and she

wanted to go home. Paris balled her fists and slammed them onto the floor. She missed Noelle so badly. She even missed her sister fussing at her about doing homework.

Paris hadn't even really thought about the fact that her mother was dead. Noelle had been mothering her for so long that she was just grateful that nothing had happened to her sister. Really, that would have been even more devastating. Paris wondered just how Noelle was going to come up with so much money so fast.

Her attention turned toward the door as she heard it being unlocked. She was praying that it was Ronald, because he was nice to her, but no such luck. It was the fat man again, with a pizza box in one hand and sodas in the other.

Paris hated him. She remembered his coming down the stairs at her house with a crazy grin on his face. He had the same exact grin now as he carried the food into the room and set it on the bed.

"Here you go, honey," he drawled as he sat on the bed near the food, then patted the bed next to him.

Paris grew very scared very fast. There was something about him that alarmed her instantly. She was one of the few kids who stayed awake during the safety videos shown at school. She knew to pay attention to that weird feeling on the back of her neck and in the bottom of her stomach.

"I said sit down," he told her forcefully.

Paris began to sit on the bed with the pizza box between them, but he smoothly slid the pizza and sodas to the other side, leaving the only available seat next to him.

Again, he patted the bed beside him and told her to sit down.

Paris didn't want to sit down, but she did anyway. She kept as much room as she could between them, which was hard, considering the man was so large.

"You are so pretty," he said, running the tip of his index finger down her cheek, which made her even more scared. There was no way she would be able to get away from him.

Please no, please no, she repeated over and over again in her mind.

When he stuck his hand out and began rubbing her leg, she jumped up immediately. It was turning into an awful situation. It was bad enough she was being held for ransom, but she was *not* going to let a man molest her. She didn't want those problems. She and Noelle watched the Lifetime Channel together all the time. She wasn't going to turn into a Moment of Truth movie of the week.

"You must not want to eat, then," he shouted, picking up the pizza box and heading for the bedroom door.

Paris put a hand on his arm to stop him from taking the pizza away and shouted, "No, I'm hungry!"

"If you're hungry, little one, let's start with dessert," he told her, then unzipped his pants and exposed himself quickly.

Paris screamed and closed her eyes as tightly as possible. She had never seen a man's private parts before, and it terrified her. There was no way he was going to make her go near that big black ugly thing. She was hungry, but she was losing her appetite quickly.

"You put this in your mouth, then I'll give you all the pizza you want," he told her with a big smile.

Paris darted for the door, but he closed it with one big hand. The door opened, however, and Ronald walked into the room just in time to sum up the situation immediately.

"Get the fuck out of here," Ronald said, and snatched the pizza box out of the fat man's hand.

Watching the fat man leave, Paris had never been happier to see Ronald. She ran up to him and impulsively threw her arms around his waist and hugged him. Because of Ronald, she could finally relax and eat. Then before she knew it, Noelle would be there to rescue her.

"He won't bother you again," Ronald said, handing her the box of pizza.

"Thank you," she replied, wiping tears from her eyes and sitting back on the floor in front of the television. Noelle had to hurry. Despite Ronald's assurances, Paris had a feeling fat man was going to be back sooner rather than later.

Chapter Fifteen

"Are you nervous?"

"Scared shitless," Noelle replied, then laughed. *Nervous was an understatement,* she thought to herself.

Parker walked up behind her and slipped his arms around her waist. He loved to breathe in her scent and couldn't seem to get enough of it. It seemed strange that they had met only a few days ago. He felt as if he'd known Noelle for years.

"You'll be fine, baby," he reassured her. "I'll be able to talk to you and see you."

Noelle pulled a black spandex shirt over her head and smoothed it down. Coupled with the black knit pants, she actually looked like a cat burglar. She had even tied a black scarf around her locs. She looked the part, but the question was, could she *play* the part?

Yes, you can! You have to for Paris!

Parker strapped a black utility belt around her waist and went over the contents again. She had done remarkably well the past two days, but repetition made for good memorization.

"I look like Batman, don't I?"

"Batman is nowhere *near* as sexy as you are," he joked. He found that joking with Noelle kept her calm.

"Thank you, Parker. For everything. I couldn't do this without you."

"All right let's get you your mic and your camera. If you have to talk to me, remember to whisper. I'll be able to hear you loud and clear."

"Okay."

"I'll get to Gray's house fifteen minutes after he calls, but you know I'll really be only three minutes away."

"Okay."

"And Noelle . . ."

"Yes?"

"Breathe."

Noelle checked to make sure she had everything. She left her purse and cell phone at Parker's house. She didn't want to risk losing something if anything happened that wasn't according to plan. She checked herself in the mirror one last time and went out the door.

"See you soon, baby. Just stick to the plan no matter how nervous you get."

Noelle nodded her head then went down the steps. The cold air hit her in the face, but she relished it. Being cold kept her from sweating from nervousness.

During the fifteen-minute drive from downtown to Pikesville, Noelle began to focus her mind and go over the plan, slowly building her confidence. She knew everything she had to do. She couldn't fuck up. She *wouldn't*. Paris's life depended on her.

She breathed deeply and thought about spending Christmas with Paris. For the first time in her life she wanted to celebrate the holiday. And she wanted a relationship with Parker. She didn't want to grieve for her mother, sister, and new relationship all at the same time.

Noelle parked around the corner from Gray's home. Parker told her not to park on Gray's street, which made sense. She didn't want Gray knowing the make of her car or her license plate number.

She cut the ignition and tucked her keys into her pocket. The block was silent and cold, but Noelle didn't hear or feel it. She kept trying to quiet the roaring in her ears and cool the inferno raging through her body.

Calm down!

Noelle took a deep breath, got out the car, and started down the street.

"I'm right here with you, baby," Parker told her through her earpiece. "Stick to the plan, and I'll be there with you very soon."

"I can't wait," Noelle whispered.

Once she made it to Gray's front door, she took out the appropriate tools to unlock the door. Unlocking the door was easy, just like Parker said it would be. Gray thought he was such a powerful man that no one would dare to break into his home; therefore, he didn't use extra precautions such as dead bolts or home alarm systems. His prized possessions were in a safe that no one knew about. For all intents and purposes, Gray felt secure.

"You're doing great," Parker whispered. "Now, make your way through the house and into the kitchen."

She walked quickly but quietly through the house. Once she made it to the kitchen she took a look around. Wineglasses and an empty bottle of vintage Merlot were on the kitchen counter.

Noelle turned suddenly when she heard laughter coming from an upstairs room. She began to panic immediately. Gray should have been asleep at three in the morning, but he was awake, and it sounded as if he had company. In fact, she distinctly heard a woman's moan, and then the woman calling out Gray's name in a high-pitched, shrill tone that would have grated on any man's nerves had he heard it at any time other than during sex.

"He's awake up there," she barely whispered to Parker. "And he's having sex with a woman."

"Stay focused and get into that safe. He won't hear you until it's time to hear you."

Noelle took a deep breath and stood at the sink, staring at the tiled backsplash. The safe that she had to get into was back there.

She pressed the painted green pear on the center tile and heard a soft hissing sound. She grabbed the bottom corner of the tile and pulled. The infamous safe loomed before her eyes.

"Now, open the safe just as we practiced," Parker instructed.

Noelle held her breath as she disabled the voice recognition program, then began clipping the wires around the safe. *So far, so good,* she thought. The hardest part was done. When she went to type in the combination, her mind went blank.

"Parker, the combination."

Parker immediately rattled off the numbers at the same time she heard Gray's voice at the top of the stairs.

"He's coming down," Noelle said quickly.

"Move fast and get the jewels."

"Gray, come back, baby," the upstairs female voice called out.

Thankfully, Noelle heard Gray retrace his footsteps. She worked quickly and finally held four black velvet pouches in her hand.

"Fifteen seconds, Noelle."

She knew that was how long before Gray would come running downstairs with a Glock, ready to fire. By removing the jewels, she had purposely tripped the silent alarm that was triggered once the weight of the jewels was removed. Now the real plan was beginning.

"What the fuck?" Noelle heard Gray shouting upstairs, and she knew he was on his way downstairs.

"He's coming," she whispered.

"Stay focused and tell him exactly what happened."

She took off toward the front door as if she were trying to escape just as Gray ran down the stairs, the Glock aimed toward her head and his finger on the trigger.

"Hold it right there, motherfucker," Gray said through gritted teeth.

Noelle immediately stopped and held up her hands. "Don't fucking shoot," she told Gray. "I had to break into your safe or he'll kill her."

"What the hell is going on?" asked the woman who stood at the top of the stairs wearing a red silk robe.

"Get your ass back upstairs, Miranda," Gray told her as he moved closer to Noelle.

She had evidently piqued his curiosity enough that he hadn't shot her yet.

"Start talking, bitch, or you're dead," Gray yelled. "Who's going to kill who?"

"Carlos killed my mother and kidnapped my little sister, Paris. I have to pay back my mother's debt, or he'll kill Paris."

Noelle slowly sat the four black velvet pouches on the floor in front of her.

"How much does Carlos want?" he asked.

"Twenty-three thousand."

"Do you know how much those stones are worth?"

"No, I don't. I'm sure it's much, much more than twenty grand. I just want my sister back home. She's only eleven."

"Why the fuck should I believe you?" Gray asked as he lowered his gun.

"How else would I know where your safe is?"

"Go into the living room and sit down," he instructed.

Noelle cautiously moved into the living room and took a seat. So far things were going according to plan. Gray seemed to believe her.

"Here comes the call, baby," Parker said through her earpiece.

She was glad that Parker was with her. It was scary enough

having a gun held on her twice in a matter of days. It felt like she was living someone else's life.

Gray picked up a sleek silver cordless phone and dialed a number. She knew who he was calling.

"Get your ass here in fifteen minutes."

Gray set the phone down and began to question Noelle further.

"How long have you known Carlos?"

"I just met him the day he killed my mother. He was waiting in my house for my sister and me to return home."

"Why did your mother take out a loan?"

Noelle shrugged her shoulders at first, but remembered she was to be as truthful as possible.

"I thought my mother was clean, but she relapsed. She wanted the money for drugs, I'm sure. While she was high, someone stole her purse, which had the money she had borrowed in it."

"Gray, is everything all right?" Miranda yelled.

"Yes, honey. Go back to bed."

Gray asked a few more questions before the doorbell rang.

"Don't move," he ordered, and went to answer the door.

Chapter Sixteen

"This will be the last time that motherfucker tries to steal from me," Gray announced.

"I know you're pissed, Gray, but you don't need trouble right now," Parker said.

"I don't have to be there, but there will be trouble. Count on it. You get anything else from the girl?"

Parker glanced over at Noelle sitting on the couch wringing her hands nervously. She was holding up like a champ.

"No, nothing more. I made a few calls. Everything she said checks out. She just wants to get her sister back. And from what I've learned, she needs to get the little one now. It seems Carlos's cousin has developed a thing for little girls."

Gray glanced at Noelle, who shuddered upon hearing about the cousin. He was getting too old for this bullshit. He regretted not taking care of Carlos years ago. But he wouldn't make the same mistake twice.

"Call Cocoa. Tell her I have a job for her," Gray told Parker.

"What time and where should I tell her to meet us?"

"One hour. But she's not meeting us. We'll meet her. She's to call me when she gets situated."

Parker pulled out his cell phone.

"Noelle, you ready to get your sister?" Gray asked.

"Yes. That's all I want."

"Well, call Carlos and tell him you have the money. Tell him that you'll be there in an hour and that you're bringing your friend Cocoa with you because she needs a loan."

"I hope you don't mind my asking," she began, "but who is Cocoa?"

"A man's worst fucking nightmare," Parker stated with a smile. Cocoa was one goddamn foxy bitch.

. . .

Noelle turned around when she heard a woman call her name. She had almost missed the sound because she was concentrating so much on keeping her legs from giving out on her. She was terrified of what was about to happen. She didn't know the whole plan, but, ultimately, Carlos was going to get fucked up. And she had to make sure Paris was safe in the process.

"Morning, I'm Cocoa."

Noelle looked at a woman who seemed as if she should be in Hollywood. She wore designer labels from head to toe. Prada sunglasses caught the beginnings of sunrise, a mink jacket kept the morning chill away, Apple Bottom jeans were tight enough you could count the change in her back pockets, and black Jimmy Choos adorned her feet. She looked damned good. And she certainly had the best weave Noelle had ever seen. That's if it was a weave at all.

That might actually be the bitch's hair, she thought, staring at Cocoa's shoulder-length curly black hair with the brownish gold highlights.

"I'm Noelle. Thank you for coming."

"When we go inside, tell the bastard you want to see your sister first, then let me take it from there."

Noelle rang the doorbell and waited. A few seconds later Ronald answered the door. She had found out that he was a friend of Parker's working on the inside to keep an eye on Carlos. She remembered his being at the house the day Carlos kidnapped Paris.

"Noelle, Paris is okay," Ronald said hurriedly. "Cocoa, good to see you, baby."

Ronald opened the door wide to let them inside. They followed him into Carlos's office and took seats in front of his desk.

"He'll be in here in a minute," Ronald told them. "Cocoa, I'll be close by."

"That's good to know, handsome," Cocoa said with a smile, and blew him a kiss.

Once Ronald left, Cocoa issued Noelle a reminder. "Remember to get Paris in here before you show him any cash."

"But I don't have any cash," Noelle whispered.

"He doesn't know that. Just get him to let you see Paris."

Noelle and Cocoa sat silently for a good five minutes before Carlos came into his office. He wasted no time, except to stare at Cocoa for an extra ten seconds before sitting at his desk.

Since Carlos wanted to stare, Cocoa gave him something to look at. She inserted her index finger into her mouth, bobbed her head up and down a few times, then made a loud smacking sound as she pulled her wet finger out of her mouth.

She batted her eyelashes, gave Carlos a smoldering stare, and said, "I'm sorry, it's just a lil' ol' habit I have to keep my lipstick from getting on my teeth. It works wonders."

"You are delicious," he said to Cocoa, then turned to Noelle. "Where's the fucking money?"

Carlos cut right to business, making himself forget that he'd just seen probably the most beautiful, erotic creature of his life.

"Let me see Paris first," Noelle told him.

"I don't have time to play any fucking games. Where's my goddamn money?"

"No money until I lay eyes on my sister, Carlos."

Carlos smiled. "If your mother was half the woman you are, she would probably be alive right now, and you wouldn't be in this situation."

Carlos picked up the cordless phone on his desk and placed a call. A few short minutes later an overweight man came in with Paris in tow.

"Noelle!" Paris started across the office but was stopped by a big grubby hand.

"Paris, baby, are you okay?"

"I'm okay."

"Touching," Carlos mocked. "Now where's my money?"

Cocoa sprang into action so fast that she actually looked like a female action hero from the movies. She vaulted over Carlos's desk, reached inside her mink jacket, and produced a syringe filled with a clear substance. Cocoa plunged the needle into Carlos's neck so fast that if Noelle would have blinked, she would have missed it.

"What the fuck are you doing?" the fat man shouted.

Cocoa pulled a 9 mm with a silencer on it from her waistband and silenced Carlos's cousin with a single bullet to the head, then turned her attention back to Carlos.

"You have been injected with a paralyzing agent," Cocoa told him, and laughed seductively. The sound was so melodious that Noelle thought she could probably sing like Patti LaBelle if she wanted.

"I'm sure you're really pissed right now, but no one gives a fuck. I'd ask you if you had any last words, but you can't talk, so fuck you."

Carlos tried to move but couldn't. Noelle could see the panic in his eyes.

"Paris, come over here."

Paris had remained frozen the entire time. She kept staring at the bullet wound on fat man's head. She was glad that he was dead. Especially because he had a thing for little girls. "Noelle!" Paris ran to her sister.

She hadn't known if she would ever see Noelle again. She went into her sister's arms and hugged her like she had never hugged her before.

"I missed you so much, Noelle! I even missed you telling me to do my homework."

"I missed you, too, baby girl."

"Carlos, you have visitors," Cocoa announced, and swiveled his chair around just in time to see Gray and Parker walk through his office door. "Go on and say hello to your friends."

Cocoa slapped Carlos on the back of his head and laughed. She loved her job so much. Being a female assassin was quite enjoyable. Especially when she got to deal with vermin like Carlos. Those were the kills she relished.

"Carlos, you sorry motherfucker," Gray said. He walked over and spit in his face.

Parker stood his ground and kept an eye on Noelle and Paris. He was glad to see the sisters reunited. His plan had worked out well. Now he was enjoying every minute of watching Carlos's soon-to-be corpse helpless in that chair.

"This will teach you to steal from me," Gray told Carlos's paralyzed body as he pulled out a Magnum .357 that would rival Dirty Harry's gun any day. "I will see you in hell."

Gray pulled the trigger and blew a hole in the center of Carlos's chest.

"What do we have here?" Gray asked as he bent down to the duffel bag beside Carlos's desk. He unzipped it and found the bag full of crisp benjamins.

Gray took his time and counted out one hundred bills, then repeated the process. He gave the first stack to Cocoa.

"Cocoa, thank you for being available on such short notice," Gray told her.

"Anything for you, Gray. I think I'll use this ten thousand to fly to Italy to pick up a few more pairs of shoes."

"That's my girl," Gray said affectionately.

Gray handed the other ten thousand to Parker. "This is a down payment. I need another safe designed."

"No problem, Gray. I'll get right on it," Parker replied.

Gray zipped the duffel bag, still full with the rest of the money, and handed it to Noelle.

"Give your mother a proper burial, put away a college fund for your sister, and have some fun. You have a lot of responsibility for someone so young."

Noelle accepted the duffel bag with shaking hands. Her mind was spinning. The bag was *full* of one-hundred-dollar bills.

"I don't know what to say," Noelle sputtered.

"Say you won't ever try to break in my house again." Gray laughed. "All right, everybody, let's get the fuck out of Dodge in case the neighbors heard that gunshot. It would cost a lot of my money to bail all you motherfuckers out of jail and even more for your silence."

"Call me the next time you need me, Gray," Cocoa said as she stood, adjusted her shades, and walked out the house.

"Parker, you'll make sure Noelle and her sister get home safely?"

"It would be my honor, Gray."

Gray winked at Parker. "She is drop-dead gorgeous, isn't she? I mean, shawty is phat!"

Parker laughed. Gray always sounded as if he belonged on Wall Street rather than in the 'hood.

"I have to agree with you, Gray. I haven't met someone as beautiful as Noelle in a long time."

"Well, don't fuck up," Gray instructed.

"Don't worry, I won't."

Gray walked out, leaving Parker, Noelle, and Paris all alone.

"Well, ladies, after you."

"How can I ever thank you, Parker?" Noelle asked, still clutching both Paris and the duffel bag.

"You and Paris can spend Christmas with me."

Noelle smiled. For the first Christmas in a long time, she had a reason to celebrate.

A Christmas Song

by Seth "Soul Man" Ferranti

Chapter One

"You know I hate fuckin' Christmas, so forget about it," Johnny Two-Fingers told his paisano, Big Vinny, who nodded in agreement. "How the fuck am I supposed to buy my fucking wife and kids presents from here?" Johnny Two-Fingers asked.

Just then Mikey P and Tommy Boy, two other New York wise-guys, walked up. Fats, who worked as an orderly in the unit, watched as he swept up the front entryway.

"Hey, Johnny, what the fuck is up?" Mikey P said, shaking hands with Johnny Two-Fingers and nodding to Big Vinny. Tommy Boy greeted them, too.

"Fucking Mikey P. We got a motherfucking problem here," Johnny Two-Fingers said.

Mikey P looked on and pushed his glasses up. "Oh yeah, well, what the fuck is that, Johnny? We gotta bury somebody or what?" Mikey P joked, and all the Italians laughed as Mikey P jabbed Big Vinny in the arm. "Sounds like a job for Big Vinny, hey, Tommy Boy?"

As they all laughed, Fats thought about his own family and what he would get them for Christmas. Johnny Two-Fingers was saying how even for those with money, it wasn't easy to get your family presents from prison. It wasn't like prisoners could buy the presents and wrap them. The Italians kept talking, ignoring Fats as he swept up cigarette butts on the walkway.

"Now look here," Johnny Two-Fingers said to Mikey P. "Youse a man with experience. Now I'm asking youse. How the fuck am I supposed to buy my fucking wife and kids presents from here? You know Christmas is right around the corner, and I gots to buy them something. They're expecting it, locked up or not. I know youse been down a long time, Mikey P, and I remember your family getting all types of nice presents every year while youse was away. So tell us, how did youse pull it off?"

Mikey P got a real serious look on his face and pushed his glasses up his nose again. He was the reputed consigliere for the Luchasse family in New York, and as he composed his five-foot-seven-inch frame, Fats could see how he had risen to his position. *It wasn't his stature,* Fats thought, *it was the way he carried himself.* The way he walked and talked. Like he knew the answer to every question. Fats didn't know the Italians real well, but he said hi and 'bye to them in passing. They were all in his unit. Fats continued to ear hustle the Italians while he swept.

"This is hows I pulled it off all these years, getting my family presents for Christmas or whatever," Mikey P shared. "I just tells my cousin Johnny G. 'Hey, Johnny, find out what the kids and missus want for Christmas and buy it for them, all right?' Forget about it. That's all you need to do, Johnny. A piece of work right?" Mikey P laughed and jabbed his partner Tommy Boy in the arm, and Tommy Boy took up the laughter, too. In a second all four Italians were laughing their asses off like what Mikey P said was the funniest thing they'd heard this year.

"So, what you gonna get 'em all for Christmas, Johnny?" Mikey P asked.

"Aw Mikey, I don't fuckin' know. I guess I better call my brother and tell him to get them something or I'll never hear the end of it. Forget about it." Johnny Two-Fingers laughed and looked over at Fats, whom he noticed for the first time.

"Hey, Fats," Johnny Two-Fingers called. "What you gonna get your family for Christmas? I saw those little kids of yours in the visiting room. You gonna get them something nice, right?"

Fats looked up, making eye contact with the chubby Italian. He wasn't used to them talking to him, but he guessed he'd been around the unit and on the compound long enough now for them to acknowledge him. It had been only eight months, but it seemed like much longer. All the Italians were waiting for him to speak.

"Yeah, I'm gonna get them something real nice," Fats answered. All the Italians smiled.

Mikey P nodded and put his arm around Johnny Two-Fingers. "See Johnny, that kid ain't even been here longer than you, and he already knows what's up. He's probably been planning it for a month already. And here we are two months away from Christmas, and you don't even know what to get your fucking family, forget about it." Mikey P clapped Johnny Two-Fingers on the back. Johnny Two-Fingers cringed from the clap, but he didn't say anything. All the wise guys laughed, and Fats walked away smiling, but honestly, he didn't know what he was going to do for his family at Christmas. Unlike the Italians, who were known as the "Big Willies" and big spenders on the compound, Fats didn't have any money to lavish on gifts for his loved ones. Actually, he didn't have any money at all.

Fats was fresh in on a ten-year bid for conspiracy to distribute crack. Twenty-four years old and not a dime to his name. Don't get it fucked up, Fats was a hustler, but he wasn't a big-time dude like the Italians, and he had no money saved up. All the money he made serving dudes from the block went to support his three kids and two baby-mamas, that is, whatever he didn't trick or gamble away. Now he was doing time in a new federal prison in West Virginia, FCI Beckley. Five hours from home and broke as a joke. He was lucky he had the twenty-five-dollar-a-month unit-orderly job that his homeboy Mel-Mel had hooked him up with when he hit the pound. And now it was Christmastime. Fats didn't even want to think about it as he made his way back into the unit.

"What up, slim?"

A downcast Fats looked up and smiled at his man, Rock. "Ain't but a thing, moe. What's up with you?" Fats asked as he pounded fists with Rock.

"You looking all sad and shit, slim! Let me find out this time killing you already?" Rock jigged at his friend.

"Naw, dawg, it's all good. I'm just thinking about my kids," Fats said.

"Well, that's all good, slim. The lil' ones coming up on the bus this weekend or what?"

"Yeah, I gotta holla at my babys' moms, but I think they coming up for sure, moe. Why, your peeps coming up, too?" Fats asked.

"You know it, baby boy! I'm trying to get my shine on up on that dance floor. It's the only time these crackers let a nigga live," Rock said seriously, and Fats agreed.

Doing time was rough. Especially up in these hills, he thought. *With all these redneck guards always sweating a brother. Getting time with the family in the visiting room was one of the only reasons dudes in prison stayed sane,* Fats thought. But for real, this Christmas thing was killing Fats. He'd never spent a Christmas away from his family before. And now his kids Maurice, Yvette, and Demitrius—who were eight, six, and five—would not only have to spend their first Christmas away from their father, they might not even get a decent present from him. *I got to come up with something,* he thought. *Hopefully I can holla at Laquesha about it on the VI this weekend.*

His homie Rock had been down a minute, but he didn't have any kids. Maybe Rock might know of a way to come up. Fats would have to holler at him later; it was still only October.

Chapter Two

It was a long trip on the crowded bus with two kids all the way from D.C. to bum-fuck West Virginia, but to Laquesha it was worth it. Fats was her babys' daddy, and when he was on the street he always provided well. It had been rough for Laquesha since Fats got locked up. She was surviving, but it was by no means easy, and it hadn't even been a year yet. She was lucky she'd had her mother to fall back on.

"Damn, girl, ain't we there yet?" Melissa asked Laquesha. Melissa was Rock's girl. She was the one who hooked Laquesha up with the bus-trip people. They picked up families all over D.C. and took them to visit at different federal institutions in Virginia, West Virginia, and Maryland, depending on the week. They charged only twenty-five dollars per person, and kids under twelve rode for free. After paying for a hotel and having money for the vending machines for two days, Laquesha could afford to do it only once a month. It was the least she could do—taking the kids to see their daddy—besides, Laquesha had a soft spot for Fats, too. *Even though he was a no-good, cheating motherfucker,* she thought. She was just glad that Kim, Fats's other baby's mama, wasn't on this trip. She hated when she had to share the visit with that bitch, even though, Kim and Fats's son, Demitrius, was cute as he could be.

It wouldn't be long, and Christmas would be coming up, Laquesha thought. She knew it would be a rough Christmas this year because, with Fats in jail, money would be tight. Laquesha would do what she could, but it wouldn't be the same. Fats had always spoiled the kids, buying them whatever they'd wanted. But this year it would be different. Maurice and Yvette would just have to face the facts that their daddy was locked up and money wasn't coming in like it used to. She hoped they were old enough to understand.

"We almost there," Laquesha told Melissa, who closed her

eyes. The bus trip had picked them up damn near in the middle of the night so that they could get there by nine A.M. before the ten A.M. weekend count. Laquesha knew if they didn't make it in before then, they would be waiting until almost noon before the count cleared and the prisoners were called. The prison staff acted like the families were the criminals, giving off attitude like they didn't even want families to visit for real. It was an experience, but for the kids it was worth it to see their daddy.

Yvette opened up her big brown eyes, which were the focal point of her little face. "Mommy, are we there yet?" she asked.

"Yeah, we almost there," Laquesha said, smoothing back her daughter's hair which was braided the way Fats liked it.

Fats always insisted on Yvette having her hair neatly braided. Laquesha thought it was cute, so she always made sure to braid both her and Yvette's hair before they visited. Maurice slept soundly in his Washington Redskins jersey. He was growing up real fast, Laquesha knew, and it wouldn't be long now before he was a man. Fats didn't want his son to follow his path, but Laquesha didn't know how she would keep him off the streets. He was already starting to run wild with the neighborhood boys. As the bus pulled onto the road that led to the prison, Laquesha started getting herself and her kids ready for the visit.

. . .

"Daddy!" Yvette screamed as she flew into Fats's arms. Maurice and Laquesha followed, and hugs and kisses were exchanged all the way around. They all took a seat off to one side.

Fats scoped out his man Rock and his girl, Melissa. He nodded at both of them saying, "What's up." "You be talking to Rock's girl on the trip?" Fats asked Laquesha. "Yeah, boo, that's my girl, why?" Laquesha said.

"Just wondering, that's all." Fats smiled. He was really wondering if Laquesha knew that Melissa was bringing in that tar for Rock. Rock had just informed Fats the night before that he had convinced his girl to bring him three grams of heroin packaged in balloons. During the visit Rock would swallow three balloons, containing a gram of heroin each, then shit them out later. He told Fats that he could make almost a thousand dollars a gram. Now that was a come up, Fats thought, heroin on the street cost seventy-five dollars a gram. If he could convince Laquesha to do the same thing, then it would be all good. But Fats didn't know how to bring it up, so he'd hoped that maybe Melissa had told Laquesha what she was doing. But, obviously, she hadn't.

"Daddy, Daddy, lookee here," Yvette said, holding something up to her daddy's face. Fats came out of his illicit moment and looked to his daughter.

"What's that, baby girl?" he asked. Yvette was holding up a little bracelet that she wore around her tiny wrist. It was one of the last gifts Fats had bought her before he got locked up, a charm bracelet from Tiffany's. His daughter held up the bracelet on her little arm, beaming with pride that she was wearing her daddy's gift. "That's beautiful, baby girl," Fats said.

"I know." Yvette grinned. "Will you get me more for Christmas?" she asked, looking into Fats's face, batting her big brown eyes. "Please, Daddy? And get Mommy one, too?" Fats felt nothing but love for his daughter as she pleaded with him.

"And I want a new bike, too, Daddy," Maurice chimed in as if on cue. Both Yvette and Maurice smiled. Fats felt all eyes on him, and he was thinking about how he wasn't gonna be able to get them nothing, but he couldn't tell his baby girl and son that.

He reached his arms around both his kids and held them close. "I'll get you all whatever you want. Just let Daddy know, and I'll make it happen." Fats smiled. "You know I got a direct hookup to Santa Claus." Yvette squealed with delight at that, and Maurice lit up, too. Laquesha gave them some quarters and told them to go get their daddy a soda and candy bar from the vending machine. When they ran off, she turned to Fats.

"Now, Felix, don't be telling them kids no lies. You know we don't have no money. How you gonna buy them presents for Christmas with money we don't have?" Laquesha scolded. She loved Fats to death, especially for the way he treated and responded to the kids, but she knew the reality of the situation. And she didn't like leading her kids on in any type of way.

"Naw, La, it ain't like that," Fats said. "You know I'm a hustler. I'm gonna figure something out."

"Oh yeah, like what?" Laquesha asked. Fats wanted to blurt it out, but he didn't know if it was the right time to bring it up. He knew that if he could convince Laquesha to bring the drugs, they'd be straight. For Christmas and everything else.

"You know I'm working on some moves, La," Fats said. "I just need to know if you with me or what?"

"Of course I'm with you, boo. You know I got your back, but you need to let me know what you're talking about." Fats looked back toward the vending machine to make sure his kids weren't on their way back.

"It's like this, La." Fats lowered his voice. "We can come up."

He looked over toward Rock and Melissa. "You see, Rock got Melissa making moves for him on the balloon tip so that he can get paper from in here."

Laquesha got a real serious look on her face and pulled her hand away from Fats. "Felix James." Her voice now stern. "I hope you're not suggesting what I think you're suggesting. With the kids and all? I won't do any such thing!" Fats grabbed his girl's hands again and held them in his own.

"Damn La." He tried to ease the tension. "Don't be getting all excited." He looked around to check on the kids again. "They doing it and it's all good, so why can't we be doing it, too?"

Laquesha saw the intense look in Fats's eyes and took a minute to consider his proposal. She knew a few of her homegirls were doing stuff like that, plus when she was just a little girl she used to take weed up to her dad while he was at USP Lewisburg. *But the kids,* she thought. If not for the kids she would be down for it all the way. She wouldn't think of subjecting her kids to that type of situation, though. What if something went wrong? Fats was asking a lot of her.

Fats saw Laquesha contemplating and figured that if he said the right thing, he could tip the scales in his favor.

Just then, the kids came back.

"Here, Daddy," Yvette smiled as Fats took his soda and candy bar. Maurice sat down and started eating his Reese's Peanut Butter Cup, and Yvette chewed down on some gummy bears. Laquesha got up in a huff like she was mad, but really she wasn't. She was weighing the pros and cons of Fats's proposal. She strolled over to the vending machine and bought herself a cherry cola.

Laquesha watched Fats with the kids and was on the verge of

deciding if she would go through with his suggestion when she noticed three COs walk into the visiting room to confer with the CO stationed at the desk. They all got up and walked over to Rock and Melissa. Laquesha knew exactly what was up.

Chapter Three

 ack on the pound the next day the whole jail was buzzing about Rock getting hemmed up on the VI. Homies stepped to Fats to find out how it went down. Foul play was suspected, but nobody was drawing any conclusions just yet. No one knew with certainty as to what really happened.

"Damn, slim," said Country. "How they get my man like that?" Fats didn't really know, but he wanted to oblige his big homie, who was one of the most respected D.C. dudes on the pound, and at least tell him something. Country had been down for over a decade and had seen time in all the pens, so this FCI shit was nothing to him; plus he'd been down Lorton back in the day, and all the young'uns had heard the war stories about Lorton. Country was known as a go-hard southeast gangsta through and through, and Fats jumped at the opportunity to be down with the big homie.

"I don't know, moe," Fats told him. "I didn't see him doing nothing suspicious with his girl. Five-oh just rolled up and grabbed dude, no bullshit."

Country rolled his eyes and screwed his face up. "Those fucking redneck crackers," he growled. "Always fucking up a nigga's move with they bamma-ass shit. You didn't hear Rock telling no-body about what he was doing, did you, slim?"

Fats double-checked Country on that one because Rock had mentioned the move to him the night before. He moseyed up into Fats and Mel-Mel's cell and could hardly contain himself knowing he was about to make a move and come up. *The stupid nigga probably ran his mouth to everyone,* Fats thought. Loose lips sink ships.

"Three grams of tar, moe," he told Fats and Mel-Mel. "Straight from the city. We gonna get that bread, no bullshit." Fats had also noticed that Mel-Mel had that glint in his eye. *Let me find out this old-timer's a dope fiend,* Fats thought at the time. But it wasn't to be. Something went wrong, and the move turned disastrous. Dudes on the pound were saying that Rock's girl, Melissa, got arrested in the parking lot, and that Rock was look-ing at a street charge if he passed any balloons in the dry cell. *And they sure as hell had him up in that motherfucking dry cell watching Slim's every move, waiting for him to take a shit,* Fats thought. The word was that they supposedly had the whole transaction on videotape from the visiting room, too. Fats knew from his limited experience in prison that dudes talked a lot of shit on the pound. Who knew what was really up?

Country was focusing in on Fats with a crazy look in his eyes.

"Did I stutter, little homie?" Country asked. "You can't hear or what, slim?"

Fats came back to the present. "Yeah, I mean, naw," Fats stum-bled. "I didn't hear Rock tell nobody nothing. No bullshit, moe."

Country seemed to accept that and hit rocks with Fats. "Check it out, slim." Country changed gears. "We balling later at the gym on the rec move, so bring your fat ass up there. You know we putting together a little team for the homies to represent in the winter league and for the Christmas tournament. I know you got a lil' game, so I wanna see you up there. I need you to get your game tight because if you can hit those trays consistently, it'll help us do something, awright?"

"Awright, moe, bet," Fats said.

Country bounced, leaving Fats in the common area of Poplar B-Upper, wondering if he should call his girl Laquesha and find out what happened to Melissa. He knew the bus had gone back that morning, and he wondered if they made it to the city yet. Fats had really enjoyed his visit, even though it was only for one day. He already missed his kids. After what happened to Rock and Melissa, Laquesha wasn't feeling that balloon shit. She wasn't having no more of that kind of talk. Just when Fats felt like he had almost convinced her, Laquesha had shut it down, period. No ifs, ands, or buts! But Fats was still scheming. He had to come up some way.

Maybe I should get in hobby craft, he thought. Then I can make my kids something for Christmas! Fats knew a lot of dudes would be making leather-craft stuff—like purses and wallets and the like—then sending them home to their families. A lot of dudes used hobby craft to hustle by making things, then selling them to other people who sent them out as gifts. They did ceramics in recreation, too. Fats had seen a lot of nice pieces, but he didn't have the funds to make any purchases. *Shit, I don't even have the funds to buy the material to get into the class,* he thought.

He was gonna have to find another way.

He did have his other baby-mama, Kim, to consider, and she

was supposed to visit him the first week of November. She was a little more gangsta than Laquesha, so Fats was thinking maybe he could put something together with her. Fats knew his big homie Country could make all the arrangements, but Fats couldn't shake the feeling from what happened to his man Rock. Somebody snitched on his boy. *But a nigga got to do what a nigga got to do,* Fats thought. Snitches or not! Fats knew the snitches in the federal prison system were vicious. He'd heard a lot of stories since he touched down on the pound, and the deal with Rock confirmed all the rap. Fats would have to be real careful if bammas were working like that. He would have to put together his plan and make sure it was tight. He wasn't trying to go out like no sucka.

"Hey, Fats, what's up there bro?" Mikey P greeted Fats as he walked down the tier. "How was your visit yesterday? I heard you had the kids up."

Fats stood up and shook the Italian's hand. Mikey P was still in good shape for an older guy, and his grip was strong. "My visit was good Mr. P," Fats said. "But you heard about my homie, right?"

"Yeah, yeah." Mikey P sighed. "Rock. He's a good dude. I've been doing time with him for a minute. A stand-up guy. Hopefully they gots nothing on him, you hear me. A guy's gotta be careful who he tells his business to in these joints. Forget about it." Mikey P slapped Fats on the shoulder and went on his way.

Fats was left there pondering. *Halloween, Thanksgiving, and Christmas I gotta get mines together. Ain't no ifs, ands, or buts about it,* he thought.

. . .

Later that day, Fats was in the gym balling with his homies. The D.C. mob wasn't looking too hot, but with Country as a motivator, they would do all right. Fats busted out with a barrage of threes, so he figured he had one of the guard spots on lock. He was a little overweight and wasn't that tall, but he could shoot and handle the rock way better than a lot of the bigger or more athletic guys. Plus, he played smart ball. Fats had run his junior high and high school teams but at age sixteen he had gotten Laquesha, then fifteen, pregnant with Maurice. So he dropped out and started hustling full-time to make ends meet, but the game never left him. He always made time to play blacktop or whatever. *If I could just get into better shape, I would be a beast!* Fats thought.

Country was thinking along those same lines. He knew Fats could score and push the rock. He was just a little heavy around the middle. Country had a couple of go-hard bangers but what the homies was lacking was a true go-to scorer. They had a couple of athletic wing-type dudes who could throw it down, but they didn't really know the fundamentals of the game. *Hopefully, between me and Fats, we can school them and win this Christmas tournament,* Country thought.

After the runs, everybody was chillin' in the bleachers while Country held court. "Man, fuck all these rats, slim," he said to no one in particular, rather addressing all his homeboys as one. "The feds is full of snitches!" Country continued. "Down Lorton, we didn't tolerate that shit. We'd run those bitch-ass bammas straight up out the yard and into PC or they'd end up with six inches of steel in they eye. That's how the fuck we was rollin' back in the day, slim. No bullshit." The younger homies like Fats listened intently. Although they had never done time in Lorton, they'd heard the stories of the notorious D.C. jail.

With complicit guards bringing in drugs and female CO's selling their bodies, Lorton was sweet for the prisoners. The violence was everyday, and it was brutal. It mirrored the violence in the city, because back in the day D.C. was known as the murder capital of the world. It was rumored that dudes on the compound even had guns to settle their differences. In a way, the younger generation like Fats were glad they'd never had to step foot in Lorton. Because it was a dog-eat-dog world, either kill or be killed. Lorton was so corrupt that the feds shut the prison down and absorbed all the D.C. convicts into the federal system and now they were flung coast to coast all over the BOP. The feds were a whole lot tamer and safe even though all the homies were much farther from home.

At recall Fats walked with his homies back to the block. A shower was definitely in order. Good prison etiquette declared that a convict didn't walk around like a Viking. The water was free, so fuck it. Fats was up on his personal hygiene anyhow, unlike a lot of these bammas whom he was forced to deal with on a day-to-day basis. A lot of them still had that crackhead mentality. After his shower, Fats knew it would be time to call Laquesha to see what was up.

* * *

Automated voice: "You have a call from a correctional facility. This call is prepaid. This call is from [voice of Fats] Fats. Please push five to accept this call; please push seven to block further calls from this person. If you accept the call, push five now." The automated voice rattled off the instructions after Fats punched in Laquesha's digits and his pin number. Laquesha pushed five.

"Hey, boo."

"What's up, La, you all made it home safe?"

"Yeah, boo, you okay?"

"I'm straight, La. What happened to Melissa?" Fats asked.

"They called the local hillbilly Five-oh and searched her and then they searched the bus and the driver, but they didn't find nothing. They just made her sit on the bus for the rest of the day," Laquesha said.

"That's good. They got Rock in the dry cell, I heard. At least Melissa made it back with you. Did she tell you if Rock was dirty?" Fats asked.

"What do you think, Fats? Melissa was real fucked up, boo. She was crying and worried for Rock the whole trip back. She said they gonna give him more time and ship him back out west to the pen. You know he was at Lompoc in Cali before? How the fuck is Melissa supposed to visit him if they send him back out there? One of the girls said that if Rock gets caught with balloons, they'll take his visits for five years. Now you see why I ain't doing no shit like that, right?"

Fats cringed at all the bullshit Laquesha was spilling on the phone. *I hope them people ain't listening right now,* he thought. *This girl trying to blow up the spot.*

"Yeah, I hear you, La. Well, how's the kids?" Fats changed gears.

"They good. I just put them to sleep," Laquesha said.

"La, let me talk to my little girl."

"Naw, boo, they *asleep*. I don't want to wake them up."

"Damn, La, just let me say hello."

"Awright." Fats heard her slam the phone down and a few minutes later he heard his baby girl's voice on the line.

"Hey, Daddy, I miss you. I love you."

"I love you, too, baby girl. Bye-bye and nighty-night."

"Bye-bye, Daddy."

Fats was all good then. . . .

Chapter Four

The next morning Fats was up early doing his orderly job. He peeped the Italians going out to the yard and overheard a couple of the gumps on his unit talking about Christmas decorations.

"Girl, you know we got to do something big here this year. We gotta put it down in this unit."

"I know what you mean, when I was in Fort Dix, they used to have this competition where you decorated a whole TV room. They used to do it up, girl. We would get wrapping paper and cardboard and make little castles with ribbons and snowmen—all kinds of stuff. For real, it was off the chain, girl."

"They not gonna let us do shit like that here. They probably won't even let us get a tree or nothing. But if they do, let's get boxes and wrap them up and put them under the tree like some gorgeous man is buying us presents." Both the homosexuals laughed.

"You go, girl! You crazy, always dreaming of some real man, when all we got is these broke-ass niggas in here with us that just be wanting us to suck their dicks."

"Yeah, you right, girl, but a bitch can dream, can't she? I need a real thug who falls in love with me and buys me presents."

"You can dream, girl, but ain't no shit like that happenin' here. Shit, they probably won't even let us put up decorations or nothing."

"Yeah, you right, but still, let's go talk to the warden at mainline and run it by her bitch ass. We might be able to convince her."

"Awright, girl."

After making their plans, the gumps bounced out the unit, too. *Probably going to some illicit rendezvous,* Fats thought. *I don't understand how some of these niggas can get with that. I'll never do no shit like that,* Fats told himself. He was repulsed by homosexuals. He could talk to them and shit like that, but he wasn't down with none of that extra shit. But he knew a lot of brothers were into that sort of thing; they were closet-type dudes. Kept their shit on the low. Fats didn't know for certain, but he'd heard that some of his homies were like that. It was just something that wasn't brought up. Fats's bunkie Mel-Mel called them homothugs. He used to hear Mel-Mel and the other old-timers joking how it was all legal after ten years. Whatever the fuck that meant. That shit would never be legal with Fats.

• • •

"Girl, you ain't heard from Rock yet?" Laquesha said as they sat in the kitchen of her mom's Barry Farms town house.

"Naw, they probably still got him in the dry cell," Melissa said to Laquesha.

"You think so?"

"Yeah, Shanice said they kept Country in a dry cell at Lewisburg for eight days before he passed the balloons," Melissa said. "Rock's a dumb-ass for doing that shit. If he woulda got me locked up for that bullshit . . ."

Laquesha gave her girl a hug when she started to tear up. *It's always dumb-ass niggas getting us girls into trouble,* Laquesha thought. And to think Fats had the nerve to ask her, with the kids and all, to try to do some bullshit like that.

"What do you think they gonna do with him, Laquesha?" Melissa asked.

"Damn girl, I don't know. That one girl on the bus said they'll probably take his visits, commissary, and phone for five years."

"Five years," Melissa said. "What the fuck am I gonna do?"

Laquesha consoled her again. "Maybe it's for the best, girl. Maybe you should dump his scandalous ass." Melissa looked up, not real sure what to say, and Laquesha was thinking that maybe she should dump Fats for even suggesting that shit to her. *But the kids,* she thought. *They love their daddy.*

Just then Maurice and Yvette rolled into the kitchen.

"Mo-mo, let me get you," Yvette squealed. Her brother ran around the kitchen table dodging her.

Just as quickly as they had appeared in the kitchen, they were gone again, laughing and enjoying the pursuits of youth. *It must be nice,* Laquesha thought. Even Melissa smiled for a second, watching the kids, before the burdens that were weighing her down resumed. Laquesha looked at her watch. "Damn, girl, I gotta get to work." It was eight-fifteen. "You'll stay with them and get them off to school?" she asked Melissa, referring to the kids.

"You know I got you, girl. Go ahead."

"Make sure they eat, okay?"

"I got you," Melissa said, and yelled to the kids, "Maurice, Yvette, come eat your breakfast. It's almost time to go to school."

Laquesha took that as her cue to leave and hurried off to work. She was a hairdresser and she liked her work, but today Kim, Fats's other baby-mama and her nemesis, had scheduled a nine A.M. appointment to get her hair done. Laquesha tried to stay civil with the girl, but she really didn't like her. If it wasn't for little Demitrius, Fats's son by Kim, Laquesha would have knocked her out by now. Only for the sake of all three of Fats's kids did she keep the peace. *If only the ho didn't try me so much,* she thought, walking out the door.

· · ·

Monique's Hair Boutique was down on MLK. Kim pulled up in front of the hair salon in her red Honda Accord. It was one of the last things Fats had bought her before he got locked up, and Kim got a kick out of parading it in front of Laquesha's face since Laquesha didn't own a car. Kim got out of the car and walked into the boutique to keep her appointment. *This bitch better be here,* she thought.

Kim was all smiles as she walked in the shop. Laquesha saw her and waved her over.

"What's up, girl, how are you?" Laquesha asked.

"It's all good. You saw Fats?"

"Yeah, I was there on Saturday. He's good. He told me to tell you hi," Laquesha lied.

"Is he doing okay?"

"Yeah, he is, but you won't believe what happened."

"What, girl, tell me!" Kim said, on the edge of her seat, thinking that Laquesha better not drop no bomb on her about Fats.

"Well, girl, you know Melissa went up on the bus with me to see Rock. They got busted in the visiting room. They put Rock in a dry cell and almost arrested Melissa. She said she had just passed Rock the balloons to swallow when they got snatched up."

"Damn, is that so?" Kim was thinking that Fats might ask her to do the same thing. She had been considering it for a while, but she was waiting for him to bring it up. She didn't want to seem like the money-hungry bitch she was. Actually, she wasn't sure if she'd do it, but she knew her brother had got his girl to do it for him before when he was locked down in Lorton, and Kim had helped her brother's girl stuff the balloons. So she knew how to do it, and the extra money wouldn't hurt. The stash Fats had left before he got sent away was drying up, and to think when Fats first got knocked he had told her to give half the money to Laquesha. Kim wasn't having that, though. She told Fats that the cops had found and took the money when they searched her apartment. She didn't like the bitch, Laquesha, and sure as hell wasn't giving her no money. That was for her and little Demitrius. The only reason she even fucked with Laquesha was because of Fats's two other children. She wanted little Demitrius to know his brother and sister. They were nice kids, no matter who their mom was.

Laquesha was nodding up and down as she started to do Kim's hair. "And guess what?" Laquesha said conspiratorially.

"What?" Kim said, ignoring Laquesha. She was thinking about Christmas coming up. Some extra money would be right on the spot.

Laquesha was blabbering on as she did Kim's hair, and all of a sudden something drew Kim's attention. "Fats asked you what?" she blurted out, startling Laquesha, who quickly regained her composure.

"He asked me to smuggle some balloons in for him." But she spoke real low into Kim's ear, because the whole salon was ear hustling after Kim's outburst.

Kim thought, *This asshole Fats! He asked her before he asked me.* She could still turn it to her advantage.

"What did you tell him?" Kim asked.

Laquesha looked taken aback by her question. "What do you think I told him, girl?" Laquesha replied. "I told him *hell* no. I think that nigga crazy. He already got himself locked up. Now he wants to jeopardize me and my kids. *Hell* no."

Kim smiled inwardly, thinking, *This dumb bitch don't want no money.*

"Hell no," Laquesha continued. "And especially after what happened to Melissa. Not this girl." Kim's smile grew outwardly now, and Laquesha noticed.

"What are you smiling about, girl?" Laquesha asked suspiciously.

"Nothing. Why, Laquesha?" Kim asked, and checked her smile.

"You're not thinking what I think you're thinking, are you, Kim?"

"What do you mean?" Kim asked coyly. Too coyly for Laquesha's tastes.

"Hell no, girl. Don't do it," Laquesha warned.

"Don't do what?"

"It's all over your face, Kim. Don't even go up there and mess it up for all of us. My kids got a right to see their daddy. Don't fuck that up, it's all we got."

Kim checked her hair in the mirror that Laquesha was holding up, took a fifty-dollar bill out of her purse, stood up, handed the money to Laquesha, and thanked her. "I don't know what you're talking about, Laquesha. Just so you know, I'll be taking lil' Demitrius to see his father this weekend. Thanks again for doing my hair." With that, Kim was out the door.

Laquesha was mad at herself for putting Kim up on what was going on. *This money-hungry dumb-ass bitch better not get Fats hemmed up.* She folded the fifty-dollar bill and put it in her bra. She then looked around for her next appointment.

Chapter Five

That afternoon Fats was playing ball with his homies in the prison gym. The games were intense and served as a stress release for the prisoners. Sometimes things got so heated, some drama would follow, but usually cooler heads prevailed. For real, dudes were just trying to get some rec and let off some steam.

"You can't check me, nigga," a cat named High-Top from Philly told Fats. *Dude was good for real,* Fats thought, but him and his homies had held the floor for three straight games and they weren't looking to give up the floor anytime soon. As long as they kept winning the games, which went up to twelve by ones, then they didn't have to leave the floor. If they lost, it would be a long wait, a rack of jokers had called next and were waiting their turn to play. Fats knew if they lost that would be it, because the CO would be calling recall soon.

High-Top had the ball and made his move. He crossed Fats up and went to the hoop, but Fats's big homie Murk had his back. Murk skied in the air to meet the Philly cat, hitting him hard, knocking High-Top to the ground.

"Foul, nigga," the Philly cat said from the floor as he watched the shot he had thrown up at the last minute roll around the rim and go in for the game-winning point. He jumped up. "That's game," he said.

But Murk quickly disagreed. "You called ball, nigga. Take it up top," Murk growled.

But High-Top wasn't having it.

"Naw, dawg," he said. "That's game. Who got next?" he screamed, looking to the bleachers. But the dudes from D.C. weren't moving off the court. Fats stepped up to the Philly cat.

"Look, moe, if you hadn't called foul, it would've been your game, but you called ball, so the point don't count."

"Naw, fuck that, that's game. Who got next?"

As the other players on High-Top's team argued his point, the team that had next walked onto the court. Fats and the other D.C. soldiers were ready to say fuck it, but their big homie Country came over and grabbed the ball.

"Fuck that, it's ball up top," he said, and stood there with the ball, daring the Philly dude or anyone else to say something. Fats and his other homies, knowing Country's reputation on the pound, decided to hold their ground, come what may. It was a tense standoff that happened almost every day in prison. Dudes drew lines and dared other prisoners to step over them. If someone stepped over the line that was drawn, things could get violent quick. That was the way it was. Sometimes a man's pride could get him seriously hurt or killed. Especially around the holidays, when some got in their feelings easier. All it took was a spark. But the Philly cats didn't take the bait.

High-Top decided discretion was the better part of valor, and said fuck it. "Ball up top," he said, and checked it to Fats. The game continued. High-Top missed the tray he put up, then watched Fats nail three treys in a row to win the game for his team. The dudes on High-Top's team were salty, but that was how it went.

Fats and his crew lost the next game anyway, and afterward they were sitting on the bleachers drying off the sweat that had accumulated from four consecutive games, getting ready to go back to the unit.

"Country, you a crazy-ass nigga," Little G said to his big homie. "You trying to start all types of shit up in here." All the homies laughed.

"Naw, fuck that, slim," Country said. "I'm about holding mine for my homies. That's what it's about. Unity. If we all stand together, then we'll never fall. I'll give these crackers what they want to see: all of us wild-ass niggas at each other's throats. I ain't for seeing my homies get roughed off for nothing, basketball or nothing else. And if we find out who dropped that note on Rock, we rolling on 'em. That's no bullshit, slim."

Fats liked listening to Country. He seemed to have his shit together. He was a good brother who looked out for his homies. Or at least that was what Fats thought at the time.

"Open up for the two-thirty one-way move from recreation to the housing unit," the PA blared. Fats and his homies rolled out of the gym en masse. Everyone on the compound knew that the D.C. mob went hard when it came down to it. It was just the Lorton in them, Fats liked to think, even though he'd never set foot in Lorton. At the block, Fats ran into the Italians Mikey P and Johnny Two-Fingers, who were playing cards in the common area.

"Hey, Fats, what's up?" Mikey P greeted him. "Say hi to Fats, Johnny."

Johnny Two-Fingers looked up and obliged Mikey P.

"Hey, Fats, how you doing? Going hard in the rec, I see." Fats stopped and pounded rocks with the two Italians.

"I'm doing okay," he said. "Mr. P, Johnny, nice to see you guys. I'll holla at you later."

"All right, yeah, yeah," Mikey P said as Fats walked over to his cell. "I'm telling you, Johnny. I like that kid. He's a good kid. I'm telling you. He's nice, respectful, and got manners," Mikey P told his friend. "Not like a lot of these kids. They're fucking animals. Forget about it." Mikey P and Johnny Two-Fingers laughed and continued playing cards for twenty-five dollars a game.

At the cell, Fats walked in and found his bunkie, Mel-Mel, sleeping. *This nigga trying to sleep away his time,* Fats thought.

"Hey, old head," Fats called out, waking Mel-Mel up. "I gotta take a shit, moe; let me use the room."

Mel-Mel got up, all cranky and shit. "Dumb-ass young nigga," he said. "Why you have to wake me up with your bamma ass?"

"Chill out, old head," Fats shot back. "You didn't want me in here shitting while you was sleeping, right."

Mel-Mel didn't say anything; he just walked out of the cell.

I guess I'm right, Fats mused, and put the towel up so he could shit in peace.

• • •

Later on Fats made a call to his babys' mama, Laquesha. He had to check on the home front to make sure everything was cool. As Fats dialed the digits and his pin number, the prerecorded message came on. Fats had heard that all this new phone shit was recent. Mel-Mel had told him that back in the nineties you could call straight through back-to-back after every fifteen-minute call, and there was no three-hundred-minute-a-month limit like there was now. Mel-Mel told Fats that it was big ballers like Rayful Edmunds, who were selling kilos of cocaine and running criminal empires from the pens, who jerked the phones off. Just Fats's luck, he had come in after these bammas fucked the whole system up. A lot of people said the feds was sweet, but Fats didn't think so. This new joint he was in, FCI Beckley, sucked for real. *Three-hundred minutes, that's only five hours,* he thought. Fats could use the phone for only ten minutes a day. Imagine that. How's a motherfucker supposed to keep good family ties with only three-hundred minutes a month? He had heard that you got an extra hundred minutes at Christmastime. That was better, but it was still some shit. The call went through, and Laquesha pushed five to accept it.

"What's up, boo?"

"What's up, La? How're you doing?"

"I'm good. You wanna say hi to the kids?"

"Yeah, put them on."

"Hi, Daddy, I love you," Yvette greeted her father.

"I love you, too, baby girl. Let me talk to your brother."

"Hi, Daddy, what's up?" Maurice said.

"What's up, Maurice, are you being good and listening to your mom?"

"You know it, Pops, it's all good."

"Awright, son, put your mom back on the phone."

"Awright, Pops, 'bye."

" 'Bye. So, La, it's all good on the home front, right?"

"Yeah, boo. But guess who I saw the other day?"

"Who?" Fats said, wondering what she was gonna drop on him now. "Kim."

The phone was silent for a second. "Oh yeah?" he said, trying to be indifferent where his baby-mamas were concerned, but it was hard because they were always trying to stir up shit with each other.

"Yeah, and Fats, you better not be trying no shit with her when she visits. I'm telling you, don't even go there. Don't mess shit up for the rest of your family. I won't put up with that bullshit."

Fats had been thinking long and hard about the move, and he'd figured Kim was his ace, but now this? For real, he didn't need this shit. He hadn't even said nothing about it to Kim yet. She was coming up this weekend and bringing lil' Demitrius, and he was gonna feel it out with her. He expected her to go for it because she was very money motivated, but he hadn't even reached the subject with Kim yet, and Laquesha was already sweating him about it. He had to dead this quick before World War III erupted between the two. If the shit was easy, though, everybody would be doing it.

"Laquesha, what the fuck are you talking about?" Fats hollered into the phone before he checked himself. "Better yet, don't even tell me. You know they record all these calls. I ain't got shit going on, so stop acting like a nigga is doing something behind your back."

"I'm just telling you, Fats. We gonna be okay. I love you, and I don't want you to do anything stupid to jeopardize your situation."

"Awright, La. I feel you," Fats said. On the inside he was mad as hell, but he decided to try to play it off. No reason to keep Laquesha suspicious. "Look, ain't nothing happening, La, for real. I gotta go. Awright?"

"Awright, boo. 'Bye."

" 'Bye." Fats hung up the phone, thinking, *That bitch Laquesha must be a fucking mind reader or something.* How does she always know his next move before he does? But for real, he needed Kim to do the move. As soon as she agreed, Fats would get with his homie Country to set it up. Fats was a man on a mission, and he was determined to make good on his promise to the children.

Back in the cell at lockdown, Mel-Mel was telling Fats about the bags that the prison gave out for Christmas.

"Yeah, joe, back in the day they used to hit a nigga up," Mel-

Mel was saying. "I remember when I was at Manchester before they transferred me to this spot, we used to get a big-ass bag with candy, shorts, socks, and some mo' shit. And them shits weren't no generic-type shit like they sell in the commissary here, either, joe. No bullshit. I'm talkin' bout Nike and shit. Nigga was styling."

Fats listened in, hoping that they would give some shit like that here, but from what Mel-Mel was saying, he doubted it.

"And, joe, they used to give out pizza and shit, too. They gave out those little-ass personal pan lunch pizzas from Pizza Hut in the little box and all. Those Italians, like Mikey P and Johnny Two-Fingers, would be going around buying all the pizzas up for a book of stamps each, no bullshit, joe. A nigga could come up by catering to them at Christmastime. They'd be buying the bags and everything. But last year at this joint, they didn't give us shit but this weak-ass little bag of candy and cookies. But still, joe, them joints were selling for a book of stamps a pop!"

Fats took it all in, wondering if he'd sell his bag. He doubted it. He had a severe sweet tooth. He was just looking forward to his visit so he could get his move on. That was the only thing on his mind. He needed some real paper. Fuck a book of stamps.

The weekend came, and so did the visit. Fats was happy to see his little boy Demitrius, and it was nice to see Kim again, too. He and Kim weren't as close as him and Laquesha, but she still brought his son to see him. He was surprised that when he brought up the move Kim readily agreed. So it was all set. Now he just had to make the arrangements with his homie Country. Fats was sad to see Kim and Demitrius leave, but he got a chance to take some photos with them. The gumps had brought in a

Christmas tree while Fats was visiting, and he got the picture dude to take the photos in front of the plastic tree. So everything was looking up.

Chapter Six

Christmas was getting closer. The environment at the prison stayed the same, but little Christmas decorations started popping up at the different units. On ESPN and BET Fats started seeing all the Christmas advertisements, but it was nothing like being on the streets. At times the staff seemed happier. Maybe it was because of the Christmas bonus or the extra pay they could get for working on the holidays, but for Fats the days all blended together. The mailbags got bigger as Christmas got closer, though, and that put smiles on a few cats' faces. In prison a lot of convicts lived for the mail. For some reason, it was the only outside communication they got. So at mail call, a lot of dudes would be down there expecting something, but it seemed to Fats that most of them never got anything. But the closer it got to Christmas, a few more dudes got mail. Not that he felt sorry for the ones who didn't. He figured you got what you gave, and thought a lot of dudes in the feds were grimy niggas who never did nothing for nobody and that was why nobody ever did anything for them.

The holidays could also be a very gloomy time for some prisoners. Fights and arguments would pop off with little to no provocation. Being in prison at Christmastime sucked all right. There was no presents, no Santa Claus, and definitely no partying. Dudes might drink some hooch or smoke a little weed, but it wasn't like there were big parties celebrating the holidays like on the street.

. . .

As Fats washed his clothes in the laundry room, Mikey P came in to do the same.

"What's up, Fats?" he asked. "How you doing, boo?"

"It's all good, Mr. P. Is everything good with you?"

"Yeah, Fats, it's going all right, except they locked up my laundry guy, so I'm stuck doing it myself. Forget about it." Mikey P laughed.

"It ain't all that bad," Fats said, looking at Mikey P, who looked lost on how to operate the machine. Fats helped him get set up.

"Thanks a lot, Fats. I appreciate it."

"No problem, Mr. P," Fats said.

Mikey P was on the verge of saying something, but was unsure if he wanted to say it.

"You know, Fats, every Christmas we make a meal, you know, to sort of celebrate the holiday and such. Why don't you eat with us this Christmas? You know, as long as you're not doing something with your homeboys."

Fats was taken aback at first, but he thought it was cool of Mr. P to ask him.

"That sounds good, Mr. P, thanks," Fats said, hoping that they wouldn't ask him to put anything in, because, for real, he didn't have anything. "But I think I'll have to pass." Fats went by the old prison maxim: you didn't take anything from anybody except your homeboys.

When he said that, Mikey P looked a little insulted. "Oh no Fats, we ain't having none of that. When a man asks you to join him at his table, you don't decline. All you need to do is bring your bowl. We're having pasta, and there'll be sodas, doughnuts, and I'm getting somebody in the bakery to make a cake. So you be ready, and I'll let you know when. I won't take no for an answer." Mikey P smiled, clapped Fats on the back, and left before Fats could object again.

At the four P.M. count, Fats told Mel-Mel that Mikey P had invited him to eat with them at Christmas.

"Damn, joe, you all mobbed up," Mel-Mel joked. "But for real, that's cool. You know them Italians do it big. They'll probably have a nice spread. You know the chow hall will have something nice, too. Probably some kind of Cornish hen or something. You know me, joe, I gotta get that bird. I'm not big on pasta, but you would be a fool not to eat with them Italians. They know how to cook for sure, joe, and they go first class all the way."

Fats felt foolish for having told Mikey P no at first; now he reveled in his good fortune. He just hoped everything else would come together as well. He really needed to get proper so that he could get his kids some nice presents. Before Fats was aware of it, he had voiced his worries aloud.

"Mel-Mel, I gotta figure out a way to get my kids something nice. I don't got no money to buy them nothing, and neither do my baby-mamas. My kids are used to getting a lot at Christmas. I can't let them down, moe."

"I hear you, young'un," Mel-Mel said. "It's rough in here." Then Mel-Mel sat up as if he remembered something. "Check it out, joe. They got this program called Angel Tree. You can sign up for it, and they'll buy your kids presents."

Fats looked up and felt some hope for a minute, but then he dashed it.

"*Fuck* that, moe. I ain't trying to get no jive charity presents for my kids. I'm trying to get them something nice, no bullshit."

"Naw, joe, my man said this Angel Tree shit is good. It's a church program and all type of big corporations donate stuff to them every Christmas, and then the churches in the local areas, by request from prisoners, call their kids to the churches and give them the presents. The kids that don't have transportation get presents delivered. My man said they give out real nice stuff. They gave his son a digital camera last Christmas. That's a nice gift, joe."

"And you don't gotta pay nothing?" he asked. It sounded too good to be true.

"Naw, joe," Mel-Mel said. "You just go up to the chapel and sign up, and it's all good. You put your kids' names, ages, and where they live, what you want to say on the card, then they take care of the rest."

"That sounds real good, moe. I'll have to go sign up for that. I need that, for real." The wheels in Fats's head were now spinning. With the Angel Tree program and the move, his kids would get all they wanted and more.

The next morning Fats woke up with two things on his mind: setting up the move with Country and signing up for the Angel Tree program. Both things involved doing something for his kids. That's just what type of time Fats was on. He would try the Angel

Tree program first. Fats saw Mikey P and decided to ask him about Angel Tree, just in case Mel-Mel was playing some kind of joke on him. *That'd be just like that old-ass bamma*, Fats thought.

"Hey, Mr. P."

"Hey, Fats. How you doing? I see you're up early and all. Another day, another dollar, right?"

Fats wished that was the case, but it wasn't, still he had pressing matters to discern. "Mr. P, can I ask you something?" Fats asked.

Mikey P gathered himself and pushed his glasses up on his nose. "Well sure, Fats, go ahead."

"You heard of the Angel Tree program?" Fats asked.

"Yeah, yeah," Mikey P said. "Isn't that the thing where they buy gifts for your kids at Christmas?"

"Yeah, that's it, Mr. P," Fats replied. "What do you think about it?"

"Well, I never used it," Mikey P said. "But I know some guys that did. Said their kids were real pleased with the gifts."

That's all Fats wanted to hear. "Thanks, Mr. P," he responded, and headed to the chapel to sign up.

"Ay, Fats, hold up. If you like, I can get you in the arts-and-crafts class. They're doing something special."

"That be great, Mr. P. What are they gonna do, make those little demonstrations?" Fats asked.

Mikey P looked perplexed. "Those what? I don't understand."

"Those demonstrations, you know, the cards."

"Yeah, that's what they're gonna make, Fats. That's it," Mikey P said.

"Awright. Count me in. Bet." Fats said, and hit rocks with

Mr. P. When security called for movement, Fats bounced to the chapel. On his way there he was on the lookout for his big homie Country.

After Fats signed up for the Angel Tree program he went up to rec, but Country wasn't there. Finally he ran into Country at lunch. They were serving fried chicken, so the chow hall was packed. Fats noticed some wreaths and holiday decorations—ribbons, cardboard cutouts of Christmas trees, and different colors of wrapping paper hanging on the walls at various points around the chow hall. He guessed the gumps had been at work. He'd seen them all up in the warden's face talking 'bout their plans the day before.

"Let me holla at you after we eat, moe," Fats said to Country, who in turn looked at his little homie, like, what the fuck?

"Awright, slim, sit down," Country said. All the homies were chowing down, and Country, in his element, was holding court as usual, telling his little homies what they needed and didn't need to do. Then somebody brought up Rock's situation.

"They said slim got caught with three of them demonstrations," one of his homies said.

"Word," Big Murk spoke up. "That's some fucked-up shit. Slim gonna be hemmed up for a minute. I hope they don't give him an outside case."

Country looked up.

"That shit probably won't happen, but Rock gonna be in the hole a minute, and he'll probably get a disciplinary transfer. Plus, them crackers will hit him for his visits, phone, and commissary hard," Country said. Fats listened intently, taking it all in.

"But for real, homies, we need to find out who the fuck

snitched on our man, no bullshit," Country said, looking around sternly at all the homies at the table. "We can't let bammas be snitching on D.C. niggas and not get punished. It makes us look soft, and we ain't soft, right, slim?" Country asked, looking directly at Fats.

"Fuck no, we ain't soft, moe. We from D.C. The chocolate city. Murder capital of the world. We go hard," Fats said, and Country clapped him on the back.

"That's right, and when we find the snitch, we got a little Christmas present for him. A shank in his motherfucking eye. Merry Christmas, bitch." Country pantomimed stabbing somebody with his fork.

All the homies laughed.

"Check that demonstration out, moe." The little homie who brought it all up in the first place laughed.

Fats hollered at Country when they left the chow hall. "I'm trying to get down, big homie," Fats said.

Country double-checked his man to be sure that he was talking about what Country thought he was. "What you mean, slim?"

"I'm trying to make a move in the visit."

Country stepped back and looked at Fats. "You serious, slim? Because I can make it happen, just say the word."

"I'm saying it, moe. How much can we get off them demonstrations?"

"Shit, little homie, you gotta bring more than one. You bring in three balloons, and we split it fifty-fifty. I set it up and get it delivered to your peeps. We can get about a grand for each joint."

That's three grand! Fats thought. *Well, half of three grand. That's a good come up for one weekend.*

"Awright, bet," Fats agreed, and hit rocks with Country. "Set it up."

"Who's coming to see you and when?" Country asked.

"My baby-mama Kim. I gotta find out when, but before Christmas."

"Awright, bet. I'll get it moving. Holla back, Fats."

"Yeah, moe."

"Don't even think about fucking this up."

Fats walked away thinking he needed to call Kim.

Chapter Seven

After Fats called Kim and gave her the 411 on the move, he went with Mikey P up to recreation to sign up for the card-making class. Mikey P's buddy, the Italian who was running the class, told Fats to show up the following Monday. Kim had to get with Country's girl Shanice. He hoped she would do her thing.

At the same time Fats was signing up to make Christmas cards for his kids, Kim was planning to meet with Shanice to get the balloons and the drugs for the move. She had called Shanice right after Fats gave her the word, and now she was waiting for her to drop by with what Kim needed to get the business right. Kim looked out the window and saw Shanice drive up in a blue Caddy.

"What's up, Shanice?" Kim said as she opened the door.

"What's up, girl. How you doing?" As they both went inside the house, Shanice took off her jacket and settled down on the couch.

"Look, girl, are you sure you're up for this?" Shanice asked.

"Yeah, I think so," Kim said, but as the moment of truth arrived, she was having second thoughts.

"You can't *think* so, girl," Shanice said. "You either gotta be all in or all out. You can't leave niggas hanging. If you gonna do it, then you gonna do it. If not, then I'm wasting my time coming up here."

Kim felt kind of offended at Shanice's words. "Naw, Shanice," Kim said. "I'm gonna do it."

"That's good, girl. You can make some good money doing this. . . ." Shanice smiled. Then she handed Kim a plastic bag with three balloons stuffed with heroin.

"All you have to do is hide them good and when you go in the visiting room before Fats comes out, go into the bathroom and put two balloons into your mouth. When he comes in and you hug and kiss him, transfer the balloons into his mouth. Have some soda ready in case he needs to drink it to help him swallow the balloons. Then at the end of the visit, you can do the same thing to get the third one off. This is heroin, girl. This ain't no joke," Shanice warned. Kim looked at the balloons in her hand and imagined doing as Shanice suggested. *Sounds easy,* she thought. But still she was having some serious second thoughts, and the indecision was killing her, but she put on a brave front to Shanice.

"What are you thinking, girl?" Shanice asked.

Kim looked up from the balloons. "It's safe, isn't it?" she asked. "I mean, this heroin being in Fats's stomach. It won't leak out, will it?"

Shanice giggled a little. "Naw way, girl," she said, "that shit is triple-wrapped in a nonbiodegradable balloon, honey. It isn't dissolving for shit. Ain't nothing gonna leak out in your man's belly, so don't worry about it."

Kim was relieved to hear that, but she still felt some trepidation. Still, she would do what she had signed on to do, or at least she hoped she could keep her resolve. Fats was depending on her.

• • •

That weekend, Fats got a surprise visit from Laquesha and the kids. Fats didn't like surprise visits, he had a basketball game; but it was all good when he got out there.

"Hey! You all surprised me. What's the special occasion?" Fats asked as he gave hugs and kisses all around.

"Grandma let us use her car, daddy, so we decided to come out," Yvette said, and Maurice nodded his head.

"Yeah, Daddy, Grandma said we might as well come visit you." Fats looked at Laquesha for confirmation.

"It was kind of a spur-of-the-moment thing. We just decided to drive up yesterday afternoon. My mom went on a church retreat and said we could use her car, so we did." Fats smiled into his baby-mama's face, then his eyes shifted to his kids. He loved them so much. As they settled down and the kids went to watch TV in the playroom, Fats decided to tell Laquesha about the Angel Tree program.

"You know they got this program here, La," Fats said. "It's

called the Angel Tree program, and I signed up for it. They gonna contact you to go to the local church to pick up presents for the kids from me."

Laquesha looked mad for a minute. "We don't need their charity, boo. I can handle it."

"Naw, La, it's not like that," Fats said. "These big corporations donate the gifts for tax write-offs, so it's all good, and all the dudes in here use the program. One dude told me his kids got gifts from the program even when he was home. They give good gifts, too. You just gotta tell them what the kids want when they call, and they'll get it for them."

Laquesha sat quizzically for a minute. "Well, it's better than what you had planned before," she said, and smiled up into Fats's face. Her smile made Fats feel guilty because he still had the move planned. Just not with Laquesha.

"I want you to get the present for lil' Demitrius, too, because Kim will forget to do it, okay?" Fats asked.

"Okay, boo, I got you," Laquesha said, knowing Fats was right. She didn't care for Kim—*that conniving bitch,* she thought—but she would make sure Fats got a present for his son, bitch or no bitch.

"Oh, yeah, I almost forgot," Fats said. "I'm in this Christmas card–making class, too. I'm gonna make cards for all of you."

Laquesha sat there admiring her man. He was such a good father. And even though the little demonstration he was trying to make didn't work out, Fats was rebounding and coming up with other alternatives so that his kids got something for Christmas. Laquesha was proud of him. "See what you can accomplish when you put your mind to it, boo?" Laquesha said. "You need to leave all that street shit behind."

Fats felt even more guilty with that remark, and Laquesha noticed the subtle change in his eyes.

"What's the matter, boo?" she asked.

"It ain't but a thing," Fats answered with a smile.

But Laquesha felt like maybe Fats was scamming her; she got a serious look on her face and looked Fats right in his scheming eye. "You better not even think of trying to do that shit with Kim, Fats!" She cut straight to the chase.

He felt like she could see through him. But he knew he had to continue to deny it; if not she would go all out trying to convince Kim not to do it. "I'm not doing nothing, La," Fats tried to reassure her. "You can bet on that."

Laquesha looked him up and down and tried to find the truth in his face, but Fats was playing it cool, and Laquesha was placated for the moment, but she still had her doubts deep inside.

This nigga better not play me, she thought. Fats quickly changed the subject. "This Italian guy on my unit was telling me about a videotape program, where you can make a videotape with a Christmas message for the kids," Fats said. "Kinda like a videotaped Christmas card. I'm gonna look into that, what do you think?"

"That sounds good, boo." Laquesha said as the kids came running up and screaming their daddy's name. *I'm glad they got all these programs in here for prisoners to make stuff for their kids for Christmas,* Laquesha thought. Because she knew money was tight, and she wasn't sure if she would be able to buy the kids anything for Christmas. She knew her mom was planning a meal, but that might be about it. If this Angel Tree program that Fats was talking about came through, and he made cards and the videotape, it might not be a bad Christmas at all. She was interrupted in her thoughts with the kids jumping up and down and pointing.

"Presents, presents!"

Laquesha looked over and saw two feminine-looking prisoners arranging gift-wrapped boxes under the Christmas tree in the corner. *That's nice,* Laquesha thought. She would have to try to at least get a Christmas tree for the house. She would talk to her mom when they got home.

"C'mon, let's go take a picture sitting in front of the Christmas tree," Fats said, motioning for the picture guy sitting in the corner. The gumps admired Fats and his family discreetly as they decorated the tree.

"Aw, isn't that sweet—a regular family guy," one gump said to the other. Fats kind of looked back at them, and they moved out of the way so he and his kids could take a picture.

"Daddy, Daddy!" Yvette squealed. "Are all those presents for me?" Fats smiled down at his little girl and picked her up. "You know it, baby girl. They're all for you."

"What about me, Daddy?" Maurice said, not to be left out. Fats hugged his son close. "You got something coming, too, Maurice, don't worry." As the picture man commenced to snapping photos of the family, Fats's kids and Laquesha beamed, just happy to be in the presence of their man.

The visit ended all too soon. *If the stupid-ass cracker COs wouldn't take so long to process people in, then maybe we could visit for longer,* Laquesha thought as she drove home. The BOP was notorious for having visitors wait for hours on end before they would let them in to visit. It made no sense to complain because then the power-tripping guards at the desk would just make the visitors wait longer. It was hell on the nerves, but when loved ones were in prison, visitors had no choice. Either wait and suffer the indifference of the prison guards, or don't visit. Laquesha always felt like they treated her as if she were the criminal. Always looking down at her and suspecting that she and her kids were smuggling drugs or something. It didn't matter that Fats was already doing time; it seemed the prison guards wanted to punish her, too. It bugged her, but what was she to do? She looked back at her kids, who were sleeping in the backseat. Laquesha still worried about Fats. No matter his reassurances, she had a nagging feeling that behind her back he was trying to do something with Kim.

* * *

The next day, with her suspicions still worrying her, Laquesha called Kim.

"Hello?" Kim answered the phone.

"What's up, Kim. It's Laquesha."

What's this bitch want? Kim thought. "Hey, how you doing? Have you talked to our man?" Kim humored her.

"Yeah," Laquesha said. "I was up there all day yesterday. He's good."

"Oh yeah?" Kim responded. She didn't know Laquesha had planned to visit Fats again so soon. She had to one-up her, though. "I'm going next weekend," she said.

Fucking bitch, Laquesha fumed. *Fats better not use up all his visiting points with her.*

"That's good, girl. I'm sure lil' Demitrius wants to see his daddy."

"Yeah, you can bet he does, and I need to see that nigga, too," Kim said, trying to cause some friction.

Laquesha ignored it. "Look, Kim, I know you two got something planned, and I'm calling to beg you not to do it."

"I don't know what you're talking about, Laquesha."

"Don't come at me with that bullshit. I know what you two are planning to do, and I'm telling you, don't do it. Don't get Fats hemmed up. I know he means well, but it's not worth it. You could go to jail, Kim. Did you ever think about that? What will happen to lil' Demitrius then?"

Laquesha threw a low blow at Kim's motherly instincts. And for real, the same thing had been playing on Kim's mind. She was scared to death something would go wrong, but she didn't know how to back out of it. She sat on the phone not saying nothing.

Laquesha took this as her cue to press on. "I'm just saying, Kim, think of the consequences. Think of the worst possible outcome. Is that something you want to have to deal with?"

Kim was quiet. She knew she didn't want to go through with it. Her own fears coupled with Laquesha's words had just reaffirmed her own doubts. She slid the phone down into the receiver.

"Kim," Laquesha said. "Kim, hello?" But Kim was no longer on the other end of the phone.

. . .

Fats was in recreation the next day working on the cards for his kids. Recreation supplied all the materials: cardboard, coloring pens, glue, little Christmas designs, glitter, Santa Clauses, Christmas trees, reindeer, snowmen, and so on. All Fats had to do was put it all together and arrange it. He was busy because the class only lasted three sessions, and Fats had to make cards for his three kids and his two baby-mamas. Plus, he had a basketball game at seven P.M., so he wasn't trying to bullshit. His homie Country saw him and came into hobby craft to holla at his boy.

"What up, slim?" Country said. "I see you jive making the little Christmas cards. What's up with that?"

Fats looked up from his work. "You know how we do, moe," Fats said. "I gotta do big things for the kids." Country smiled admiring his homeboy's tenacity. "So what's up with that demonstration?" Country asked, referring to the move. "You got it all set up or what, slim?"

Fats looked back at his homie. "It's all good for this weekend, moe," Fats said.

Country clapped him on the back. "Good deal, good deal, slim. You ready for the game or what?" Country asked.

Fats nodded. "I'm ready," he replied. The game was big, but to Fats his kids were bigger.

Don't get it twisted, he was ready to do his thing with the rock. It was the first game of the Christmas tournament, and the whole pound would be out to see what mob was up to win the whole thing. Dudes would be betting mad cheddar on the games, and all the homies would be out representing for the D.C. mob. Fats knew he had to do this thing, he was being counted on to distribute the ball, run the point, and hit the trey when needed. But Fats was confident in his game. So he would just ball. His mob stood a good chance to win it all if the things fell right. Although they didn't have one dominant player, the D.C. dudes played together. Everyone played their role and hustled. Plus, Country was a good motivator and wasn't afraid to call his players out when needed. *It will be what it will be,* Fats thought, and got back to finishing his cards.

Chapter Eight

The next morning, the gumps were decorating the unit with more cardboard designs of Santa Claus and the like. *These gumps really get into this shit,* Fats thought. But he didn't give a shit for real. Actually, he was shining like a motherfucker. The glow from last night's game was still on him. He and his mob had put on a show. Fats hit two crucial treys in the last two minutes to give his team the win over the dudes from Baltimore. They had one of the best players on the pound, a kid they called DJ, who had Superman cuts and a game like lightning. DJ dropped thirty-five on Fats's mob, but he was the only threat on his team, and the chocolate city team prevailed in the end after trailing most of the game. The homies won mad books, and they were all on Fats's jock for his game-winning efforts.

Fats saw Mikey P and went over to join him.

"Hey, hey!" Mikey P said. "It's the basketball star. Hey, how you doing?" Fats nodded to Mikey P and the other Italians playing cards at the table.

"What's up, Mr. P," Fats greeted, pounding rocks with the old mobster.

"Will you look at this guy?" Mikey P said. "Forget about it. Look at this kid." He told all the other Italians, "This kid is a helluva ballplayer. Who would of thought? I mean, look at this kid." All the Italians laughed at Mikey P and nodded to Fats.

Fats didn't know if they were laughing at him or with them, but he didn't care. He knew Mikey P was a good old dude, so he could take the ribbing if that's what it was. A lot of dudes underestimated his athletic skills because of how he looked. Fats was a little rolypoly-looking dude. That was how he got his name Fats in the first place, so it was all good.

"Mr. P, I wanted to ask you if you know who's running the videotape program?" Fats asked, getting down to more serious business.

Mikey P looked at his buddies again, and Johnny Two-Fingers held up his hands.

"Damn, Mikey, you letting this guy in on all our rackets or what," he joked.

Mikey P looked at Fats and pushed his glasses up on his nose.

"Well, let me introduce you to these guys," he said, and looked to Fats. "This is a friend of ours." And all the Italians laughed again. It was an inside joke.

"But hey, really Fats, I know the guy who runs the program. You want to make a videotape to send to your kids? I'll set it up for you, all right?" Mikey P smiled. "We can go down to rec this afternoon and do it, is that good?"

"Yeah, that's good Mr. P, thanks a lot," Fats said, and was about to turn to leave.

"Hey, Fats, did you bring those cards you were making back to the unit?" Mikey P asked.

"Yeah," Fats said. "I got them upstairs."

"Well, bring them down and show the old lugs what you got."

"Awright," Fats said, and went up to get the cards he made for his kids. On his way back he heard Mikey P telling the guys, "This kid is really talented. I'm telling you. He could be some type of designer. Here he is. Show 'em the cards, Fats."

Fats showed the Italians the three cards he'd made for his kids.

"Those are nice," Johnny Two-Fingers said. "Are you sure you made 'em?"

All the Italians looked to Fats and laughed again.

"Shut up, youse lug," Mikey P said. "I watched him make them with my own eyes."

"Hey, Fats," said Big Vinny. "You ain't trying to sell none of them cards?"

Mikey P and Johnny Two-Fingers looked at Big Vinny sharply.

"Naw, you big lug, he ain't trying to sell those cards," Mikey P admonished. "He made them for his kids."

"Oh," Big Vinny said, and Mikey P and Johnny Two-Fingers shrugged, as if to apologize to Fats.

"I can't even invite my friends over with this guy," Mikey P said, nodding toward Big Vinny.

"Naw, it's okay, Mr. P. It's all cool," Fats said, trying to soothe over the matter.

"Lookee here," Johnny Two-Fingers said. "Fats is always the gentleman. Bravo, bravo." He did a little golf clap with his hands.

"Don't mind these guys, Fats, they're just a bunch of morons. Forget about it." Mikey P laughed out loud at his joke, and all the other Italians started laughing, too. "I'll see you after chow, and we'll go up to rec, okay, Fats?" Fats nodded and made his departure.

Fats ran straight to the jack to call Kim. After Fats pushed all the necessary numbers to place the call, Kim answered the phone.

"What's up, Fats?"

"What's up? How's my lil' dude?"

"He's all good. He's at school right now."

"That's good, and how's my baby-mama?"

"I'm good, Fats, and looking forward to seeing you this evening."

"That's good, is everything all good with that little demonstration?"

"Yeah, it's all good Fats," Kim said, but in her heart she knew she wasn't going through with it. She couldn't tell Fats that over the phone, though. She would just have to tell him in person and keep lil' Demitrius close to her in case Fats got mad. Surely he wouldn't flip out on her if their son was right there. Kim didn't even know what to do with the balloons. She wanted to get rid of them. She had become increasingly paranoid since her conversation with Laquesha. Her mind was playing tricks on her. She wanted to call Shanice and give her the balloons back, but she was scared of the big girl. She felt it would be better for Fats to take care of everything and get her off the hook from inside. He was the one who set it up and pressured her into doing it, so he could handle the fallout.

Fats hung up with Kim and looked at the clock. He had to wait half an hour before he could call Laquesha because of the way the phone system was set up. It sucked, but that is the way it was. Exactly half an hour later and right before lunch, Fats called his other baby-mama. She scolded him again and reminded him not to be fucking up. Fats wanted to lash out at her, but he held his tongue and maintained that he wasn't doing anything wrong. She told Fats that the Angel Tree people had contacted her and that she was supposed to go next week to pick up the presents for the kids. Fats was happy to hear that.

When Laquesha got off the phone, someone was at her front door. Her girl Melissa was the unexpected visitor.

"What's up, girl?" Laquesha said in greeting.

"What's up?"

"Did you ever hear from Rock?"

"Yeah, he called me the other day. He can only use the phone once a month from the hole. He said they got him under investigation, and when I tried to ask him if they got the balloons, he said he didn't want to talk about it."

"Well, girl, at least you talked to him and he's all right."

"Yeah, but it is what it is, right?" Melissa resigned.

"Yeah, that's right. It is what it is," Laquesha echoed. "You know Fats signed up for this Angel Tree program and they called me this morning about getting some presents for the kids? That's nice, isn't it?"

"Yeah, girl, I heard about that program before," Melissa said. "This girl I know from Northwest got some stuff from Angel Tree one year when her man was down Lorton. She said they called her up and told her son and her to come to the church. The little boy wanted a bike, and they didn't have no bike on the premises, so the church lady got in the car with them and took them to this big-ass bike factory down in Virginia. They went in and there was like a thousand bikes all lined up. Different colors and types. The church lady turned to the boy and said to go get a bike. The kid was like which one, and the church lady said, 'Whatever one you want.' My girl said watching her little boy run around the bike factory and trying all the different bikes was the best present ever for him and her, and when she told her man down Lorton, he was really happy about what happened, too."

Laquesha was eager to see what would happen when she took her kids to the church. Something like that would be fascinating. She just hoped something half as good would happen to her family.

"That's a beautiful story, Melissa. I would have loved to see the look on that boy's face."

* * *

That weekend Kim and little Demitrius visited Fats. It took forever for them to get processed in. Fats was up on the tier stressing. He was already nervous as it was, with plans to do the move, and now that they hadn't called him yet, Fats was hot. He sat and looked out the door watching dudes from other units go to the visiting hall.

Mel-Mel saw his bunkie pacing. "Damn, young 'un, chill out. They gonna be here," he said.

"I know, I'm just mad 'cause I know they probably sitting out front with some jive-ass crackers fronting on them," Fats replied.

"I hear you, joe," Mel-Mel said, and just then the CO came out of the office and looked down the tier.

"James," he called. "You got a visit." *About fucking time,* Fats thought. All his pent-up anxiety left him as he walked to the door of the unit and waited for the big fat-ass redneck CO to let him out.

"We got one to the visiting room," the CO said into his walkie-talkie. When the compound officer responded in the affirmative, the CO unlocked the door and let Fats go.

Only two more weeks to Christmas, Fats thought.

As he entered the visiting room his little boy ran up and jumped him. "Daddy, Daddy, hey Daddy!"

Fats grabbed his son and hugged him tight. "What's up, little man?" he said, then turned to Kim. He could tell something was wrong because Kim had that look on her face. Fats frowned at her. "What's up, Kim?"

"Nothing, Felix." She gave him a hug and a kiss. Fats was expecting her to push the balloons into his mouth, but there was nothing. Only Kim's tongue. When Kim pulled away from him, he knew that she hadn't brought the balloons. It was all in her face. To say the least, Fats was mad. The look he gave his girl was so severe that lil' Demitrius noticed.

"What's the matter, Dad?" he asked. "You got gas or something?" Fats looked down at his little son, like, what the fuck? But he smiled and picked the boy up again and moved to sit down. Kim used that as an excuse to walk over to the vending area.

"I'll get you guys some sodas," she said, and made her escape.

Fats looked on in displeasure.

Lil' Demitrius sat on Fats's lap, studying his dad's face again. "Daddy, Daddy, what's wrong?" he asked, and grabbed Fats's hand. Fats looked down and felt fucked up for his son. He was mad, but it wasn't his son's fault.

"Ain't nothing wrong, little man. It's all good. Mommy just makes me mad sometimes," Fats told his son.

"Why's that, Daddy?" Demitrius asked.

Fats looked down at his ever-inquisitive son. "Well, Demitrius, that's for me to know and you to find out." Fats started tickling his son, who screamed, got up, and dared his dad to chase after him. The CO sitting at the guard station glared over at Fats. Fats returned the glare. Fuck that cracker.

Kim came over with some Cokes and candy bars.

Fats brooded, refusing to look at her.

"Felix, look at me," she said.

Fats mumbled something under his breath.

"What'd you say?" Kim asked, and Fats looked up into her eyes.

"I said, why didn't you bring it?"

Kim looked over to see Demitrius running around with two little white girls.

"Well, Fats, I was gonna bring it, but then I talked to Laquesha, and she told me I better not. She said if I got you in trouble that I was in trouble with her. I was scared, Fats. I'm not trying to fuck with your psycho hood-rat baby-mama." Fats couldn't believe Kim was telling him this bullshit. Kim was looking into his eyes to see if he was buying it.

Finally he said something. "Kim, you were never gonna do it, you shouldn't have agreed to it in the first place. Now you put me in a bad spot. I set something up with someone, and they're expecting something, and I don't have it." Fats squared off with Kim. "That's just not how you do things around here. All you got in here is your word and your balls, and now, because of you, it's gonna look like my word is some shit because you didn't bring me that little demonstration."

"Blame it on me," Kim said, grabbing Fats's hands.

"You really think that jive-ass shit is gonna work in here? I'm supposed to go to the dude and tell him, 'Oh, she decided not to do it.' Get the fuck outta here," Fats said. He spent the rest of the visit in brooding silence. He was too busy sweating what he was gonna tell Country. He knew his big homie was gonna be pissed. Kim had left Fats in a real bad spot. She could just go home and not think about it, but Fats had to deal with the situation head-on. He tried not to be in his feelings for his son's sake, but it was hard. When the visit was over, it wasn't a minute too soon.

Later on, during count, Fats told Mel-Mel what was up and asked his advice on what he should do. Mel-Mel told him the best thing to do was to be straight up with Country and hope for his mercy.

That night, Fats and his homeboys had a second-round game in the Christmas tournament. Fats didn't say anything to Country before the competition, and luckily Country was too hyped by the game to press Fats about the balloons. But Fats could tell as the big homie kept looking at him that he was waiting for him to say something about the move. Even though Fats was fucked up and feeling sick on the inside at having to explain the fuckup to Country, he played real well and the D.C. mob won again to all their homies' delight. Dudes were running around the gym like they won the NBA championship after the game, and then came the moment that Fats was dreading.

"Little homie, what up, slim," Country said. "You played real good, but what's up with the work? It went good, right, slim?"

Fats looked up at his homie. "Country, for real, the shit's fucked up. My girl didn't bring it."

Country double-checked his homie for a minute, mean-mugging him. "Don't say that slim."

Fats nodded, confirming the bad news.

"Damn, slim, then shit's fucked up." Country started to walk away before adding, "You better come up with a plan and get that shit straight because I gotta have my shit. This ain't a joke." Fats just stood there, waist-high in deep shit.

Chapter Nine

The next morning Fats was reading over the holiday flyer that the institution had put out. It was done up all fancy like they were really doing something special. It listed the Christmas meal they would be having: Cornish hen, corn on the cob, applesauce, green beans, muffins, and Italian sausages. *Sounds good,* Fats thought. But he knew the reality of prison, that although the meal might be better than normal, it would still be some shit. Nothing like the spread Fats would be eating if he were on the streets. Another flyer listed the activities that were planned for the holidays. They had all types of Christmas tournaments like the one Fats was playing in basketball, including a pool tournament, Ping-Pong, three-point shot, and a dunk contest. Not to mention the concert put on by the prison bands, the talent show, the soccer shootout along with an indoor soccer tournament, a volleyball tournament, and various board-game and card-game tournaments, too. There would be plenty for the prisoners to do. Fats figured the prison tried to keep the inmates busy during the holidays—the busier they all were, the less violence or trouble they'd get into. The administrators must have figured that out from experience.

They also gave out little prizes, like twelve-packs of soda and bags of candy for the victors in all the holiday activities.

Fats was trying to get that case of soda that they gave out to each member of the basketball team that won the Christmas tournament. Bragging rights and that case of soda is what most dudes played for. They could either drink up with their homies or sell the case to one of the big willies for a book of stamps. *It was something,* Fats thought, *but he'd be drinking his.* There was also a holiday-movie list, but most of the movies were some pure garbage. The BOP had this policy that grown men in prison couldn't watch rated R movies, so they got all this Harry Potter–type shit. Fats never understood the logic of it. They had some type of feel-good Christmas movie. Fats wouldn't be watching that shit.

Fats turned around in the unit and saw Johnny Two-Fingers and Tommy Boy putting down bids for dudes' Christmas bags. They were offering a book of stamps a bag. Mikey P had told Fats that the Italians liked to buy up all the bags to send them home to their kids. It was like a regular thing they did year after year. But just like he wanted to drink his own soda, Fats wanted to eat his bag. He didn't have it like the Italians, who would be spending their limit every month and going to the vending machines to buy sodas, sandwiches, and pastries every day. The bag of candy would be a treat to Fats and most of his homies, too. They weren't getting that much money in at all, and when they did they usually spent it on shoes. D.C. dudes liked to keep their gear fresh.

Fats decided to give Kim a call. He walked over to the phone and punched in his girl's digits. He thought, *This girl really got me in some shit. A nigga could end up getting shanked because of her bitch ass.*

"Hello," Kim said, after pushing five to accept the call.

"What's up?" Fats asked.

"Oh, you want to talk to me now?" Kim replied.

"Yeah, you need to come back and handle that, for real, Kim."

"I can't believe you, Fats. I told you I'm not doing it. So why you calling me with that shit?" Kim said.

"Look Kim, you about to get a nigga hemmed up in here."

"I'm sorry Fats, but I ain't doing it."

This fucking bitch! Fats thought. "Well, what'd you do with that demonstration?" Fats asked. He was getting nowhere with Kim; therefore, he had to come up with an alternative, fast.

"I still got it," Kim said.

"Well, since you won't do what you said you're gonna do, you need to give that demonstration to Laquesha."

"Laquesha? Why would I give it to that bitch?"

"Because she's gonna do what you too scared to do."

"Fuck you, Fats."

"Fuck you, Kim. Who the *fuck* you think you're talking to?"

"Who the fuck you think *you're* talking to," Kim said, before crying, "Fuck you, Fats, don't be calling me no more."

Ain't this some shit. Fucking jive-ass bitch. Fats would have to call Laquesha later and beg her to help him out. If she wouldn't, then the alternative wasn't going to be nice. Fats didn't like his chances with Country. He knew Country would go hard for his. Not that Fats was some type of sucker, but his big homie was like that, and deep down Fats knew he was in the wrong.

After lunch Fats went up to rec to chill. He saw Mikey P in the hobby craft.

Mikey P waved him over. "Check it out, Fats. Look what I got my wife and daughter for Christmas." Mikey P showed Fats two leather purses and some ceramic figurines that were displayed on the table. Fats checked them out. They were nice. He wished he could have gotten Laquesha, Kim, and his daughter some. Well, maybe not Kim. *Fucking jive-ass bitch.*

"Those are nice, Mr. P," Fats said. "I bet they were expensive."

Mikey P pushed his glasses up on his nose. "Not that much," he said. "I had a guy owed me some favors." Fats wished he had some dudes who owed favors and could do work like that. But all of Fats's homies were broke just like him. All of them except Country, that was. And the homie who had the most was the one breathing down Fats's neck. *I guess that's why he has the most,* Fats thought. *He be about his business.* Fats's choices were limited; he knew that he had to convince Laquesha to do the move. She either did it or he'd get fucked up. But Fats was still skeptical. And if he had to get fucked up, then so be it. He just hoped his homie wouldn't murk his ass. He just wanted to be able to provide his kids with gifts from their daddy. That wasn't a crime, was it? Fats felt Mikey P staring at him.

"Fats, you all right?" Mikey P asked.

"It's all good, Mr. P."

But Mikey P sensed that something was wrong. "Well, look, kid, if you need something, you let me know, okay?" he said, and shook hands with Fats.

"Awright, Mr. P," Fats said. "I'm about to bounce."

"Oh yeah, Fats. I signed you up for that videotape program. You have to do it tomorrow. They said they'll put you on the call-out. All right?"

"Awright, thanks Mr. P." Fats walked off thinking about what he was gonna do and how he was gonna pull it off. It always seemed in Fats's life that everything he tried to do always fucked up no matter how good his intentions were. As he waited for the announcement so that he could move back to the unit, he walked by the band rooms and saw some white dudes jamming. Fats stopped for a minute. They were playing "Jingle Bells" really fast, like a heavy metal version. Probably practicing for the concert. In the next band room some brothers were singing Christmas carols a cappella. It sounded pretty good. He wondered if they would win the talent show.

Back in the unit Fats overheard some of the Nation of Islam dudes talking about the celebration of Christmas. Fats listened in to see how these brothers were kicking it.

"Christmas is the result of WASP capitalist beliefs," said one NOI brother to the other. Both of the dudes wore their khakis pressed and fitted. "You see, my brother, there is nothing Christian about it. It is a made-up holiday for the WASP capitalistic elite to get the masses to spend money. They aren't celebrating anything religious, they are celebrating the spending of money, plain and simple."

The other brother nodded and looked over to Fats like he was eavesdropping or something. "How you doing, brother?" he said.

Fats nodded and walked away, not wanting to disrespect the NOI brothers. He wasn't feeling what they were saying anyway. *Shit, Christmas is Christmas,* he thought. *It is what it is. Buying presents for your kids is cool; fuck all that bullshit they tripping off.*

Fats went in his room and decided to get the cards he made for his kids ready to send. He would put them in the mail today. It was only a week before Christmas, and he wanted the cards to get to them on time.

The gumps were busy at work retaping the Christmas decorations that they had plastered all over the unit. Some of the ribbons and stuff had been ripped down by unruly prisoners. Naturally, Fats's homeboys, but it was all good.

"Why these dumb-ass niggas rip down the shit we work so hard to put up?" one gump said to the other.

"These little-dick niggas don't got no Christmas spirit," the other one replied.

"You right, girl, you right." They both giggled as they continued their work fixing the decorations. Fats watched and laughed, thinking about what little-dick niggas they were talking about. *They don't wanna fuck with this Mandigo,* Fats thought. But he wasn't serious. He wasn't on that type of time. But there were plenty who were. He didn't understand how a man could get off with another man. *That shit is sick,* Fats thought. Fats still wasn't sure what to tell Country. He had a game that night, and he knew tomorrow he would be on the callout to do the videotape message for his kids.

Fats lay down and took a nap to try to forget about his problem and the pressure that was closing in on him.

That night at the game the homies advanced to the semifinals. It was all good for the D.C. mob. Country was really standoffish toward Fats, but he was happy the homies won since he was the coach. He didn't really talk to Fats during the game except to pass on game instructions. After the game he called Fats over while all their other homies were running around the gym, crazy with energy and mad hyped because they'd won.

"Fats, you gotta make that happen or face the consequences," Country told him. Fats didn't know what he was gonna do, but he didn't tell his big homie that. "I got you, big homie. I got it all smoothed out, it's in the works for this weekend," he lied. "My bad, moe. It won't happen again." Country looked at Fats like he wanted to believe him, like he wanted to trust him, but he didn't say anything. He just gritted on Fats and turned to celebrate with his other homeboys.

Chapter Ten

Fats was really in a jam. He was fucked up, and he only had one person to turn to. Laquesha. He called her up.

"What's up, boo?" Laquesha said.

"What's up, La." Fats decided that he might as well break it down to her straight. "Look La, I'm in a serious bind, and if I don't get straight some drama might be jumping off, and it ain't looking good for me."

"Tell me what's up," Laquesha said with concern in her voice.

"Well, it's that thing with Kim. Since it didn't happen, it looks like I'm the fall guy, and dudes are getting ready to fuck me up if I don't come up with the demonstration or the paper."

"Oh, Fats, I told you so. I told you that shit was nothing but trouble."

"I know, La, but I really need your help. We gotta make this work, or shit's gonna jump off."

Laquesha was upset at Fats but she also recognized the severity of this situation. She knew when push came to shove she would hold her man down however and whatever way she could. But she didn't just want to come out and say it; she wanted to make Fats sweat a little. *Serves the nigga right,* she thought. Fats was waiting for her to respond to his predicament, but Laquesha went another route.

"Fats, you know the church contacted me about the presents. I told them Maurice and Demitrius wanted bikes and that Yvette wanted a dollhouse. They said it would be no problem and told me to bring the kids to pick up the presents on Christmas Eve. Isn't that great?"

"La, didn't you hear anything I just said?" Fats screamed into the phone, clearly desperate and at the end of his rope. Laquesha realized that the situation was more serious than she'd thought and worked quickly to defuse it.

"I'll handle it, boo. I'll come this weekend. Who got the demonstration, Kim?" Relief flooded Fats. He felt the weight of the world lift from his shoulders. Laquesha would make everything all right, just like she always did. Thank God.

"Thanks, La! Yeah, Kim got that so get it from her, and I'll see you on Saturday," Fats said. "And La?"

"What, boo?"

"I'm sorry for yelling at you. You're the greatest, La, and I mean that."

As Fats hung up the phone, Laquesha thought to herself, *Yeah, I know, but what the hell have I just gotten myself into?*

Later that day Laquesha went over to Kim's house. Kim had been expecting her so she wasn't surprised to find Laquesha at the door.

"What's up?" Kim said. "You came to get that?"

"Yeah, girl, I came to get that. Since you couldn't handle yours, now I gotta handle mines."

Kim couldn't believe the nerve of the bitch. "You the one who convinced me not to do it, Laquesha, so why you coming at me like that. What happened to all that don't fuck it up for me and my kids shit?" Kim said.

Laquesha wanted to lash out but didn't. It would only make matters worse. The situation was already complex, and Laquesha knew if she let Kim get her in her feelings then they would all end up losing.

"I don't want to do it, Kim, but Fats said if I don't then something might happen to him. I can't let him go out like that."

Kim looked up at Laquesha and realized she was right. She started crying, and Laquesha consoled her, hoping that she was doing the right thing and that everything would turn out all right.

That Saturday Laquesha took the bus up. She didn't bring the kids. If anything went wrong she didn't want them around to experience it. She was a chick on a mission, and she was flying solo. It was her and Fats against the world, or at least that was Laquesha's attitude. She would ride or die for her man. Fuck the consequences. She couldn't bear the thought of something bad happening to Fats, the father of her children. When she got on the bus she was surprised because Shanice, Country's girl, was taking the trip, too. It struck Laquesha as kind of funny because Fats hadn't said nothing about her coming up to see Country, and it seemed to her that on the trip Shanice was mad-dogging her like she'd done something wrong. Laquesha tried to holler at the girl, but Shanice brushed Laquesha off and acted like she was all up in her feelings for some reason. *What is up with that?* Laquesha thought.

As they got closer Laquesha was thinking about something Melissa had said about Shanice one time. It was something that Shanice had said to Melissa that struck her as kind of odd. Shanice had told Melissa when she gave her the balloons that if Melissa and Rock fucked up the move then she would have to start making the trips again. But she was trying not to make the trips because of something that happened before. A close call or something like that had taken place when Country was in USP Lewisburg. Supposedly she told Melissa they had got hemmed up, but Country had gotten them out of it someway. Now as she was thinking about it Laquesha wondered how it was that they got out of it. *If Shanice is on this trip at the same time as me, could she be doing the same thing I'm doing?* Laquesha thought. *Is that why she's mad at me, because she feels it's Fats's fault that she has to make this trip?* Laquesha couldn't shake the feeling that something was definitely up, and whatever it was it wouldn't be good news for her or Fats.

At the prison Shanice was first off the bus to be processed. Funny thing was that she kept looking back to Laquesha like she was making sure that Laquesha was coming in, for some reason. While Laquesha was waiting to go in, she got a sudden premonition that she was about to be set up. She was spooked, and she didn't pass it off as being paranoid. She panicked right before going in the visit and decided to ditch the drugs. She went into the ladies' room, took the balloons out, and flushed them down the toilet. She hoped that she was doing the right thing, because if her premonition was wrong, then Fats could end up getting hurt really bad because of her being spooked. Laquesha trusted her instincts, though.

When Fats entered the visiting room, she could tell he was nervous and kind of tense. But he was determined to make the move. When he saw Country and Shanice in the visiting room, his eyes lit up. He nodded to his big homie, who nodded back. Fats walked over and gave his girl a kiss, expecting her to push some balloons into his mouth, but again, like the ordeal with Kim, it didn't happen. Fats disengaged from the kiss and looked inquisitively at Laquesha.

"I couldn't do it," Laquesha said. Fats looked at her. Mad at first, but then resigned to his fate. *Fuck it,* he thought. *I'll do what I gotta do. Come what may.*

"It's awright, La. I'll make do," Fats said, as a thousand possibilities ran through his head.

Laquesha looked up to see Country and Shanice staring at them intently. *What are they up to?* And as she looked away, she noticed that some COs were rolling in and coming right toward her and Fats. It looked like a repeat of what had happened to Rock and Melissa.

Laquesha was so happy she'd trusted her instincts and hadn't brought in the drugs. She knew their visit was over and that they'd put Fats in a dry cell, but she knew that Fats wouldn't pass anything. As the COs escorted Fats away and got ready to take her out of the jail, Laquesha glared at Country and Shanice. She couldn't prove it, but she knew in her heart that her and Fats had been set up by them.

Chapter Eleven

*L*aquesha didn't have any drugs on her, so even though she was searched and detained by the local police for a minute, they didn't have anything to hold her on. She waited on the bus the rest of the day with the driver in the parking lot, and when all the people came out for the return trip to D.C., Laquesha wanted to bust Shanice in her face, but she restrained herself and decided to play stupid and feel Shanice out. She was pretty sure the whole thing was a setup, but it was better to play it cool. Maybe Shanice would let something slip. But on the bus trip back Shanice ignored her like she didn't even exist. Every time Laquesha tried to make eye contact Shanice would look away.

All right, then that's how it's gonna be then, bitch, Laquesha thought. With Shanice's avoidance Laquesha was sure that she and Fats had been set up to take the fall. Some of the other girls on the bus asked Laquesha if she was okay, and she told them it was all good, but she still worried about Fats's being subjected to those white people's wrath in the hole when they found out he didn't have any drugs. She also worried about how Fats would react when he hit the compound. She knew her baby's daddy wasn't no killer, but Fats was known to handle his own.

When she got back to the city the first person she called was Melissa. "What's up, girl?" Laquesha spoke into the phone.

"What's up? How was your visit?"

"You'll never believe what happened, girl."

"Tell me then, girl."

"Fats is in the dry cell."

"Is he clean or dirty?" Melissa asked.

"He's clean. I flushed the balloons down the toilet before I went in. I just had a funny feeling, and I was right. And guess what the worst of it is?"

"What?" Melissa said.

"I think that Country set Fats up." There was silence on the phone for a minute. "Damn, girl, say something."

"That's funny," Melissa said. "I just got a letter from Rock today, and he said the same thing. He thinks that Country set him up, too."

"Is that so?" Laquesha said. "Is that so."

. . .

Fats was in the dry cell tripping. They had him stripped to his underwear in a cell with no toilet, no sink, and a metal bed with no mattress and only a sheet to sleep with. There was a CO sitting and watching Fats through a big window and videotaping his every move. The lights were glaring, and Fats couldn't turn them off. They fed him and let him drink water but they wouldn't even give him a toothbrush, a facecloth, or anything. It was the next day and Fats was ready to shit. He knew he was clean, so he didn't have anything to worry about. The lieutenant had told him he needed to shit like five to eight times and if he didn't pass anything they would let him out. The lieutenant told him it could take anywhere from two to five days. Fats was like, fuck that, I'm gonna get my shit on. He banged on the window.

"Hey, CO, I gotta shit, slim. Let's do this." The CO got a look on his face like, what the fuck. "Hey buddy, I'm almost off. Why don't you wait for the next shift," he told Fats.

"Naw, slim, I gotta shit now, no bullshit." The CO looked resigned and got up to enter the dry cell with Fats. He had a little plastic bedpan, some plastic gloves, and a wooden tongue suppressor. The CO called the lieutenant and two others. They all entered the room with Fats and held the video camera on him while he squatted down and shit in the little plastic bedpan.

"I need some toilet paper, slim," Fats said. There was a scramble because the COs had forgotten to bring some. Fats watched as the one CO used the tongue suppressor to mash through his shit looking for balloons.

"It's clean, Lieutenant," the CO said, and they all exited the cell and disposed of the shit. Fats had four or five more shits to go.

Later that same day, Fats saw his homie, Rock, who was an orderly in the hole. Fats motioned him over, but Rock shook his head and looked around. He continued doing his orderly duties and slowly made his way over by the dry cell.

"CO, I'm gonna clean up right here," he said, motioning to some debris in the corner.

"All right," the CO said. "But no communication with the guy in the dry cell." Rock nodded and started cleaning up, waiting for his opportunity to talk to Fats, which came a minute later when one of the other COs called over the CO who was watching Fats.

Rock crept over, keeping a constant watch for the CO, who would return in a minute.

"Damn, homie," Rock said. "We in here for Christmas."

Fats shook his head. "I'm not dirty," he said. "They got me fucked up, moe."

"Oh yeah," Rock said. "You didn't talk to Country about doing something, did you?"

Fats nodded.

"Damn, slim, that's fucked up. I think I'm in here because of that nigga."

Fats looked at Rock quizzically, making sure he'd heard him right.

Rock nodded. "Yeah, slim, it's true, Country set me up and probably tried to set you up, too."

Fats could only shake his head as the CO came back over glaring at Rock, and Rock made a quick retreat from the dry cell.

Three days later Fats was back on the pound. He knew he had some business to take care of, but he wasn't sure as to how to go about it. One of the first people he bumped into when he came out of the hole carrying his bag was Country. Country looked surprised as hell to see Fats.

"What's up, little homie," Country said to Fats, trying to hide his surprise.

"What's up, Country." Fats said, thinking, *This nigga got a lot of nerve.* Fats didn't know whether to jump on the dude right then or to wait and think things through. He wasn't 100 percent sure in what he thought, but what Rock had told him had a lot of merit. *I gotta rock this nigga to sleep,* Fats concluded.

"I'm glad you made it back out. You know we got a game tonight. The final, slim," Country said, and Fats nodded. "We'll talk about that other shit later. You gotta let me know what the fuck is up."

Fats nodded again and walked away to his unit. As he entered the block and made his way to his cell, he was at a loss as to what he needed to do, but that all changed when he walked in his cell and saw Mel-Mel nodding. "What up, moe." Fats said.

Mel-Mel looked up, scratching his head. Mel-Mel was whacked out on heroin.

"Merry Christmas, joe," Mel-Mel said, and broke out into a wide grin. "You know Country hooked me up with a little something, something."

"Oh yeah, is that so?" Fats said. *So Country made his move and I got busted,* Fats thought. He looked up to see Mikey P at his door, motioning him out of the cell. Mikey P shook Fats's hand, and they exchanged greetings.

"Good to see you, Fats," Mikey P said. "I thought you were gonna be gone for a while."

"Naw, Mr. P. I was clean. They didn't get nothing on me."

"That's good. That's real good, but I got something to tell you," Mikey P said real serious-like. "I didn't want to say anything before, because I didn't really know you, but when I was doing time in Lewisburg, they said your homie Country was setting dudes up to get his heroin in. I'm not saying anything, but it seems to me that he did the same thing to you and Rock."

Fats hadn't wanted to accept the truth of the matter, but now he had no choice, it was staring him in the face point-blank.

"Thanks for letting me know, Mr. P.," Fats said, and hit rocks with the old mobster.

This nigga got some serious problems now, Fats thought. He knew he had a game that night, and he would play. He would make Country think that nothing was wrong, but after the game Fats would get his. *At least my kids got some presents from the Angel Tree program,* Fats thought. *Because after I do what I gotta do, they might not see me for a minute.* All because Fats wanted his kids to get something for Christmas. Fats felt good knowing that they got something even though he didn't come up. *That's what I get for fucking with treacherous niggas,* Fats thought. All that bullshit about finding the snitch and giving him a Christmas present. *I got a motherfucking Christmas present for that bitch.* Fats started planning the night's activities.

Chapter Twelve

After dinner Fats went up to rec to see the Christmas concert that was put on by the prisoners. They had a rap band, a heavy metal band, an R&B band, a country band, some Jamaican MC's, and Fats's favorite: the go-go band. Fats sat with his homies and watched them all. He noticed that Country hadn't shown up yet. Fats had gotten a shank from Mel-Mel earlier, who copped it from some other old heads. Fats was ready to put in some work; he wasn't fucking around. He didn't know what Country was saying about the whole affair, but he wasn't waiting to find out.

As far as Fats was concerned Country had put his family in jeopardy, and Fats didn't fuck around where his family was concerned. After the concert it was game time, and on the move Country showed up in the gym. He was psyching the homies up for the finals. The D.C. mob wasn't favored to win. They were playing a team comprised of North Carolina dudes that was led by the Monkey-Man, a fan favorite. Monkey-Man could shoot the lights out and was considered the best player on the pound by far. As the game tipped off, Fats was just thinking about what he had to do after its completion. He kept seeing Country looking at him like he was trying to feel him out, but Fats didn't really say nothing to the dude other than what he was expected to during the game. *Maybe he doesn't suspect anything,* Fats thought. The Monkey-Man's team jumped out to a big first-half lead, but with Country exhorting his team the D.C. mob clawed back to within five points. Big Murk was grabbing boards like crazy and putting back all misses.

In the second half the Monkey-Man came out on fire, and his team looked to win for sure, but in the last eight minutes of the game Fats found his shot and the Monkey-Man went cold. Fats drained five threes to end the game, giving the D.C. mob a one-point victory to win the Christmas tournament. The homies were going crazy, running all over the gym and screaming. It was pandemonium. Just the cover Fats needed. He took it all in stride. The congratulations and accolades. Fats had only one thing on his mind. Retribution. Country came up to Fats and slapped his homie five. Apparently all lost love forgotten. He was all on Fats's dick, talking with that that's his man and shit. All the homies were gathered 'round, and there was a big cheer for D.C.

"Merry Christmas," Country told all his homies. "I told you we could win this shit. Chocolate city all the way." Congratulations went around one more time, and everybody ran around wildly celebrating. When Country turned his back, Fats went and got the shank out his gym bag.

In the crowd it was easy to approach Country from behind. Fats was focused. More focused than at any time in his life. He closed in on Country from behind. All the cheering and noise receded in Fats's mind as he came upon Country. Country turned around with a big smile on his face. When he saw the shank, his smile quickly vanished. Country put his hands up, but it was too late. Fats sank the shank swiftly into Country's chest.

"Merry Christmas, moe," Fats said as the shank bit deep.

Charge It to the Game

by J. M. Benjamin

Chapter One

As he rode shotgun in the passenger seat of his Beamer, occupied with rolling a dub sack of Sour Diesel weed, Supreme was interrupted by the sound of his cell phone. "Hmm?" he answered, holding the phone up to his ear with the help of his shoulder since his hands were preoccupied while he licked and twisted the cigar paper full of weed to form what he called a perfect L, ready to get his chief on.

"You have a collect call from . . . It's me, Victorious. Accept the call! This call may be recorded or monitored. To refuse this call, hang up. To accept this call, dial one. To block future—"

"Peace, sun. What's good? Where you at?" Supreme asked, turning down the volume of the Harmon Kardon system in his midnight blue 2007 convertible 645i, bringing the latest DJ Phat Rodney Club CD to a minimum.

"I'm in Union-muthafuckin'-County Jail, bee!" an upset Victorious replied.

"For what?" Supreme asked as he sparked up the blunt he had just finished rolling.

"I don't really wanna say over the jack, but it ain't a good look. These devils caught me on some humbug shit," replied Victorious as he recalled the incident.

"Word? How the fuck that happened?"

"Like I said, I don't really want to go into details over the jack like that, but, yo, you hear me."

"Yeah."

"I don't know how the fuck they knew, but them muthafuckas found the Self-Truth-Allah-Self-He in da Benz, feel me?" Victorious stated, using a street lingo he knew Supreme would understand, referring to the stash spot compartment in his CLS 500.

"Get the fuck outta here. How they get up in ya shit?"

"Yo, they pulled me over on some fake shit. On a bullshit traffic violation, talking about I switched lanes without using my blinker," Victorious explained. "But like I said, that's bullshit, though."

"Word is bond. That sounds like some bullshit right there, sun. What they say was probable cause for them to be searchin' ya piece, though? What, you ain't have ya credentials on you or somethin'?" Supreme asked, passing the blunt to the driver.

"How you sound? You know I always travel legit, kid."

"So how they get in ya whip then? I know you ain't give 'em permission."

"Now you really buggin'," Victorious said. "Never in the history of the game would I do that. Nah, them mu'fuckas ran down on me like they was tipped off or somethin'."

"That sound like illegal search right there, unless they was already onto you, but I don't know. You sure they wasn't squattin' on you?"

"You know ain't nothin' slow about me but my walk. Trust me, kid, they were squattin' on me," Victorious answered, still trying to decipher the mayhem in his mind even as he spoke. "Oh, yeah, and check how they gonna hit me with the bullshit, talking about they smelled Equality in my joint," Victorious added, using Five Percent terminology to refer to the imaginary smell of marijuana the arresting officers used to justify the search of his vehicle.

"Come on, sun. You know that's bogus right there. A muthafucka couldn't get in my piece if they were travelin' like that, you know that. You, my manz, and I still ain't let it go down like that, nahmean."

"True," Supreme answered. For some reason Victorious's words made Supreme think about how he was traveling in his own whip blowing trees. The thought of what Victorious had said almost made him dud the blunt he was smoking out, but the weed had already begun to take its effect, so he brushed the notion off, refusing to let Victorious's statement get him paranoid.

"But, yo, why you think they was tipped off, though? And by who?" he asked.

" 'Cause they knew exactly how to get up in that shit. They tried to fake me out like it was on some ole coincidental-type shit, but believe me when I tell you, kid, they knew the official steps it took to finagle their way into the box. How? I don't know. Who? I don't know that, either. What you thinking, though?" Victorious asked Supreme, hoping that he would somehow be able to shed some light on the situation.

"I don't know, beloved. We'd have to build on that when you touch down, but anyway, check it," Supreme said, changing the subject, feeling that Victorious was going too deep into details over the phone.

He had hoped by doing that, Victorious would catch on, which he did. "Yo pardon self, sun. I know I'm kinda reckless right about now. This shit just got me real vexed."

"I smell you my dude, but you gots to keep a level head up in there, you follow me?"

"Indeed, sun, no doubt," Victorious agreed, regaining his composure.

"Yo, kid, what's your ransom anyway?" asked Supreme, referring to Victorious's bail.

"That's why I hit you up. It's a buck-fifty, no ten percent. I already hollered at the bondsman to see what the damage was on that earlier, and he said he wanted fifteen thousand eighty-eight dollars and two signatures. I been trying to reach Meeka ever since I got knocked 'cause she got access to that, plus I need her signature." Victorious was becoming frustrated behind the fact that he was unable to get in touch with his girlfriend, who was the only one besides himself who knew the combination to the safe at his condo.

"But, yo, I can't get in touch with her ass. That's why I need you to swing by the crib and see what's good, 'cause she should be there. She probably all treed up and shit and fell asleep. She don't be hearin' shit when she like that. If the truck there, then she home; if not, then I need you to get at the bondsman and handle that for me before the day out, and I'll see you back on that when I touch."

"Say no more, I got you. I'ma dip over there right now as soon as I hit the town."

"Yo, where you at now?" Victorious asked, concerned about the length of time it would take for Supreme to do what he asked of him.

"Right now I'm on one and nine," Supreme answered. "Yeah, me and Math just coming back from New York doing some shopping. I just rode past the Budweiser factory."

"Math? Math who?"

"Mathematics." Supreme had completely forgotten about the history between Math and Victorious.

"Yo, sun, what you doin' with that joker?"

"I seen sun over there when I was on two-fifth. He caught the train over, so I gave 'em a ride back, that's all." Supreme prepared himself for the lecture that was to follow, fully aware of Victorious's dislike of Math, but he was surprised when he wasn't given the third degree.

"Anyway, sun, just take care of that for me, a'ight? You know jail ain't my thing. I can't believe they finally got me to pay a visit to this hellhole, and on some ole fluke shit, too." Victorious was still in disarray over the whole ordeal.

"I know, dawg, but just fall back and chill. I got you. Everything's gonna be everything. I'ma locate wifey, and we gonna come snatch you."

"I think sun could be the cause and effect of this chaos and confusion," Victorious blurted out.

"Who?" Supreme asked.

"Mathematics."

"How you figure, god?" Supreme questioned, wanting to hear the logic in Victorious's accusations.

"No, I'll elaborate on that more when I touch, but yo don't let the nigga leave your sight. Keep sun close until I get there, a'ight?"

"Done deal," replied Supreme. "I'ma locate wifey, don't worry, but if I don't connect with her, that ain't about nothing, I still got you, a'ight, sun?"

"True indeed, god, that's love. Yo, I'ma hit you back up later after I holla at the bondsman again and let him know what's good. This jack should be about to cut off in a few min—"

"You have one minute remaining," the recorded operator stated, cutting in.

"—uck that nigga!" was what Victorious thought he had heard just as the recording of the one-minute warning was ending, and he could have sworn that the words came from a female, but with the Akon cut "Go Better" now playing in the background on Supreme's end, he wasn't for certain.

"Yo, sun, I only got less than a minute left, so I'ma go 'head and holla at the bondsman again and let 'im know you gonna be comin' through, but, yo, who else wit' you?" he asked, unable to shake the thought he just had seconds ago.

"I told you. Why? What's up?" Supreme asked.

"It sounded like I heard a chick in the background."

"Naah, suun, you buuggin'," Supreme replied, sounding as if he was trying to hold his breath and talk at the same time.

Victorious didn't have to be a genius to figure out that Supreme was smoking weed. He couldn't help but grin at the thought. He figured being as though that was the case, then the voice that he had heard before had to be how Mathematics sounded when he smoked. But who was he referring to when he had said "uck that nigga," or rather "Fuck that nigga?" That couldn't be possible. He knew there was no way that his man Supreme would allow that to go down in his presence. Maybe it was his own paranoia from this being his first time in jail.

As if reading his mind Supreme said, "Them walls is talkin' to you, kid. Just sit tight, I got you. You'll be out in a minute," he added, exhaling the smoke.

"You right, sun, I'm buggin'. Just hurry up and get me outta this muthafucka."

"I got you."

"A'ight, sun. Peace."

"A'ight. Peace," Supreme replied, bringing their phone conversation to an end.

Victorious was just about to hang the phone up and dial the bondsman's office again when the sound of Supreme's voice made him pause. "You's a stupid bitch!"

"Hello?" Victorious called out into the receiver, but his question went unanswered. The phone line had already gone dead, and all he heard now was the busy signal from the disconnection. Supreme had just called somebody a bitch, but the sixty-four-thousand-dollar question was who? Furthermore, why?

As his mind began to race with thoughts, without hesitation, Victorious rapidly began dialing Supreme's number back with the voice of the anonymous person playing over and over in his head. Before, neither the words nor the voice were really clear to him, but as he punched the last three digits of Supreme's cell phone number, both the identity and the familiarity of the voice instantly registered as if it had been hovering over him in midair the whole time, waiting for him to just reach out and grab hold of it.

"You must wait before placing your next call," the recording announced.

"What the fuck?" Victorious snapped. "Un-fuckin'-believable!" Out of all the times in the world, how could the phone decide to start acting up then? It wasn't a good look for him, Victorious decided.

"Ayo, fam," Victorious called out to another inmate who had just gotten off the phone across from him. "Yo, that phone you was just on still working?"

"Yeah. Why? What's up?" the inmate responded.

"I don't know, but I just tried to make another call on this one, but it wouldn't go through," he told him.

"Oh, you gotta wait an hour before you can make another call," explained the fellow prisoner.

"Word life? A whole fucking hour?" Victorious asked in disbelief, becoming agitated.

"Yeah. This is a fucked-up spot, kid."

Victorious couldn't agree with him more, but for him, not only was he in a fucked-up spot, he was also in a fucked-up predicament—one that he was unable to look into, at least for another hour.

"Damn!" was all he could say.

Chapter Two

"Who the fuck you calling a bitch, muthafucka?"

"Yo, what I tell you about calling me outta my fuckin' name, Meeka?" Supreme shot back.

"What, nigga? What about me? My mother mighta called me a bitch, but she ain't name me one, so I ain't gonna let you disrespect me and call me out my name either," Meeka stated, firmly standing her ground.

"So why you actin' like one then?" Supreme spat back.

"Preme, I swear to God, you say that shit again I'll kill us both up in this muthafucka," Meeka screamed, jerking the steering wheel of Supreme's quarter-to-eight Beamer, causing the car to swerve on the highway.

"Yo, what the fuck you doin'? You bugging the fuck out, shortie," Supreme yelled, holding on to the dashboard.

"I ain't buggin', nigga. I'm for real. I don't appreciate that shit, Supreme. All my life I grew up hearing that shit, and I ain't having it no more," Tameeka said.

"Oh, and you think I'm havin' you playin' fuckin' games while I'm on the phone with my peoples?" Supreme replied, disregarding what Meeka had just said.

"Oh, that's your peoples now, huh?" Meeka shot back with attitude. "Nigga, please. Was he your peoples when you was fucking me and I was sucking your dick? Or what about him being your peoples when you agreed to go along with this shit?" Tameeka said, throwing Supreme's violations toward Victorious in his face.

"Shut the fuck up. You don't know what the fuck you talking about," was Supreme's only comeback.

"Whatever, nigga. Your peoples!" Tameeka remarked sarcastically, letting her words hang in the air.

Supreme just let Tameeka's comments ride because now was not the time for him to get into an argument with her, especially after he had technically chosen her over his man.

Although he tried to dead it by remaining silent, Tameeka would not let it go.

"Tsk! You know what? You kill me!" She started back sucking her teeth. "You swear you this righteous-ass nigga with all this 'my peoples' shit, always talking about Victorious you're A-a-like, B-a-like, and C-a-like, when the fact and truth of the matter is that you ain't respecting that shit. You don't really give a fuck about that ABC shit. Nigga, you ain't no Five Percenter, you's a Five Pretender," Tameeka yelled, cutting Supreme deep.

"You got me fucked up, yo. I'm a *hundred* percent," Supreme shot back, taking offense to Meeka's statement.

"No, you got your own self fucked up, sweetheart. Get it right."

Supreme had finally gotten fed up with Tameeka's mouth and was determined to bring her comments to an end.

"Yo, I'm tired of ya smart-ass mouth," he barked. "Keep talking slick, and I'ma be the one to kill us up in this piece my muthafucking self. Every time I say something, you gots to pop shit. Say some more shit and see if I'm joking out this muthafucka or not." Supreme stared at Tameeka stone-faced. He meant every word of it.

Tameeka knew that she had gone too far with Supreme. She knew that he was far from being a weak individual when it came to his handling his business. In fact, the only weakness she was aware of was the one he had for her. She was trying to get him to focus on their plan and not on what he had actually done to his man Victorious. There was always that possibility that if he thought about it long and hard enough that he would have a change of heart about seeing things through. She knew that if they were going to finish what they had started, then she had to smooth things out.

"Supreme, why we even going through this, boo?" she asked in an attempt to break the ice.

Supreme sat silently on the passenger side as if he hadn't heard a word Tameeka said.

"Oh, you ain't speaking to me now?" Tameeka asked in her most innocent voice as she reached her free hand over toward Supreme's lap.

"Get off me," Supreme said in a semihostile manner, affected by Tameeka's words.

"I can't touch you now either?" she asked provocatively.

Tameeka's words came right out of her mouth and traveled straight to Supreme's manhood. Normally that's all it would've taken for Supreme to throw in the towel, but not this time. Supreme already had an urge to choke the life out of Meeka for the blatant disrespect she had displayed and the misconception she had of his man.

Victorious and he had a bond, which made it that much more difficult for him to go against the grain like he had. He had allowed Tameeka to get him to let his guard down, and because of that, things had reached a point of no return.

Had Victorious been home that one particular day almost two years ago when Supreme stopped by his crib to check for him, things may have been different, Supreme thought, and he probably wouldn't be in the position he was in.

He remembered as if it were yesterday when Tameeka answered the door with only a bathrobe covering her body, partially revealing her butter pecan–toned breasts and one of her smoothly shaved slender legs. At first, Supreme had lowered his gaze at the sight of her half-nakedness because she was his man's shortie, but Tameeka was by far one of the baddest, if not *the* baddest, women he had ever seen in his life, and he just couldn't resist another look, especially since she had no problems showing it. As he redirected his attention to her, he could see her curvaceous physique, even through the robe.

She was indeed one of God's gifts to men, and since he considered himself to be a living god, he reasoned that she was also a gift to him.

"Vic home?" he had managed to ask as their eyes met.

"No, he ain't here, he just left about an hour ago. I think he went to go take care of some business," Tameeka had told him as she looked Supreme up and down.

Supreme's dick had stiffened as her eyes traveled down below his waist and zeroed in on what she was looking for.

Supreme was no stranger to Tameeka. She had known him just as long as she had known Victorious. She recalled the first time she had laid eyes on Supreme. Supreme had pulled up on her and Victorious on a summer day by the basketball court at Cedarbrook Park in his money green Cadillac Escalade truck sitting on chromed-out twenty-four-inch Davins.

In her mind, she had deemed him fuckable the first day Victorious introduced him as his right-hand man. She was instantly attracted to Supreme as soon as he hopped out of his SUV wearing a New Jersey Nets' throwback, matching fitted cap, and Evisu capri jeans, not to mention the white, orange, and blue Air Force Ones that completed his hookup. To set his I'm-doin'-big-things look off, he sported a thick platinum chain with an iced-out medallion that read BIG PREME and a matching flooded wrist piece. Supreme's light bill was definitely paid up, Tameeka had thought, referring to how Supreme's shines added extra lighting to the day, giving the sun a run for its money.

He stood before her that day similarly dressed, looking like a chocolate candy bar just waiting to be unwrapped.

"A'ight then, let him know I came by," Supreme had said, wishing he had said more, but instead spinning around and stepping off before he said the wrong thing. Meeka stopped him in his tracks.

"You want to come in and wait for him?" she had asked.

Supreme had turned around, and when he did, he could have sworn that Meeka's robe had loosened a bit. It was as if Tameeka's robe had deliberately opened more. He knew that was a warning sign for him to decline her offer, but, instead, he disregarded his instincts and accepted it.

"A'ight, yeah, that'll be peace."

Tameeka had slid to the side just enough to let Supreme into the house. As Supreme proceeded through the doorway, he unconsciously brushed up against Tameeka's body, and she had smiled. Tameeka had closed the door behind him.

"You want something to drink?"

"Yeah, you got Coronas?" he had asked.

"You know I do. I don't know why you and Vic like them nasty shits."

" 'Cause they smooth, and they a nice chaser behind that Henny."

"Vic says the same thing," Tameeka had said, heading for the kitchen to get Supreme's beer.

What the fuck you doin' Preme? Just get the fuck up and leave before she comes back, his conscience spoke to him, and with that he headed for the door.

"Supreme, where you going?" Tameeka had asked, reentering the living room.

"Yo, I gotta go," was all Supreme had said as he continued toward the door.

Sensing something, Tameeka had walked over to him. "Here, at least take your beer with you," she had offered as she got close to him. Supreme had taken the Corona and attempted to turn back to leave, but Tameeka had jumped in front of his path.

"You gonna leave without saying 'bye?" she had asked, wearing the sexiest expression Supreme had ever seen on a woman.

He had smiled at her comment. "See you later, Meeka," he had replied, thinking she would move out of his way after that.

"Dag, you all in a hurry like that? You just gonna leave a sister all by her lonely?" she had asked him with a devilish grin.

"Yo, I gotta bounce. I'll come back through again some other time and check you," Supreme had said, not believing what he had just said.

He knew that he was in a major violation, but he was hoping that he could make it up out of there without things going any further. Hopefully his man wouldn't find out about the incident. Supreme just wanted to put the little mishap behind him, but Tameeka was making it real hard for him to do.

"Okay, well, at least gimme a hug before you go," Tameeka had suggested.

Against his better judgment Supreme had agreed, only because he wanted to get out of the house before Victorious happened to show up, forcing him to explain why he was there while his man wasn't home. Supreme had extended his arms as Tameeka stepped into him. As he had wrapped his arms around her, Supreme instantly smelled the Chanel fragrance illuminating from her body. He had felt his manhood slowly rising from the intoxicating scents. Tameeka had embraced him, squeezing him tightly, pressing her breasts up against his chest and her pelvis into his dick. That was all Supreme could take. He had tried to break free of Tameeka's hug, but she wouldn't release him. There was no doubting that she felt good to Supreme—real good to be exact—but he knew that if he didn't break loose of the hold now, things would lead into something that he wasn't sure he was ready for.

"Meeka, let me go," Supreme had said, but Tameeka didn't comply. Instead, she had raised her head from his shoulder and looked into his eyes.

"Don't leave. I don't want you to go."

Supreme had just stared at her, bewildered. He could see in her eyes that she meant what she said. Before he could get the words out of his mouth and ask why, Tameeka had kissed him. He kissed her back passionately, as she allowed his tongue to part her lips. For a moment Supreme had gotten caught up, but, as the realization of what he was doing set in, he broke their lip-lock.

"Yo, shortie, this ain't right," he had said, still trying to break free of Tameeka, who had her arms around him. She wouldn't release him. Instead, she kissed him again. This time she had managed to slide her hand into his sweatpants and grab his dick.

Supreme had felt the heat and moisture that was generated from the palm of Tameeka's hand as he kissed her back again, and, before he knew it, once again he had been caught in the rapture. Letting his guard totally down, he began to take control of the situation, taking Tameeka's robe off, revealing her nakedness.

Supreme had guided Tameeka's nude body to the floor as they continued to kiss. He glanced down at Meeka spread-eagle on the living room floor, and he began to undress. *A work of art*, he thought.

Meeka had watched with lustful eyes as Supreme undressed. When she had wrapped her hand around Supreme's manhood earlier, she could tell that he was bigger than Victorious, but actually to see it told it all. The way Supreme was hung reminded Tameeka of her ex-lover, causing her to moisten at the thought.

Supreme had no clue as to when the next time an opportunity such as this would come around again, so he decided that if he was going to go through with it, to go all out. After he had undressed completely, he had knelt down to where Tameeka lay.

Tameeka reached out to him with the intent of guiding him inside of her, but Supreme moved her hand. He had other plans. Instead of giving Tameeka what she apparently wanted, Supreme intended to give her something else; he continued to travel down her body until his mouth reached its destination.

This was definitely a surprise to Tameeka, who had no complaints. As Supreme's tongue began to massage and caress her inner thighs, Tameeka began to realize just how much she was in desperate need of a tongue-lashing. It had been quite some time since a man had gone down on her. Early into their relationship, Victorious had made it perfectly clear that he was not down with the whole oral aspect of sex, at least not giving it, anyway. The last time she had received any type of lip service was when she'd been with her partner before him, who was expertly skilled in the craft, but unfortunately for her he had been unavailable for some time now.

Supreme was not surprised at how delicious Tameeka tasted. He had gone down on many women in the past—some because he wanted to while others he felt it necessary in order to sex them for the night—but with Meeka, it was more than that. Whether he wanted to or not, he felt that it was mandatory, and since they were already taking a risk, he wanted the experience to be complete. He was determined not to come up short in any way.

After her orgasm, Tameeka had just heated up. She knew it was now her turn to show Supreme what she was working with. She had grabbed Supreme's head, indicating that she wanted him to stop, though she would have preferred that he continued, but she knew that if she didn't stop him then, she never would.

As Supreme had come up for air, Tameeka had rolled him onto

his back, and all in one motion she began going to work. She started out by planting kisses on his neck and then began running her tongue down his chest, licking one of his nipples as she traveled down until her tongue had met up with his dick.

When she had taken him into her mouth, it had taken all the willpower that Supreme had possessed to refrain from exploding right then and there as she deep-throated him. Let her tell it, her head game was hands down among the top five chicks in the tristate area who professed to have super head skills. She actually enjoyed going down on men because she was so much of a control freak. She felt that she could make a man do anything for her after she had him in her mouth, but what she really enjoyed even more was the reaction that she got once she began licking their sacks and running her tongue between their ass cheeks. What she got a kick out of most was sliding her finger into their butt holes. She loved the way men squirmed when she did that.

Not everyone she tried this with was receptive to her freaky methods, but most of them were, including Victorious. Now it was time to put Supreme through the test to see whether he got down like that.

Supreme couldn't keep still as Meeka licked his male G-spot. Every time he had felt her tongue lightly brush across his anus, he would flinch, unable to control his nerves. But at the same time it felt like heaven to him, and he didn't want her to stop.

As he tried to relax and enjoy the pleasure of her tongue, he felt something foreign to him, and he became alarmed.

As she had slid her middle finger inside of his rectum, Meeka had slipped Supreme's dick back into her mouth, in hopes that he was receptive. Slowly, she cautiously slid her finger in and out of Supreme's butt as she continued to suck the helmet of his joint.

By now Supreme had realized what was taking place, and anger overswept him for a split second, but just as quickly as it had come it went. His anger turned into pleasure, and before he could even decide whether he wanted Meeka to stop, she had taken her finger out of him and his manhood out of her mouth, and expertly straddled him.

There was no doubt in Supreme's mind as to why Victorious had allowed Tameeka to move into his crib after only a month of dealing with her. In his whole thirty-one years of living, Supreme felt that he had never paid for a piece of ass as good as what he was getting at that time, nor could he compare the pleasure that Tameeka was giving him to any he'd ever had before. The way that he felt inside her was like a match made in heaven, Supreme had thought.

It was from that day on that Supreme had a hard time resisting Tameeka whenever she called on him, committing the ultimate betrayal of going behind his man's back.

"Like I said, you don't know what the fuck you talking about. You don't know what me and my man been through. Matter of fact, hurry up and get me to Asbury," Supreme said, annoyed about the situation.

His only concern was to get to the house of his son's mother, Gina, in Asbury Park. He was going to snatch up the three hundred grand he had stashed there. The 360 Gs that Tameeka had taken from Victorious was in the trunk of the car.

Supreme began to think of a way to eliminate Tameeka from

the equation and keep all of the paper for himself. Supreme thought to keep it all was the best solution as Tameeka continued to drive in silence.

Supreme had no desire to be with Tameeka anymore, having seen her true nature, behavior, and disrespect toward him. The more he thought about it, the farther away he wanted to get from her. But he also knew that he couldn't allow his personal feelings to get involved while he was handling his business, so he decided to cross the bridge of getting rid of Tameeka when he got to it.

Tameeka, nervous about Supreme's attitude, accelerated on the gas pedal. She figured by turning Supreme on, getting him aroused, he'd make her pull over so he could drive, like he had done many times before, while she performed oral sex on his magic stick. But her plan didn't work out the way that she expected, and now she, too, had an attitude.

"When we get there, I hope you gonna be in and out. Don't make me have to come up in there and hurt that bitch," Tameeka spat with venom in her words, no longer able to hold her tongue.

"Yo, just drive," Supreme commanded, as he reclined his seat and continued to puff on the remainder of the L.

Chapter Three

"Pardon self. Yo, good looking on that. What's ya name?" Victorious asked the inmate who informed him about the status of the phone.

"Hasan, but everybody calls me Has, and yeah, that was nothing as for the phone. I know how it be," Has replied, extending his hand. Has had gone through these types of formalities a million times. He had been in the county so long that he was used to meeting cats who came and went, whether making bail or being shipped to prison. "What do you go by?" Has asked.

"Victorious," was the response given as Victorious shook Has's hand.

"You God-Body?" asked Has, familiar with Victorious's attribute.

"True indeed," Victorious answered, wondering if Has was Five Percent himself. "You deal with the lessons?" Victorious asked, referring to what they called Allah's Truth.

"Nah, I'm not G-O-D, but I'm familiar with the teachings of the one-twenty." Has then began to explain to Victorious how his cousin Bilal Rose was a PRT (poor righteous teacher) and taught him some of their teachings.

"So you from Plainfield?" asked Victorious, familiar with Has's cousin and where he was from.

"Yeah, I'm from the Field," replied Has, using his town's street nickname. "Where you from?"

"Out here. I'm from the E-Port section. Eastwick. And my cousin's name Bilal, too—Bilal Pretlow. You hear of him?"

"Oh, no question, sun was a beast throughout his era. Ain't a joker in Union County from the streets that never heard of sun," Has said with admiration in his tone. "Yo, is it true that he hung himself right here in the county?"

"Nah, that's emphatically now-cipher, sun," Victorious answered, speaking from his Five Percent alphabets to emphasize the word *no*.

"So how that go down then?" Has asked, curious to know.

"All I can say is that shit is deeper than what people can fathom," was the response Victorious gave.

"I feel you, kid, but whatever the situation, it was a fucked-up one. Cats losin' soldiers left and right in this war and shit. Like my man Shap, from out my way."

"Yeah, I heard about sun. Somethin' about a motorcycle accident, and it was supposed to have been a big-ass riot or something out there over that, right?"

"Something like that. His peoples from Third was wildin' out over his death. They loved the dude like dudes loved the kid Bilal out here."

"No doubt, and I know if my peeps Sean and Vinnie was in town when the shit happened with Bilal, ain't no telling what they would've did 'cause they was some wild brothers when they was home," Victorious said.

"They still knocked off?" Has asked.

"Yeah, they both down Fort Dix. They got almost eighteen in. I just sent them some flicks and shit two days before I got knocked off."

"That's what's up," Has replied.

"Yo, you know these two brothers name Pete and Squirm from out your way?" Victorious asked, testing to see what type of dude Has really was, knowing the caliber of the two names he made mention of.

"Yeah, I know them, but not know them know them, I just know of them. They from the new projects on Second Street. I heard they some good dudes," Has answered.

"Yeah, no doubt. I met them back in the day when Echo Lanes was still open. I be hollerin' at them when I be dippin' out there to Liquid Assets," said Victorious, satisfied with Has's answer about the two brothers. He, too, had heard nothing but good things about them and felt the same.

Once it was established that Victorious was from Elizabeth, New Jersey, and Has was from Plainfield, New Jersey, the two talked for quite some time, name dropping street legends and any and every high-maintenance chick they could think of. Victorious grasped from their conversation that Has was about his business and was a somebody in the town. He also gathered that Has was extremely intelligent and inquisitive. He reminded Victorious of himself, judging from his conversation during the short period of time they talked. After about twenty minutes of conversation and feeling Hasan out, Victorious was comfortable enough to ask him about his incarceration. "Has, how long you been in here, kid?"

"I spent the last two Christmases in this spot," replied Has, seeing Victorious's facial expression change.

"Damn, sun, two years? How you do that much time in this piece?" Victorious asked sympathetically.

"I just happen to luck up and get this orderly job so I could make moves as opposed to being stationary. That's how I'm able to come here and use the jack and chill over here with you. I get mad extra trays and work out when I want, but the best benefit is being able to have access to the jack so I can stay on top of my shortie."

"Yeah, that's probably how I would do my time if I had to be in here that long," Victorious said, understanding Hasan's methods. "Yo, what's the latest a muthafucka can get bailed up outta this spot?" Victorious asked.

"Anytime, as long as your peoples get the paper to the bondsman. That's what I'm waiting on now," Has answered. "How much is your bail?"

"A hundred and fifty Gs, no ten percent," Victorious answered.

"That's nothing for you, right?" Has questioned.

"Nah, it's just a matter of my people hollering at the bondsman. I would've been out already, but I can't get in touch with my fucking shortie," responded a frustrated Victorious. Hasan listened attentively. "That's neither here nor there, though. What's your bail?" Victorious asked, wondering what amount of money could have kept Hasan stuck in the county for two years.

"It was half a mil cash, but then they dropped it to two hundred fifty Gs cash, like six months ago. I was trying to get out then, but the only one I can really rely on is my shortie, so you know it ain't easy to come up with that type of paper, even though I already had almost half of that put up out there. Still, it ain't easy to come up with a hundred something Gs when you ain't hustling, especially when you a female, but baby girl went on the grind and been scraping shit up, feel me?" Has said with both passion and admiration for his girlfriend.

"Yeah, I feel you, sun. Your shortie sound like a trooper, kid," Victorious replied, thinking about the lack of communication he'd had with his since he'd been there.

"No doubt."

"Lock down! Lock down!" a correctional officer yelled.

"Damn. I didn't even get the chance to dial my peoples back or wash my ass," Victorious said, becoming mad at himself for getting caught up in a conversation with Hasan rather than handling his business.

Seeing the anger in Victorious's eyes, Hasan tried to calm him. "Yo, if you want, I can try your peoples for you while you locked in until I go upstairs. As far as the shower, just take a birdbath in the sink. Make that dude in the cell turn over."

Not thinking of either one of those ideas, Victorious was grateful for Hasan's suggestions.

"Yo, I'd appreciate that, sun. I'ma hit you with—"

"Yo, my man, let's go," the officer spoke to Victorious and walked away with a warning stare.

"Yo, go ahead. That guy a dickhead right there. I'll come over and get the info."

"A'ight," Victorious replied, walking over to his cell.

Chapter Four

"Why you gotta park around the corner? It ain't like I don't know where the bitch stay," Tameeka said, referring to Gina's house.

"Yo, didn't you say you didn't like being called a bitch?" Supreme asked.

"You know I don't," Meeka shot back.

"Well, why you keep calling my son's mom one like she like it?"

Tameeka didn't answer him; instead, she sucked her teeth and rolled her eyes. Still not in the mood for the bullshit, Supreme hopped out the BMW with the intention of returning with his money.

"Hurry up!" Meeka yelled just before the car door slammed, but Supreme paid her no mind.

Just as he turned the corner, Tameeka's cell phone vibrated.

• • •

"Yo, take this for you and lil' Preme. This should hold you for a minute. I'll get at you to see if you need more in a couple of months," Supreme said, giving Gina sixty thousand dollars of the three hundred thousand he had taken out of the bedroom closet floor safe after he had looked in on his four-year-old son, who was sound asleep. He was tempted to sex Gina like he normally did whenever he went down to south Jersey, especially now, with her standing before him in just a wife beater, coochie-cutter jean shorts, and a pair of bunny slippers, but he knew that it was not a good time. For one, he and Tameeka had to make their move to Atlanta before Victorious realized what had really happened, and second, because he knew that if he did try to sex Gina right quick, Tameeka would smell her scent all over his body and flip out, causing him to really have to hurt her. As Tameeka crossed his mind, the thought of her possibly becoming impatient and coming to Gina's door caused Supreme to conclude his visit. It was not a matter of fear of what Tameeka would do to Gina, because he believed that, if it ever came down to it, Gina would be able to handle Tameeka. It was more about his not wanting to bring any unnecessary drama to his son's mother's house.

"Supreme, why you giving me all this money like this, and why you so in a hurry to go?" Gina asked.

"Yo, stop askin' so many questions. Just take the money like I said, and I'll get at you later when I can, a'ight?"

"Okay," Gina said, sighing. "But what's up? You ain't got time to gimme some?" she asked, as if she were a little girl asking for her favorite candy.

As much as he wanted to, he knew that he had to decline Gina's offer and get out of the house before he both compromised and jeopardized his plans, especially since he had made an error by leaving Tameeka in the car with the keys and the other money. He cursed himself for being so reckless, knowing that this was not the first time that day.

As Gina tried to approach him in an enticing manner, he held her back by the shoulders.

"Yo, I gotta go, but I promise I'll come back through. I got you," he said as convincingly as he could.

Gina knew that he was lying, but still she accepted his answer. In a way, she felt somewhat ashamed about how she was acting. Her craving for a man's physical attention overpowered her integrity as a woman.

Supreme could see the hurt in her eyes from the rejection, and guilt overcame him. Had things been different, he knew that he would have stayed, but the fact of the matter was that he had to go. He kissed her on the forehead. "You know I love you, right?" he said, trying to restore her pride.

"Yeah," she said softly.

"What?"

"I said yeah," she repeated with more feeling.

"Oh, a'ight."

She smiled, and Supreme returned her smile with one of his own.

"Yo, tell my son I love him, too."

"Okay."

"You better tell him," Supreme enforced.

"I said I will."

"A'ight, I'm out. Be good, and don't be having no nigga around my son either, you hear me?"

"Yeah."

"A'ight then. I love you."

"I love you, too," she said, truly meaning it. She was kinda upset that her son wouldn't be able to spend Christmas with his father, but that was the life of fucking with a hustler. She had to charge it to the game.

Chapter Five

"Oh, I gotta go," Tameeka whispered, hanging up her cell phone, hoping Supreme hadn't seen her. Supreme was already halfway to the car with the knapsack over his shoulder by the time Tameeka spotted him.

"Who was you just talking to?" Supreme asked, getting in the car.

"What?" Tameeka responded, stalling for an explanation.

"You heard me. Don't play fucking stupid. Who was you talking to?" Supreme repeated.

"What the fuck is you talking about, Supreme? And don't be calling me stupid," Tameeka said, still thinking of an answer.

"Yo, whatever. So you tryin' to tell me that I ain't just see you on the phone talking to somebody?"

"No! What your nosy ass did see was me checking my voice mail, if you really want to know," she said, finally coming up with what she hoped would be a suitable answer.

"Yo, pop the trunk."

Tameeka reached down and hit the trunk button, relieved.

It really didn't matter at this point who Tameeka was talking to, Supreme thought, and wondered why he had even brought the phone call up. What mattered was the six hundred Gs they now had in the trunk of his car and getting on 95 South headed to ATL, where he was sure he could get rid of Tameeka once and for all.

"You know what, I ain't even trying to argue with you. Just hit the highway," Supreme commanded, forgetting about the cell phone. "Matter of fact, let me drive. I know a quick way to hit the turnpike from here."

Chapter Six

Supreme had been driving for the past five hours and now noticed that the fuel gauge was a little over a quarter tank. He really didn't want to stop, but he knew that there was no way he could make it to North Carolina on a quarter tank of gas, let alone all the way down to Atlanta. He saw the Richmond exit sign for restrooms, restaurants, and gas stations, and pulled off the highway.

"Meeka, wake up," Supreme yelled, shaking Tameeka.

"I'm up," she replied, still half asleep. When Tameeka wiped her eyes, she looked over at Supreme, who was checking his cell phone. "Where we at?"

"Virginia."

"Damn, you been doing some drivin'." How coincidental, Meeka thought, recognizing the familiar area. They were actually in her hometown of Richmond. She hadn't visited the state in quite some time, seven years to be exact, since she had moved up to Jersey after graduating Virginia Union College to be closer to her ex. Supreme had no idea that this was where she was originally from, and she was tempted to tell him but thought better of it. Right then, time was of the essence, and she didn't want to say or do anything that may deter her from the set agenda that had been planned.

"Who was that on the phone?" she asked.

"Nobody."

"Oh, you trying to be funny?"

Supreme laughed for the first time since everything had been going on. It had just dawned on him that he sounded like Tameeka did when he had asked her who she was talking to on the phone back in Asbury.

"Nah, yo, that was the nigga Victorious."

"What he say?" she asked, now fully awake hearing Victorious's name mentioned.

"He ain't say shit."

"What you mean he ain't say shit?"

"Just what it sounds like."

"So the two of you just sat on the phone and said nothing?" Meeka asked, finding that hard to believe.

"Nah, I ain't accept the call."

"Why not?" Meeka asked, surprised.

"For what? We outta Jersey now."

Supreme had a point, Meeka thought. "You think he know something's up?"

"Probably. He been hitting my phone up every hour since we left Asbury."

"Maybe that's been him calling my phone, too. I kept feeling my shit vibrate in my sleep."

"Most likely, but fuck it. What's done is done. We halfway there now," Supreme said.

"Yeah you right, boo," Meeka said, both happy and relieved to hear Supreme sounding better.

"Yo, if you gotta use the bathroom or want something to eat, get it now 'cause I ain't stopping until we get to ATL."

"No, I'm okay."

"You sure?"

"Yeah, I'm sure."

"A'ight, I'ma go take a leak right quick and then we out."

Chapter Seven

"Yo, sun, I tried both of them numbers you gave me again, and I ain't get no answer on neither one of them pieces," Has told Victorious, referring to Supreme's and Tameeka's cell phones. A total of six hours had gone by.

"A'ight, yo. That's good-looking, though." Victorious thanked Has for his efforts. "You think you'll be able to try back later for me?" he asked, sounding stressed.

"Yeah. No doubt, that's nothing. I'll keep trying until they lock me down or until I hear something about my bail, which should be soon. Most likely I should be up outta this raggedy muthafucka and up in some pussy before the sun come up, feel me?" Has smiled at Victorious.

"I feel you, sun. I'm trying to do the same thing, kid."

"Yo, hopefully shit go right for you, and we can link up out there. Like I said, I know some niggas from Elizabeth, and you know some heads from out my way, so it ain't nothing to ask somebody how to find each other, or we bound to bump heads somewhere."

"Yeah, no doubt."

"A'ight, yo, I'ma shoot upstairs for a minute. I'll probably be back down in about a half, and I'll try back for you again."

"That's peace, beloved. I appreciate that."

"Yeah but, yo, I'ma bring you some honey buns and shit back just in case, but hopefully you won't be here long enough to eat 'em all."

"Word," replied Victorious. He hoped the same thing as he

lay back in his cell bunk. He was grateful for meeting someone like Has, but knew with all that was going through his mind at the moment, he was in no mood to eat any honey buns or anything else for that matter—maybe later, but not now. Hopefully, there wouldn't be any later, but as strange thoughts continued to play in his head he knew that there was a strong possibility. . . .

Chapter Eight

"*S*upreme, pull over," Tameeka requested, waking out of her sleep.

"For what?" he asked, looking at her as if she were crazy.

"I gotta pee."

"What? Come on, yo. Didn't I ask you back in Virginia if you had to use the bathroom?" he said, agitated.

"Yeah, but I ain't have to go then. I gotta go now."

"Can't you hold that shit?"

"Why? Where we at? We almost in Atlanta?"

"Nah we in North Carolina."

"Boyee, is you crazy? I can't hold this shit for six hours."

"You gonna have to do something 'cause I ain't trying to pull over," Supreme told her.

"A'ight I'ma just piss in this muthafucking seat, that's all. You can smell the shit for the next six fucking hours if you want," she threatened.

The thought of Tameeka urinating on the seats of his brand-new eighty-thousand-dollar ride was enough for Supreme to re-consider. He knew that she was actually cocky enough to do it, so he had no other choice but to submit.

"Yo, chill! Don't piss in my muthafuckin' car, I'ma pull over."

"Yeah, I figured you would," Tameeka remarked.

After driving another five minutes, Supreme came across a rest area and pulled in.

"Damn, it's dark as hell in this piece," Supreme noticed as he parked. As soon as he stopped the car, Tameeka jumped out and ran toward the restroom, following the blue-and-white sign that read RESTROOM and had a female figure on it.

"Hurry up!" Supreme mocked Tameeka from when they were in Asbury Park.

Through the darkness he could see her middle finger go up. He laughed to himself. Looking around, he noticed that his was the only car at the rest stop. He began flipping through his CD selection until he came across one of his Dirty South favorites, Ludacris. How appropriate, he thought, being he was ATL-bound. He then reached in his glove compartment and pulled out another Phillie with the intent of rolling up another twenty-dollar bag of Sour Diesel.

After listening to a few songs Supreme realized that Tameeka had been gone nearly fifteen minutes, which was way too long. He blew his horn, hoping that she'd hear it and come out. Supreme had been so busy smoking the blunt and thinking about ways to get rid of Meeka that he hadn't even realized that nearly another ten minutes had gone by.

When another five minutes had gone by he became worried a little.

"Shit!" he cursed as he got out of the Beamer. "Stupid-ass bitch."

Before going off into the dark, Supreme reached for his stash box to get his two chrome .45s. After three unsuccessful attempts to get the hidden compartment opened, he chalked it up as a minor glitch and proceeded to the ladies' room. As he walked, he could feel the effect of the potent weed he'd smoked. It had fully kicked in, and he was feeling as if he was floating to the restroom rather than walking. The December air was sharp even down South. Mad behind the fact that he had to go look for Tameeka in the cold, Supreme wondered why he just didn't pull off and leave her ass. After all, he did have all the money in the car. *Wasn't that what this was all about?* he asked himself. With that thought, he almost turned back to head toward his whip and bounce on Meeka, but he had already reached the bathroom.

"Meeka! Meeka!" Supreme yelled. He received no answer.

Though it was dark up front where he was parked, it was even darker where he stood. The only light that was in the area was the one coming from under the bottom of the women's bathroom door.

"Meeka!" he yelled again, knocking on the door.

He reached for the door handle and slowly pushed it open, peeking his head in first. Unable to really see anything, he stepped in to take a closer look. Had he looked to the right instead of the left first, maybe he would have had a chance to react, but that was not the case.

Tameeka could not believe that she was actually going through with this. She had coached and prepared herself for this at least a thousand times, she figured, but to think or say it is one thing, to act on it is another. She had definitely amped herself up, talking the talk, but now that it was crunch time, she wasn't sure she could walk the walk. Each time she heard Supreme call out her name, it was as though the bass of his voice echoed through her entire body as she nervously stood behind the restroom door. On the third time he called her name she knew that he was right outside the door, merely inches away from where she stood on the opposite side. Only the metal door separated the two, and Meeka had hoped that it was soundproof or else Supreme was sure to hear her heart beating. She heard the handle jiggle and held her breath as the door opened. Then she saw the back of Supreme's head. With her finger on the trigger, Tameeka hesitated on the squeeze, but just as Supreme turned to face her she knew that it was now or never.

Boom! Boom!

The two shots ripped into Supreme's face, the impact splitting his head like a coconut. He never knew what hit him.

Still a little shaken, Meeka placed the chip back in the fuse box in order to operate the stash compartment. She did the necessary three-step maneuver she had seen both Victorious and Supreme do many times to open it. After putting both Desert Eagles back into the box, Tameeka closed it and pulled out of the rest area. Instead of hopping back on I-95 South, she jumped onto I-95 North, headed back to Jersey. At first, she thought she was going to be sick as images of what she had done to Supreme began to haunt her mind. She had never killed anyone before and felt a little remorseful, but the six hundred Gs in the trunk had her feeling a whole lot better as she drove with caution on the highway. Besides, the hard part was over. . . .

Chapter Nine

Daylight had just revealed itself when Tameeka first reached the New Jersey Turnpike, and now she was exiting off the highway where the sign read 13A, ENTERING ELIZABETH.

It had been a long night, but she had finally tied up all the loose ends and was now headed to her initial destination. Had it not been for the time-consuming trip to the South, where she had to get rid of Supreme, she could have already handled her business affairs in Jersey, but Supreme's death was a must. He had served his purpose, and now he was no longer needed. Besides that, it was a gift to Victorious, because, in her opinion, he was too good of a man to have someone as grimy as Supreme on his team. In spite of what Supreme's mouth said, Tameeka knew that his words were a contradiction to his actions, and he did not deserve Victorious's friendship. With that in mind, Tameeka pulled in front of the bail bondsman's office with the intent of taking care of what she had set out to do.

Chapter Ten

"Hold on. Lemme get a minute right quick. Yo, sun! Yo, sun!"

"Oh, what up, kid?" Victorious responded.

"Yo, I'm outta this muthafucka, bee."

"Word?"

"Yeah, sun, they just told me to pack up like five minutes ago."
Has couldn't contain his smile.

"Damn, kid, that's a good look for you right there. What time
is it?"

"It's almost eight-thirty."

"Shit! I been up all muthafuckin' night. I just dozed off like a
few hours ago," Victorious said, climbing out of the bed, still half
asleep.

"Sterling! Keep standing there, and you'll stay up in here with
him. Now let's go!" the CO shouted at Has.

"A'ight, I'm coming now. Yo, I gotta go, but I left you some
shit with my man Mustafa. He gonna get that to you. Yo, stay up,
kid."

"Yeah, no doubt. You, too. I appreciate everything, sun, that's
my word. I'ma come check for you when I touch. I should be out
today, too." Victorious was not 100 percent convinced of his own
words.

"Yeah, do that," Has suggested as he walked backward toward
the door.

"Hold it down out there," Victorious yelled as he watched
Hasan exiting the tier. Just before Has stepped off the unit, he
pumped his fist in the air to Victorious and grinned, then he was
out the door.

Chapter Eleven

Hasan waited patiently for the metal door to open—he had butterflies in his stomach. It had been a long two years up in the county jail, but now it was over. He was moments away from being a free man. The clothes he wore were now too small for his newly built physique. All types of thoughts ran through his mind as he waited. There was so many things that he wanted to do when he got out, but first he wanted to take a long, hot bath to get the jail stench off of him, put on some fresh gear, eat a big hearty meal, and sex his girl. Without her, he knew he'd still be sitting upstairs with the rest of the inmates who wished they were in his shoes.

At first Hasan thought long and hard about what he was asking her to do, not even knowing whether she'd agree to it or not. But he knew that it was his only chance at any freedom, especially facing murder charges. He remembered as if it were yesterday when, with a straight face, he proposed it to her on a visit. He thought after she heard him out she was going to hang the phone up and leave, but surprisingly, she stayed, and after five well-thought-out visits, she agreed. It was then, and only then, Hasan realized the depths and extent of the love she had for him. The CO opened the sliding doors from the control booth, and Hasan walked out of the county jail.

"See you when you get back," one of the officers said to him as he exited.

"I doubt it," was Hasan's comeback with a smile.

Chapter Twelve

"Yo, you Victorious, right?" the inmate at the door yelled, walking up to Victorious's cell.

"Yeah. Why, what's up?" Victorious asked, jumping out the bed thinking he had made bail.

"Yo, I'm Mustafa, Has's people. He got bailed out. I got some shit for you."

"Oh," Victorious replied, disappointed that he hadn't hit the lottery himself.

"Yo, I'ma gets the CO to bust the slot for me. Hold up," Mustafa said before walking off.

Victorious was glad that the kid Hasan who he had gotten cool with had made bail, but it made him stress more because he knew that he should have been in the same situation.

He had stayed up all night thinking about the last time he had spoken to Supreme. A whole bunch of maybes and what-ifs crossed his mind because he just didn't want to believe the obvious. He still had hope that either Supreme or Tameeka would come to get him out. Slowly but surely, though, the light of Victorious's hope was dimming by the hour.

Within two minutes Mustafa was back with the CO.

"Don't take long," the officer said to Mustafa, walking off.

"A'ight," Mustafa replied. "I told Has I'd get this to you this morning," Mustafa said, sliding the junk food and cosmetics through the porthole.

"Damn, I don't need all of this, kid. This too much. I should be out today, too. Take some of this shit for yourself," Victorious insisted.

"Nah, I'm good. He left me mad shit, too. Has was strapped in this muthafucka. That was love, how you was holding him down out there. Ain't too many real dudes like that no more," said Mustafa, under the impression that Hasan and Victorious were friends from the streets.

Catching the misunderstanding, Victorious attempted to correct the assumption, but Mustafa was getting called from another direction.

"Yo, Mu, hurry up. Check this shit out," one of the inmate orderlies yelled.

"Hold up for a minute, kid," Mustafa told Victorious.

"What up, sun?"

"Yo, this dude Has doing it real big out here," the orderly said, while looking out the window down to the front of the county jail.

Mustafa took a look out the window.

"Damn! That piece hot!" Mustafa said in reference to the whip outside the jail.

"You think that's his joint?" the orderly asked.

"Nah, that's probably his man's piece, 'cause that's his man's shortie right there," Mustafa clarified.

"Oh, I was wondering why he ain't kiss her. After all that time I woulda been all over that piece. Shortie bad as hell. Yo, he looking up here."

Both Mustafa and the orderly threw their hands up as they noticed Hasan waving up to them just before he hopped in a Beamer.

Chapter Thirteen

As soon as Hasan stepped from around the corner of the county jail's back entrance, he saw her leaning against the brand-new vehicle. He had waited too long for this day to come when he would be able to be close to his girl again without being separated by Plexiglas. He knew that as bad as he wanted to just run up on her and snatch her up, he had to wait just a little while longer to touch her, just until they were away from in front of the county jail.

Tameeka didn't see Hasan walking up on her, but when she heard his voice, it took everything in her power not to jump all over him. She fought to hold her tears of joy back and smiled with her eyes instead. Hasan warned her that she could not show any form of affection because there would be a lot of eyes on them.

"I told you I'd have you out by the morning," she said to him.

"I never doubted you, baby," he replied.

"You better not had," she said, flashing him a half smile.

"Chill," was Hasan's reaction, catching the smile as he turned around and waved to the inmates who were standing at the fourth-floor window, where they house new commits. "I told you all eyes would be on us. You should've waited for me in the car."

"I know, but he don't know nothing, right?" Meeka asked.

"Nah, not about us, but I can tell he was putting the pieces together with you and his man, though. Speakin' of his man, did you take care of that nigga like I told you?"

"You know I did. That's what took me so long getting back. I had to go all the way to North Carolina and back," Meeka answered.

"That's nothing, as long as you handled that," Hasan said, reaching for the car-door handle. "Yo, let's get the fuck up outta here," he said, opening up the passenger's door.

. . .

"Yo, I just seen my dude Has leaving."

"That's what's up," Victorious said, happy for Has.

"That's your Beamer, right?" Mustafa asked.

"What Beamer?" Victorious replied, confused by Mustafa's question.

"The blue six series."

"Nah, why you think that?"

"I mean . . . that was your shortie driving," Mustafa tried to explain."

"My shortie? Yo, kid, you mistaken. You don't even know my shortie," Victorious said, wondering who Mustafa thought he was.

"Nah, you right. Ain't no disrespect, kid. I just thought that was your shortie you was hugged up with in all the flicks you sent Has," Mustafa replied, not realizing just how powerful his statement was.

"Flicks?" Victorious asked, puzzled. But even as the word came out of his mouth, the pieces began to come together. Taking a shot in the dark, Victorious said, "Oh, the flicks? Yo, I'm buggin'. This jail shit got me fucked up, sun. You talking about a tall, light-skinned chick with long hair and a nice body?"

"Yeah, that's her," Mustafa answered.

"Was the six midnight blue with twenty-fours and tinted windows?"

"Exactly. That's the one."

Un-fucking-believable! This can't be for real, I gotta be on the muthafuckin' Punk'd show or somethin', Victorious thought as he tried to appear unfazed by the new developments, compliments of Mustafa, but the burning sensation in the pit of his stomach was making it difficult to do so. Seeing Mustafa looking at him strangely, Victorious tried to play it off.

"Yeah, that's my shortie's whip," he said, knowing who the car really belonged to.

"Damn, kid, you must be doin' it up real big out there if wifey got the new quarter to seven. What you pushin', a Maybach or somethin'?"

"I got the new 745," Victorious replied, still keeping up his appearance so Mustafa wouldn't suspect that he was milking him for information.

"Yeah, that make sense," Mustafa said. "Yo, them was some hot minks you and your shortie had on in the flicks in front of Madison Square Garden. What was those, chinchilla?"

"Yeah, no doubt," Victorious said, remembering when he and Tameeka had gone out for her birthday sporting matching furs. That had been the most recent picture he and Tameeka had taken.

"Yo, you and your wifey was definitely livin' it up out there, from what I saw in the flicks Has showed me. That's all he used to talk about. But yo, I gotta bounce, but I'll come back through to see if you still here later. Hopefully you not. They should be callin' you next, right?" Mustafa said.

"Should be," Victorious replied dryly.

Misinterpreting Victorious's vibe, Mustafa added, "Yeah, I know how they be bullshittin' around here, so anything's possible. Yo, let me roll though."

"A'ight, yo," Victorious said, letting Mustafa's words marinate.

Yeah, shit happens, he thought to himself as he jumped back in his bunk, nauseated by the situation.

"Muthafucka!" he yelled after Mustafa was far enough away. He began thinking about how he had just been played like a mark. So many thoughts and unanswered questions raced through his mind. He couldn't help but notice the roller-coaster sequence of events.

"Ayo, fam, you a'ight down there?" Victorious's cell mate asked.

But Victorious was so heated that he didn't even bother to answer. "Damn!" he yelled, this time with a lot weighing heavy on his mental and his gut twisted up in knots. "Why me?" Victorious asked himself, his hands on his head massaging the migraine that just came on. How could he not have seen this coming? he thought. Could it be that his girlfriend of two years had been playing him the whole time? And if so, how could his man he had known since he'd been in the game and been through thick and thin with cross him for a chick? Was Supreme only pretending to be his friend? Was it a setup all along? Was Has really who he said he was? Was his girl and Has's girl actually one in the same? And how did Has and Supreme know each other? These were just some of the unanswered questions floating around in Victorious's mind as he drifted off into a tormented sleep.

Epilogue

"Mail call!" the CO yelled as the inmates began to ritually gather around the dayroom table, seeing the stack of mail in the officer's hand. After all, this was one of the highlights of the day for all inmates. Not to mention, it was two days before Christmas.

"Charles Brent, mail!" was the first name the CO sounded off.

"Ayo, Karim, Chuck-a-Luck!" two inmates began shouting out.

"Yo, what's that, mail? Get that for me. I'm in the shower," inmate Brent yelled back as he stuck his head out of the unit shower. As requested, one of the inmates grabbed the letter for Brent, who was referred to by two different names.

"Andre Davis, Hussam Williams, mail," the CO continued.

"Yo Bisquit, Hu," another inmate yelled over to where inmates were playing a game of spades.

"A'ight, we heard it," said Davis, who was referred to as Bisquit, and Williams, who was referred to as Hu.

"Wayne, Akbar, Prey!"

"Right here, CO," said inmate Prey, who was known to all as Akbar, as he stood in the front of the dayroom table.

"Corey Grant!"

"Yo, right here. Pass that back," Grant, who was known as C-Understanding, replied.

"Damn, kid. Sue stay floodin' you," another inmate said to C-Understanding as the mail was passed back.

"Yeah, that's my baby," Grant replied.

"Shawn Hartwell, mail!"

"Yo, CO, I'm on the phone," Hartwell yelled. "Somebody snatch that for me."

"I got you, dawg," another inmate yelled.

"Antwuan Johnson, mail!"

"Pass that," a friend of Johnson's called out.

"Yo, Chet!" he yelled up to the top tier, where Johnson's room was.

"Wiz, you called me?" the inmate referred to as Chet asked, sticking his head out of his cell. "Hold up Harris, you got mail, too," the CO said to the inmate referred to as Wiz.

"A'ight. Yeah, you got some love down here," Wiz called back up.

"A'ight. Bring it up for me."

"Drake Barksdale, mail!"

"Yo Blue, Big Blue, Blue!" one of the inmates yelled up to the top tier, where Drake slept.

"What's up?" Big Blue asked as he stuck his head out of his cell.

"Yo, you got some love down here."

"A'ight. I'm comin' down now."

"Listen up! Mail call is every day at five P.M. Y'all know that, so for all you guys that be expecting mail and know that your family members and friends write you, you should have your asses over here during mail call. Not on the phone, not playing cards, not in the shower, and not in your room. Now the next time I'm going to just send your shit back, and you know how long it'll take before you receive it again," the CO reprimanded. "Now let's start this again. Vincent Jackson, mail!"

There was no answer.

"Here we go again with the bullshit. Y'all holding me up. Jackson, Vincent Jackson, inmate number 803050," the CO called out, becoming frustrated as the inmates looked at one another, wondering who Vincent Jackson was.

"I think he got bailed out," one of the inmates from the back yelled, frustrated behind the fact that the inmate the officer was calling was holding mail call up and he was expecting an important letter that he was anxious to receive. Every letter during the week of Christmas, due to the long holiday schedule for mail delivery, was an important one.

"Aye, V, ain't that you," an old-timer asked Victorious, who was preoccupied with his next strategic move on the chessboard.

"Don't try to throw me off, old head. You goin' down today," Victorious said as he continued to contemplate his next move, thinking that the old-timer was trying to distract him.

"Nah, young blood, I'm serious," the old-timer replied.

Hearing the tone of the old-timer's voice caused Victorious to look up. When he finally did, he saw the expression on the old-timer's face, which indicated that he was, in fact, serious.

"Me, what?" Victorious asked, having no clue as to what the old-timer was referring to, since his attention had been focused solely on the chess game.

"Your name Vincent Jackson, right?"

"Yeah, why? What's up?" Victorious asked, wondering why the old-timer was calling him by his birth name.

"They just called you for mail," the old-timer told him.

"Mail?" Victorious questioned, thinking that the old-timer might have been mistaken. He had been in the county jail for a little over a year and had never gotten a visit or used the phone, other than to call his public defender, let alone received any mail, so the thought of receiving any now had him puzzled.

"You sure?" he asked.

"Yeah, 803050, right?" Before he had the chance to answer, Victorious heard it for himself.

"Last call, Vincent Jackson, mail!" the CO repeated for the third and final time.

"Oh shit!" Victorious said as he hopped up from the chess table. "CO, right here, Jackson!"

As soon as he said it, everyone in the whole dayroom instantly had turned their attention in Victorious's direction. As many of the inmates who knew Victorious or knew of him, no one had given it any thought that the name Vincent Jackson could have belonged to him, not even the other older heads with whom he interacted daily, like Akbar, Donnie Ray, and old head Claude from Plainfield. Victorious was known as a laid-back, quiet individual, and was considered to be an old head himself by the other inmates, in spite of his being only thirty-three years old. Everybody knew that he had time-in in the county and was fighting his case, but that was as far as they knew because he didn't discuss his situation, which everyone respected. And just as Victorious had thought to himself, no one had ever seen him get any visits, play the phone on a regular, or receive any mail, which was why it came as a surprise to everyone when he came up and got the letter that had been delaying mail call. Even the CO was surprised when Victorious came up.

"Jackson, you didn't hear what I said?" the CO asked, not wanting to come down on Victorious too hard because he had been working the unit for the past few years and had never heard Victorious's name called for anything, so he figured that this had to come as a surprise to the inmate and may have possibly been his first letter since he had been in.

"Nah, honestly I didn't," Victorious replied as the CO handed him the letter.

"Just listen up for your name the next time, all right?" the CO said with a little authority in his tone, not wanting the other inmates to think that he was being soft or showing favoritism, being that he had just given them all a lecture.

"Yeah, pardon me," Victorious replied just before he stepped off, knowing that the CO could have been a dick if he wanted to be.

"Keith Wooten!" the CO continued.

Victorious was curious to know who had written him as he checked the return address. The heading of the letter read, "Guess Who?" But Victorious was far from being in the mood for playing guessing games, so he opened it up. As soon as he began reading the first few lines, he already knew who had sent him the letter without having to see her name.

> *Dear Victorious,*
> *I know that you're probably surprised to be hearing from me . . .*

"Yo, old head, I'm goin' up to my room for a few; I'll be back down later," Victorious called over to the old-timer he was playing chess with.

"A'ight, young blood, handle your business, I'll catch up with you later," the old-timer responded, understanding more than Victorious probably thought he did. Victorious climbed up the steps that led to his cell, went inside, and closed the door behind him as he sat at his room's desk.

Dear Victorious,

I know that you're probably surprised to be hearing from me, but nonetheless, this letter is long overdue. I hope that when you receive this missive, in spite of all that you've had to endure, you are holding up in there. Knowing you, I'm sure that you are. Anyway, I wish that things could have been different between us, but like they say, it is what it is. I didn't write you to throw anything up in your face or anything. My only reason for reaching out to you really is because overall I feel that you deserve to know how it got to where it went, which I'm sure has been puzzling you for the past thirteen months.

First I want to start out by saying that it was not my idea or my doing setting you up. That was your man's work. The only thing that I am guilty of, as far as that is concerned, is fucking him too good, which caused him to do what he did to you. But if it's any consolation, he and I are not together, and because of his actions, he got what his hands called for. In my opinion, he did not deserve your friendship. With friends like that, who needs enemies? You're probably saying that same thing about me right now, but like I was saying, I saw to it that you never have to worry about seeing or hearing from him ever again, and I do mean never. As far as us, you must believe me when I tell you that I did love you and I still do, but what took place had nothing to do with how I felt about you. It only made it more difficult to do. It was never anything personal, even though my feelings were never supposed to get involved. It was just business!

As for Hasan, what I'm about to say doesn't justify how and why things turned out the way they did, but it may give you a better understanding. Just as I loved you, I also loved Has. In fact, he was my first true love. Where you and I only had two and a half years in together, he and I had nearly twenty. All that happened was on the strength of both my love and loyalty to him.

He told me how he had gotten close to you up in there and how you were going through it, and for a minute I felt fucked up, but I knew that there was nothing that I could do about that. Had I not thought that you would have tried to find me when you got out, I would have paid your bail, but knowing the type of individual that you are, I knew that you wouldn't rest until you found me, so I couldn't take that chance.

By the way, for what it's worth, Hasan and I are no longer together, either, in case you were wondering. For some reason he just couldn't accept the fact that I fucked both you and your man, which he suggested, with his insecure, ungrateful ass, so like Supreme, he, too, had to go!

Well, that's basically all I wanted to say, so I guess I'll bring this notation to an end.

But in conclusion I want to say that I hope that you don't hate me, because, like I said, it was nothing personal, just business. If you do, then I don't blame you. But if that's the case, then I think that it would make you feel a whole lot better about the situation or at least a little if instead of you chargin' what happened to my heart, you simply charge it to the game, sweetheart.

From You Know Who

PS. To try to trace this postmark would be useless and a waste of time 'cause it's bogus. You'll never find me when you get out. Oh, yeah. Merry Christmas.

Victorious couldn't believe what he had just finished reading. He was amazed at how Tameeka had the audacity to write to him after the snake shit she had pulled on him more than a year ago, but at least now he had more clarity on his situation and could put what happened behind him—for now anyway.

He got up from the little six-by-nine cell desk, turned toward the stainless-steel toilet, threw the letter in the commode, and began urinating on it. He could see Tameeka's handwriting on the envelope fading as he stood there relieving himself.

"I can't believe this bitch!" he said to himself, letting out a somewhat psychotic laugh as he shook his head in disbelief. As the letter continued to dissolve from the combination of water and urine, Victorious couldn't help but to think about the predicament Tameeka had played a major part in getting him in. And now he was practically being forced to sign what he thought to be the rest of his life away to a thirty-year plea bargain for the five kilos of crack cocaine that were found in his Benz. Remembering Tameeka's ending words, as much as he would have liked to disagree with her, he knew that there was no way that he could, because she was absolutely right.

At his own expense, getting caught with his pants down, Victorious had no other choice but to charge it to the game.

Acknowledgments

K. Elliott · I want to thank God and my parents, Otis and Margaret Douglas. Thanks also to Nikki Turner for the opportunity to be a part of this project.

Mo Shines · First and foremost, I have to thank God, creator of Heaven and Earth. Thanks to my wife. Thanks to all my family. Thanks to Nikki Turner for believing in me and giving me this opportunity. Thanks to all my friends, present and past. With God all things are possible!

Dee Blackmon · I would like to thank Nikki Turner for her vision, her patience, and for allowing me to take part in such a great project.

Seth "Soul Man" Ferranti · I would like to thank my wife, Diane, Kevin, Tiffany, Tuck, Bing, Supreme, Lil' Bob, Eyon, Wahida, Joe Black, Kwame, Tut, Fridge, Ben, Ethan, and of course the queen herself, Nikki Turner.

J. M. Benjamin · To The Most High. You continue to protect and guide me on the straight path, both personally and professionally. To the one who made this possible, "The Queen" of this genre, Nikki Turner, "I told you I was gonna come home and do it." Thanks for believing in me. My mother and children, I love you. My brother, nothing or no one can ever come between us or change history. My partner of Real Edutainment Publishing, Kev, Dawg love is love. Nancey Flowers, to thank you would be an understatement, friends 4 life. To my man Randy Kearse, we've proved that two brothers can plan to do something positive together, come home, and follow through; let's keep doin' it!

Hood Ornaments

K. Elliott resides in Charlotte, NC. He is the author of many bestselling novels, including *Entangled.* He has contributed to a few anthologies and was selected to launch the first series of G unit novellas with his work *The Ski Mask Way,* which will be a G unit film.

Mo Shines was born in Brooklyn and raised in the Bronx. His writing reflects the harsh and grim realities he saw growing up. He's a former NYC corrections officer who has been on both sides of the law but chose to walk a righteous path. *Brazen* was his first novel and his next novel, *Eye for an Eye,* will hit bookstores in the fall of 2007. Visit his website at www.moshines.com.

Dee Blackmon's down-to-earth style has made her a favorite among fans with her debut novel *Fallen Snow*. She is also a playwright and lives in Maryland where she is currently working on her next novel.

Seth "Soul Man" Ferranti is the founder of Gorilla Convict Publications and is the bestselling author of the underground hit *Prison Stories*. Seth is also a journalist who contributes to several urban magazines. Find out more about Seth at www.gorilla convict.com.

J. M. Benjamin is the author of *Down in the Dirty* and *My Manz and 'Em*. He is also a contributing author to the anthology *Menace II Society* as well as a nonfiction piece titled *Changin' Your Game Plan*. Visit his website at www.allaboutjm benjamin.com.